PROMISES
BOUNTY HUNTERS 1

A.E. VIA

PROMISES

Promises – Part One
Bounty Hunters I
Published By: Via Star Wings Books
Copyright © September 2015
Edited By: Ally Editorial Services
http://allyeditorialservices.weebly.com/
Cover Art By: Jay Aheer of Simply Defined Art
Formatting & Illustrations By: Fancy Pants Formatting
http://www.fancypantsformatting.com
All rights reserved under the International and Pan-American Copyright Conventions. No part of this book may be reproduced or transmitted in any form or by any means, electronic or mechanical, including photocopying, recording, or by any information storage and retrieval system, without permission in writing from the author, Adrienne E. Via.
No part of this book may be scanned, uploaded, or distributed via the Internet or any other means, electronic or print, without permission from Adrienne E. Via. The unauthorized reproduction or distribution of this copyrighted work is illegal. Criminal copyright infringement, including infringement without monetary gain, is investigated by the FBI and is punishable by up to 5 years in federal prison and a fine of $250,000 (http://www.fbi.gov/ipr/). Please purchase only authorized electronic or print editions and do not participate in or encourage the electronic piracy of copyrighted material. Your support of the author's rights and livelihood is appreciated.

PROMISES

Trademark Acknowledgments

The author acknowledges the trademarked status and trademark owners of the following trademarks mentioned in this work of fiction:

Academy Award: Academy of Motion Picture Arts and Sciences: adidas: adidas America Inc.
Amazon.com: Amazon.com, Inc.
Armageddon: Touchstone Pictures, Jerry Bruckheimer Films, Valhalla Motion Pictures
Arrow: Berlanti Productions, DC Entertainment, Warner Bros. Television
"At Last": Mack Gordon and Harry Warren : Audi: Audi of America
Bleu De Chanel: CHANEL, Inc.: Bluetooth: Bluetooth SIG, Inc.
Catfish: MTV Networks: Chevrolet Nova: General Motors
Chevrolet Silverado: General Motors: Clarks: C & J Clark America Inc
Coke: THE COCA-COLA COMPANY: Crown Royal: The Crown Royal Company
Dallas Cowboys: NFL Enterprises LLC.: *Deadliest Catch*: Discovery Network, Original Productions
Die Hard: Twentieth Century Fox Film Corporation, Gordon Company, Silver Pictures
Dockers: LEVI STRAUSS & CO.:
Dodge: Chrysler Group LLC.: Dolby: Dolby Laboratories
Ford F350: Ford Motor Company : Glock: GLOCK, Inc.
Google: Google Inc.: *GQ*: Condé Nast
Ice Road Truckers: Original Productions, A Fremantle Company, History Channel
Ideal Home: Time, Inc. (UK) Ltd Homes Network: Jell-O: Kraft Foods
Macy's: Macy's, Inc. (formerly known as Federated Department Stores, Inc.)
McDonald's: McDonald's: *Men's Health*: Rodale Inc.
MTV: Viacom International Inc.: Netflix: Netflix, Inc.
Northmen: A Viking Saga: Elite Filmproduktion, Jumping Horse Film, Two Oceans Production (TOP), Anchor Bay Entertainment
Parker Duofold: Parker
Person of Interest: Kilter Films, Bad Robot, Warner Bros. Television, CBS
Polo: Ralph Lauren Coproration: Ralph Lauren: Ralph Lauren Coproration
Range Rover: Jaguar Land Rover North America, LLC: Sig Sauer: Sig Sauer, Inc.
Solo: Dart Container Corporation : Superman: DC Comics, A Warner Bros. Entertainment Company
TASER: TASER International, Inc.
The Late Show with Stephen Colbert: Spartina Productions, CBS Television Studios
To Catch a Predator: NBCNEWS: *To Kill a Mockingbird*: Harper Lee

PROMISES
Vicodin: AbbVie Inc.

PROMISES

ACKNOWLEDGMENTS

    I'm so glad I was able to finally give Duke the HEA he so deserved after Judge left him to follow his own path. Duke holds a very special place in my heart so I had to put him with a man that wasn't as hardcore and rough as what Duke was used to being around. Welcome…Vaughan Webb, Esquire. But because of their age difference and of course, Vaughan being Duke's best friend's son, I had to develop a situation that would make Vaughan undeniably the best thing to happen to Duke. I hope you enjoy their story.

    As usual I had a lot of help putting this story together from a group of very talented people and long list of friends.

    I have to thank my family for all their support and understanding of the long days and nights closed up in my office. My husband is the most patient and understanding man in the world and I love him with everything I have.

    Tina Adamski of course is the most amazing editor, not to mention the most amazing *person* I've ever had the pleasure to work with. She doesn't even blink at my ridiculous deadlines and I appreciate her most for that. You don't find many editors that respect or even give a damn about deadlines or release dates. I'm really fortunate to have this very talented lady on my team.

    Casey of Fancy Pants Formatting, as always, thank you for coming through and putting everything together into a beautiful

PROMISES

package. You were also extremely patient and lenient as always. Thank you so very much

Of course, the biggest thank you I can express goes to Jay Aheer for the amazing cover. It's unlike anything I've ever seen. Thank you! It's absolutely perfect to start out the series. The graphics, posters, teasers, just everything you do always blows my mind. You are an amazing artist and so easy to work with. I look forward to working with you a lot more.

Thank you to Andrea Goodell, River Mitchell, Jennifer Wedmore, Pam Ebler, and Stephanie LaSalle of Man2Mantastic Blog for beta reading for me. You are the ladies I run to for advice with every book. You know my passion, you love my guys, and I trust your opinions. Thank you very much.

To my dedicated fans and the new ones. I love you to pieces. I hope you enjoy this book and continue to watch for more real soon.

PROMISES

CONTENTS

Acknowledgments

Chapter One

Chapter Two

Chapter Three

Chapter Four

Chapter Five

Chapter Six

Chapter Seven

Chapter Eight

Chapter Nine

Chapter Ten

Chapter Eleven

Chapter Twelve

Chapter Thirteen

PROMISES

Chapter Fourteen

Chapter Fifteen

Chapter Sixteen

Chapter Seventeen

Chapter Eighteen

Chapter Nineteen

Chapter Twenty

Chapter Twenty-One

Chater Twenty-Two

Chapter Twenty-Three

Chapter Twenty-Four

Chapter Twenty-Five

Chapter Twenty-Six

Chapter Twenty-Seven

Chapter Twenty-Eight

Chapter Twenty-Nine

Chapter Thirty

Chapter Thirty-One

Chapter Thirty-Two

Chapter Thirty-Three

Chapter Thirty-Four

Chapter Thirty-Five

PROMISES

Chapter Thirty-Six

Chapter Thirty-Seven

Chapter Thirty-Eight

Bonus Scene

Also by A.E. Via

CHAPTER ONE

"Get 'em before he goes in that house Duke!" Quick's deep voice could be heard a half block away. Knowing that his long-time trusted friend was there always made doing the job that much easier. Quick was not only his best friend, but his most efficient bounty hunter. He rarely made mistakes and his retrievals were almost always clean.

Duke saw his bail skipper clear the four-foot fence, running full speed towards a small, ranch-style home whose front yard was littered with toys. *Oh no. Not kids.* Duke only had a second to decide if he could clear that gate. He wasn't a spring chicken at forty-five years old and aging–what felt like every day. Duke pumped his legs faster and leaped into the air, his back foot just grazing the top of the fence. He landed harder than he wanted, losing speed as he righted himself. *Fuck me, that hurt.*

The young bail skipper dodged a few toys but face planted into the kiddie pool when he turned to gauge Duke's distance. Double-timing it, Duke hurled himself forward and collided with the kid's back, sending him back down to the wet grass with an angry thud. Air left Duke's lungs with the impact, but he didn't have time to rest. He scrambled to get the scared kid's hands behind his back.

"Stop fighting, Troy," Duke hissed. "It's over. It's over."

PROMISES

After tussling for a few more seconds, Quick was there, coming down on one knee and helping secure the skip's other arm. "Easy kid. Easy," Quick grumbled, his voice like something out of a scary movie.

Duke let Quick take over and crab walked backwards, plopping down on his ass to drop his head between his knees, still gasping for breath.

"You alright over there?" Quick laughed, his green eyes glistening with humor, while zip tying their skip's hands behind his back.

"Yeah, I'm good, man. But that fuckin' fence wasn't a great idea." Duke huffed a breath.

When they heard the sound of tires squealing, Duke and Quick both rolled their eyes. "Why the fuck does he always do that?"

"Beats the fuck out of me." Duke shrugged. "It's like the cliché scene in action movies; when the cavalry comes barreling up the street, lights and sirens blaring—after all the shit has already gone down."

Quick pulled their skip up to his feet. "When you gonna let Charlie go, man? He's not feeling this anymore, Duke, and you know it. He hardly shows up to the office, much less for recon; which is his damn job."

Duke raised his hand, cutting off Quick's tirade, because he knew the man could go on for days. "I'm not firing him. He was my dad's right hand man, and when I took over this business I swore that Charlie would always be welcome."

"This is a business, Duke. Now that Judge is gone and you're back in the field again, we all need to be capable, or someone's gonna get hurt. This ain't a barbershop, dude. No loitering," Quick urged.

"Shut up. Here he comes."

"Duke."

"We'll talk about this later. Now shush."

PROMISES

"Boss, you okay? Got here as fast as I could. There was traffic on Cascade Ave," Charlie said, out of breath, like the short walk from the truck to the yard where they waited took a lot out of him.

"You do know you can put the siren on and go through the traffic, right?" Quick said sarcastically. Duke shot his friend a warning scowl.

"I didn't want to scare anyone," Charlie said defensively.

Duke stood up. "It's cool, Charlie. Here. Load our skip up and get him ready for transport. Call County and let 'em know we're coming in."

"Duke, please. I was gonna go to court. I swear," Troy whined.

Duke shook his head sadly. Troy was only twenty years old. He'd been arrested more than a few times on petty drug charges since he was seventeen, and Duke had bailed him out every time. But this was the fourth time in two years that Troy hadn't shown up for court, and instead of Duke taking Troy's mom's car – which she'd used as collateral this time – he chose to pick him up. Bail skippers were the most unpredictable defendants they dealt with. They made a million promises to get out on bail, but once they were released they had no loyalty.

"Your court date was nine days ago, Troy. You are breaking your momma's heart. She hasn't seen you in days. Getting off these streets is the best thing for you right now, buddy. You're gonna have to stay behind bars until your next appearance is scheduled."

Quick and Duke stood there talking while Charlie ambled over to the large, gutted-out Silverado and loaded Troy into the back.

"He should've retired ten years ago." Quick checked his weapons while they walked back to Duke's truck.

"Maybe. But everyone doesn't retire at sixty anymore," Duke said wearily.

PROMISES

"No. Most people retire from this job by fifty. He can't run at all, his reflexes are nonexistent. He shouldn't be in the field like that. It's dangerous," Quick retorted. "Hey. Maybe we can throw him a surprise retirement party and just have him show up to realize he's the guest of honor."

Duke laughed, slapping his friend on his broad shoulder. "I don't think that'll work."

"You'd better think of something." Quick got in the passenger side of Duke's F350. They followed Charlie, driving less than forty miles per hour, to the jail so Duke could make sure the paperwork was done correctly. As much as he hated to admit it, Quick was right. Charlie was having a hard time pulling the hours needed to do the job. His eyesight hindered him when using the computers and especially doing surveillance. He'd have to come up with a tactful way to retire Charlie. If his hunters didn't want to have Charlie in the field covering their backs, he had to do what made his employees feel safe.

"That's fucked up about Troy, huh?" Quick threw his last dart, this one hitting in the outer ring of the bull's-eye. He pumped his fist and went to the board to count up his points. Duke drank another gulp of his dark lager and took up his spot to throw next.

"Yeah, it is. Never thought he'd skip on me. He used to always show up for court, but he's changed the last year or so."

"He's caught up in that crowd."

"I really feel for his mom, ya know. That woman's been through enough." Duke stood about eight feet back and aimed to throw his first dart. This was their ritual after securing a bail skipper or bounty. They needed to unwind and have a little fun. Since they were both older and single, their night of fun usually consisted of beer, darts, pool; sometimes watching a game at

their favorite sports bar. Random conquests never made the list. Duke had been there, done that. That ship had sailed when his last chance to fall in love hightailed it out of his bed and into the arms of a hotshot detective right here in Atlanta. Speaking of...
"Judge was supposed to be meeting us here."

Quick snorted. "He can't get away from that hottie long enough to meet up."

Duke jerked his head back, a coy smile curving his lips. "You think Detective Michaels is hot?"

Quick flicked him off. "Not in that way. Well if I went that way... you know... He's no Brad Pitt. I-I mean, he's not ugly. If I was that way... But I'm not... Soooo...."

"Shut the hell up." Duke threw the dart, not really caring where it landed. "He better get in here soon so he can update me on the new case."

"I still can't believe you let him run your PI business after what he did to you."

Duke threw his last dart and sat down next to his friend. "He didn't do anything *to* me. He met someone and fell for him. What did it have to do with me?"

"But weren't y'all sleeping together at the time? You were practically in lov—"

"Hey!" Duke cut Quick off. "I wasn't in love with Judge. I liked him. We had a comfortable arrangement. That's it. It was nice for a time and then it was over."

"Mmm hmm."

"He's a good man and a damn good business partner. A real man doesn't let petty shit— like the loss of good sex—fuck up his money. I needed someone to run that side of my business and Judge was... is the best man for the job."

"Mmm hmm," Quick hummed again, with his beer bottle to his lips.

Quick's tone said it all. He was calling Duke on his bullshit. But Duke needed to say those things about Judge out loud over and over. *I don't need Judge. I especially don't need love.* Anything to get through the long, lonely nights. He'd had to admit to himself though, that he'd probably liked Judge a whole lot more than he let on, but the man had made his choice and it wasn't Duke. How could he compete with a guy that was twenty years his junior? He was guessing; he had no clue what Michaels' actual age was – with his perfect hair and exciting job. He was smart, adventurous... *What the fuck am I doing?* Duke frowned. He didn't need to think about them.

"Anyway. He had better let us know what's up soon. I'm a partner in this business, too, and I don't give a damn if he has David Beckham in his bed. He needs to keep us up to date with what's going on over there. Monthly reports were a stipulation when he agreed to run the Atlanta PI office." Quick signaled for the waitress, ordering them another round of beers.

Duke grinned, watching his friend.

"What?" Quick grumbled.

"You think David Beckham is hot too, huh? You know. Not being gay and all, you sure do have an arsenal of guys in your mental bank that you think are hot."

"You're an asshole." Quick threw a few bar nuts at him, making him laugh, and forget about his loneliness, if just temporarily.

"On another note. Guess who's on his way home this weekend?"

Duke stopped his beer midway to his mouth. "Who?"

"Vaughan." Quick smiled proudly.

"No shit! He's done with school already?"

"Man. He was done with school six months ago: he's been studying to take the bar. Which he just passed, so he's coming home."

"Wait. How come I wasn't invited to the graduation?"

PROMISES

"He graduated during the summer, so he opted out of the ceremony. You know Vaughan. He's all about just getting shit done and moving forward."

Duke chuckled softly. "I think I do remember that about him. How old is he now?"

"Thirty-one going on sixty-one. That boy has always been too damn mature."

"I remember that, too. So, he's coming to Atlanta. He knows you left Charleston with me, right?"

"Yep. Says he wants to spend more time with his old man now. Possibly look for work here."

"And Remy is cool with this?"

"She's his mom, man. Remy's had him his whole life, while I got scraps. Some weekends and occasional holidays. Then only a year after high school, he was off to college and then Europe to study abroad and right into a rigorous law program. It's like I'm finally getting a chance to have some time with him now."

Duke nodded his head in understanding. Vaughan was Quick's sole purpose for living. His son was everything to him, so Duke was happy for him. Damn, he hadn't seen Vaughan in a few years. Every time he came to visit during school breaks, Duke was gone on a retrieval or out of town.

"He's really something, Duke. A chip off the old block. Wait until you see him." Quick beamed.

PROMISES

CHAPTER TWO

"Sounds like everything is going good, man." Duke sat at his desk searching for an appropriate graduation gift while Judge updated him on the status of the PI side of his business. He'd been "Duke's Bail Bonds" for almost fifteen years, but last year he added on "and Private Investigations" along with a separate office in downtown Atlanta. Even though he'd moved his businesses from Charleston, North Carolina because of their ancient laws regulating bounty hunting, he still rarely saw Judge. Which was okay with him. Atlanta was plenty big enough for the both of them.

"Yeah, we're good. I'm going over this contract for a sales consulting firm. They suspect embezzling within their upper ranks."

Duke's eyebrows rose and he paused his Amazon perusal. "No shit."

"Yeah, man. They're offering a shit ton of money to retain us and even more if we find evidence."

"Nice. You gonna outsource this job? All the guys are on other assignments, right?" Duke murmured.

"I'll handle it. Don't worry. I'll find the right guys for this one."

"Sounds good, man."

"You alright, Duke? You sound a little... I don't know."

PROMISES

Duke shook it off. Tried to add some pep to his voice. Talking with Judge – though it happened rarely—always messed with Duke's head. Not a lot, but some. That dark, brooding timbre that used to make his cock weep was wafting through his phone intercom system in Dolby. Made it sound like Judge was in the room with him. Duke wasn't hard, but he sure missed those days sometimes.

"I'm gonna let you go, Judge. Sounds like you got everything handled."

"Naturally."

Duke laughed.

"Hey, you wanna come over to the house? Austin is having his team over for fight night on Saturday. You haven't seen all the renovations we've made to our place yet."

Our place. Duke pinched the bridge of his nose. "I know. I've been meaning to. You guys have done a lot over there. But Quick's son just came home and he wants me to get up with them on Saturday."

"Well let me know when you wanna come by, alright."

"Sure thing," Duke said, and ended the call. He liked to think he wasn't bitter. Judge had found someone who made him happy. Made him a different man if Duke was being honest… a better man. He wouldn't hate on that just because it left him high and dry. Duke didn't do jealousy.

With a resigned sigh, Duke turned back to his desktop and looked through graduation gifts. He wondered for the millionth time if it was a silly idea. Vaughan wasn't some eighteen-year-old graduating from high school. The guy was a lawyer now. Duke turned his executive chair to face the full-glass patio door. He opened the top drawer of his wet bar and removed a fresh Cuban. He stepped from his home office out onto the deck that overlooked a dark, dense forest. He'd been working from home for the past few days. He'd sent a couple of his other guys on

PROMISES

some bonds, but thank goodness they hadn't had any jumpers this week. Duke needed the time alone.

He'd gotten a call from Quick that Vaughan's flight had arrived safely and they were having dinner at one of Duke's favorite restaurants, but he'd declined the invitation to join them, wanting to give them some bonding time. Which meant Duke was left to do what he usually did on any given night. Turn on an old movie and cook a meal for one.

It was after two in the morning and Duke had enough of Die Hard for one night. "Damn. How many of those movies did he make?" he murmured, moving around his condo turning off lights and locking up. He could still hear the quiet, soothing sound of jazz music filtering through his neighbor's wall and into his bedroom. From what Duke knew of his young neighbor, he played concert piano and saxophone, and was a music major at Clark University. Some variety of music could always be heard wafting from his place and Duke just thanked the gods that his neighbor wasn't an aspiring rapper. Jazz he could handle.

He turned on the high-powered showerhead in his master bathroom and stepped in while it quickly heated up. He washed up efficiently, pausing just briefly to pay extra attention to his sensitive balls. Leaning against the warm tiles, he leaned his head back and let the water beat on his chest while he gently stroked himself. It wasn't done with real purpose; it was simply make him feel a hint of euphoria. He hadn't beat one off in weeks. Not in the mood. He actually wouldn't mind a damn good release right then, but a part of his brain kept reminding him how pathetic he'd become and then like clockwork… there went his erection.

After drying off, he pulled back the covers on his king-sized bed and climbed in naked. Lying in the dark, listening to muffled sounds of jazz, his phone buzzed with a missed message. It was almost three a.m. It had to be a bond request. Scrubbing his hands over his face, he woke up his phone and saw it was a message from Quick. Not bothering to read the message, he immediately dialed his number, hitting the speakerphone.

"Hello, Duke. Long time no hear."

What the... "Who's this?"

The sexy, deep chuckle that came through his speaker and resonated in his groin had him frowning at his body's reaction. *It's been way too long.*

"It has been a long time. My father is in the bathroom so I picked up when I saw your name on the screen."

Shit. It's Vaughan. Nope. Definitely not the young-sounding, scrawny high school geek he remembered. "Damn. Sorry, Vaughan. I didn't recognize your voice. You've grown... I mean you're older. No. You just sure sound different." Duke rolled his eyes at his ridiculous rambling.

"Interesting," Vaughan said sensually, his voice a deep, melodic purr. "Although it's been three years. You sound just like I remember, Duke. So how have you been?"

Duke's mouth was hanging open and it took him a second to realize he was talking to his best friend's son, not some phone sex operator. He had to clear his throat before he could continue. "I've been real good. Business is good, of course. I'm sure your dad told you all about it."

"Yes, he did. But I'd like to hear it from you."

Duke frowned again. Either it'd been a while, or he was imagining the flirtatious tone of the conversation. Had to be. Duke remembered those days. Guys or girls. It made him no difference. Vaughan was in his early thirties, he'd flirt with a damn mailbox if it was designed prettily enough. Duke finally got himself together. "So what was Quick calling me for at this hour?"

"He wanted you to come join in on the fun. We're at Harry's, but I think we're gonna call it a night. I have an interview and I'm sure y'all have work to do."

PROMISES

Duke couldn't get over how mature Vaughan sounded. He'd been in the kid's life since he was a teen. Since his freshman year in high school. He knew the guy would grow up to be amazing. He'd always had a level head. Never got caught up in the bullshit that so many kids did these days. He looked forward to talking to him again.

"Yeah. I'm going into the office tomorrow to wrap up for the week. I won't keep your dad long, though. I'm sure y'all have plenty to catch—"

"Hold on one second, Duke." Vaughan cut over him. He heard the smooth man talking to someone who he presumed was their server. "Thank you, honey. You were great." Then that deep sexy chuckle. "Naw. I'm good. Just the check, love. Thank you... Okay. I'm back. You still there, Duke?"

Damn. Was he. Yep. Just like he thought. Thirty-year-olds loved to flirt and see if they could get a rise from you. "Yeah, I'm here." Duke was ready to end this conversation; he was feeling some type of way for having wood while talking to Quick's son. "I'm gonna hit the hay. I'm exhausted."

"Mmm. I see. Boyfriend keeping you up late?"

Duke smirked. How cute. "Can't exactly say that. I sure wish, though."

His comment was met with silence and Duke thought that maybe he'd grossed the kid out until a moan almost too soft to hear reached his ears, and Duke wondered if Vaughan was doing something... maybe with someone else while he was on the phone. Until he spoke again.

"What else do you wish for, Duke?"

"W-what?" Duke stammered in response to the loaded question.

"Oh, never mind. I'll find out soon enough," Vaughan said casually.

PROMISES

Duke laughed, more so from nervousness rather than anything striking him as funny. There was no mistaking Vaughan's coy tone.

"Good night, Duke. Sleep well."

The next thing he knew, the line was dead. Duke was speechless. *Fuck*. And hard.

PROMISES

CHAPTER THREE

Vaughan didn't bother telling his dad that Duke had called. He laid in bed that night thinking about his plan. He'd been attracted to his father's friend since he first brought him around. Even then, Vaughan knew his true orientation, because Duke could make him hard as steel just by entering the room. All that before the man spoke a word in that deep-southern-down-home-drawl. He didn't sound like a hick, but sort of like a hot cowboy. Vaughan shook his head as he ran his large hand down the smooth patch of hair in the center of his chest, all the way to his cock. He pulled on his considerable length a couple times, imagining Duke kneeling next to him, watching him pleasure himself.

When he was a junior in high school, he'd come over to his dad's on the weekends praying that Duke would come by. Whenever he did, Vaughan would have to restrain himself from confessing his love, knowing Duke wouldn't reciprocate. Would have nothing to do with a kid. At that age, Vaughan couldn't have taken being laughed or cooed at for having a—what grownups considered—puppy love crush on the older man. Instead, he'd observed Duke from afar. Touched himself as he watched Duke and his dad play catch in the backyard. Daydreamed about Duke sneaking into his room while everyone else was downstairs enjoying the barbeque. Shit. He had a ton of

PROMISES

jerk off material. He paused mid-stroke, his back arching from the intense feeling of anticipating having Duke soon. He wouldn't beat off. Not now. He'd wait. Let all the pent up want and need for the man he was destined to have build until he got what he had desired for so long.

He'd just known that when he came home Duke would be playing house with that big bastard, Judge. Imagine his surprise when he called during finals last year and his father told him that Judge had fallen in love with someone else and chose to end the "arrangement" he had with Duke. Vaughan had wanted to pump his fist in victory, knowing that Judge had been his only real competition. But his celebration was short-lived when his dad told him how upset Duke was. He'd told him that he tried to hide it from everyone, but when he thought no one was looking, Duke got a real forlorn look on his face. It took everything in Vaughan not to leave school right then and run back to Atlanta to comfort Duke. He couldn't, not then. He had to be a man when he went back, wouldn't give Duke an excuse to associate him with the kid he was when he saw him last. He was tall like his father, six-two, built strong, with tightly packed muscles, cropped dark hair that required little product, and then his best asset… his mind. He was brilliant. "A force to be reckoned with," his law school mentor would say.

Now he was back to finally claim his reward. While he wasn't a virgin by any means—he needed to be good when he got Duke, wanted to know how to give him the pleasure he deserved, but Vaughan had never given his heart to anyone.

"You want breakfast?" his father called out from the kitchen after Vaughan had poured himself a cup of coffee.

"Sure. Just something quick. I have to be there by nine." Vaughan smoothed down his pale pink and ivory striped tie. He opened up the newspaper already on the table and went for the finance section first to check on his stocks, that would be quickly followed by the real estate section, so he could find his own place.

"You're dressed like a model, not a DA," his dad said, setting a plate of fluffy scrambled eggs and toast in front of him. "Where'd you get that suit?"

"Barcelona. Why? What's wrong with it?" Vaughan looked down at the charcoal gray, immaculately tailored suit. His light pink, collared shirt matched the tie perfectly. His gray Donna Karan lace-up oxford dress shoes set off the entire look.

"Nothing's wrong with it. It's nice. Real sharp."

"You think Duke will like it?" Vaughan said cheekily.

His dad groaned loud, plopping down in the chair next to him. "You're still intending on going through with this plan."

"I most certainly am, and you said you wouldn't intervene."

"I know what I said. I just… I don't…."

"Spit it out, Dad."

"I don't want you to get hurt."

"I can handle this."

"Duke's had eyes for only one man as long as I've known him. And even though Judge is gone, I haven't seen Duke date anyone else, even glance at another man. He might still be pinning." Vaughan watched his father run his hands through his overgrown hair. "I don't want him using you as a rebound guy or some boy toy."

Vaughan frowned, setting down the paper. "You really think that's the kind of man your friend is?"

"No." Quick sighed.

"Okay, then." Vaughan went back to eating, careful not to get any crumbs on himself. "Just leave it to me, I'll gauge if he's still hung up on that dumbass."

PROMISES

"Judge is far from dumb."

"He left Duke for someone else... that spells dumb to me."

"Boy, you've got it bad." His dad laughed at him. "I can't believe I gave you all those updates on Duke when I should've been discouraging this whole crush thing."

Vaughan poured his dad some more coffee, getting his attention. "First off. This is not a crush. Second. I need you to support this, or else Duke will fight it." Vaughan looked at his dad pointedly. "You promised."

Quick waved him off. "I know. I know. I'm not against it, okay."

"Not against doesn't mean support."

"Vaughan, I said okay. Go now. You're gonna be late."

Vaughan grabbed his briefcase. "Remember. Don't tell Duke I'm coming by today."

"You're a tool." His dad laughed again.

"Shut up," Vaughan yelled on his way to the front door. "Catch you later, Pops."

Vaughan drove back on I85 in his rented Audi taking the Peoplestown exit and heading towards Duke's new office. He was glad to hear they'd relocated to Atlanta, because he wasn't excited about going back to Charleston or being that close to his hovering mother, either. It's why he chose to leave home right after high school, and why he chose a college in DC instead of Duke or UNC. He'd always wondered if his mom resented him for looking so much like his father. No mistaking she took good care of him, but she wasn't physically affectionate. Couldn't hug him, kiss him; hell, couldn't stare at him too long without looking away. His dad had hurt her bad when he left, but Vaughan understood. They'd had a one-night stand that ended with her pregnant and her father holding a shotgun at Quick's back while they stood in front of the justice and the peace. Quick

PROMISES

had decided after Vaughan turned sixteen that he could still be a good father while not being married to Vaughan's mom. As a kid, he had always been mature, so his dad explained it to him, and he quickly understood.

He parked in the almost empty parking lot. He recognized his father's Range Rover and a large F350 with Duke's logo on the tailgate. Had to be his truck. He was about to see Duke again, for the first time in… He was breathing heavily and trying to calm his racing heart. He couldn't walk in and start swooning.

It's game time. Get yourself together.

PROMISES

CHAPTER FOUR

Duke went into the kitchen to grab another soda from the refrigerator. His head was pounding and all the caffeine probably wasn't helping, but it was giving him a boost since he'd gotten very little sleep the night before. Quick got in around ten and was all smiles, singing Vaughan's praises like he was up for sale at an auction.

He looked around for Charlie, but didn't see him at his desk. Their spacious office was a gutted-out warehouse that they'd had renovated. Now each guy had his own workspace sans any walls. Only Duke's office was closed off in the back. Quick was at his desk going over a contract with another bail bondsman that they sometimes hired as an outside contractor to retrieve their bail skippers.

Duke walked over to him. "Hey. Where's everyone at?"

Quick took off his reading glasses and looked up at him. "Dana, he's sick. Called off this morning. A couple of the guys are out doing surveillance and Charlie went to County to bail out Ricardo and his girlfriend again."

"Again?" Duke barked a laugh.

"Yep. They got picked up last night on 13th street for disturbing the peace and indecent exposure." Quick laced his hands on top of his head and reared back in his chair, his thick arms bulging underneath his white Polo, Duke's logo on the breast.

"Damn. Those two can keep me in business by themselves."

"Tell me about it." Quick yawned. "At least they show up for court, though."

"True." Duke got up and headed back to his office. "You look worn out, buddy. Why don't you head out, start an early weekend? I got this covered."

"That actually sounds pretty good. But...."

Before Quick could finish his sentence their front door opened, and Duke almost dropped his soda when his eyes feasted on the gorgeous male specimen that had just stepped through it. Just about the same height as him, but decked out like a GQ model. Even his aviator sunglasses looked expensive. Who the fuck was this guy? His lip was turned up in a half-smile, half cocky smirk as he stared just as hard back at Duke.

Duke finally pried his eyes off the man to look at Quick for an explanation. His friend was shaking his head at him like he'd lost his mind. "It's been that long since you seen my boy, Duke?"

Shit. Boy, my ass. "There's no way that's Vaughan," Duke said, more so to himself.

Not realizing he'd said it loud enough for anyone to hear, Vaughan began walking towards him. His gait was full of masculine confidence and maturity. Duke swallowed when Vaughan completely ignored his father's work area and came straight in his direction. He pulled off his sunglasses and Duke just controlled his gasp. Beautiful, bedroom hazel eyes framed by long, dark lashes, locked solely on him. His beard was perfectly trimmed, but still gave his beauty a bit of ruggedness.

Fuck.

"Hello Duke."

Oh shit. There was that voice. The same one from the phone. Only there was no background noise and no filter from the phone lines. Duke didn't think it possible for Vaughan to sound any sexier than he did the night before. He was wrong.

Instead of Vaughan giving him the handshake Duke was expecting, Vaughan gathered him in his arms and pulled him in tight. Duke instinctively brought his arms up and hugged him back. He refrained from closing his eyes, although the smell of fresh, clean-scented cologne assaulted every one of his senses. When Vaughan spoke again, his deep voice was right at the base of his ear, and Duke was that he felt his lips tickling the fine hairs on his neck. "It's really good to see you, Duke." The words were spoken so wistfully they made him want to moan. Vaughan's strong hands rubbed down his back, lingering before squeezing right above his hip. Duke forced a step back, remembering the kid's father was in the room with them. Chancing a peek over Vaughan's broad shoulder, he saw that, sure enough, Quick was watching them, his expression unreadable. Duke dropped his arms and put some distance between Vaughan and himself, backing almost into his office.

"Yeah. It's good to see you too, Vaughan. It's been a long time. I hardly recognized you."

Vaughan unbuttoned his suit jacket and tucked one hand inside his pants pocket. He nodded his head, his eyes boring into him. He needed to say something, anything, to clear the tension in the air. Duke turned and looked back in his office at the black box with the gold ribbon sitting on his desk. "I, uh. I got you something." Duke nervously ran his hand through his salt-and-pepper hair. "A sort of belated graduation gift."

Vaughan's smile was downright sinful. "How sweet of you."

Duke tried to shrug nonchalantly. "I'll get it for you." He turned and walked into his office, had just reached his desk when he heard his door shut behind him. With the small box in his hand, he spun around and saw that Vaughan had closed them inside. He took his time looking around at the books and picture frames on the wall-to-wall shelves. Long, graceful fingers skimmed the bindings of one of Duke's favorite books: To Kill a Mockingbird. "I've read this too many times to count." Vaughan finally spoke. "We seem to have similar taste."

Ignoring that statement, Duke chose to talk about something else. "Your dad said you had an interview this morning. How'd it go?"

"Looks like I'm gonna be working in the DA's office. It was my first choice after passing the bar, so I'm happy about it."

"Wow. Congratulations. You must be…." Duke's voice tapered off as Vaughan walked over to him. His rear was against his desk so there was nowhere to go. He held the box in front of him, thinking again that it was boxed like a diamond bracelet was inside and wrapped like something you'd present to a lover. Vaughan stood only a few inches away, so Duke extended the box to him.

Vaughan's gaze never wavered from his as he pulled gently at the bow until it unraveled, and slowly lifted the lid off. When Vaughan finally looked down in the box, a soft, genuine smile appeared on that beautiful face. "This is great, Duke. I like it. A lot." Duke watched Vaughan remove the monogramed, Parker Duofold black ballpoint executive ink pen and read the elegant cursive script along the side, Vaughan Webb, Esquire.

With his eyes back on Duke's, Vaughan took the pen and slid it easily inside his suit coat pocket. "My only graduation gift. I'm glad it was from you."

Duke went to open his mouth but Vaughan inched in closer, his eyes appearing to be obsessed with Duke's lips. His voice was raspy and low when he spoke again. "I've traveled all over Europe for two years, Duke. In Eastern Europe, they kiss on every occasion. They kiss to say hello, goodbye, to congratulate, to comfort, and especially to say thank you."

Duke's eyes fluttered slightly as Vaughan's chest barely touched his. That damn scent was causing his dick to quickly take interest. He should've pushed Vaughan back, but he didn't want to overreact. He wasn't even sure Vaughan was gay. There was nothing wrong with saying thank you for a gift, right?

Next thing he knew, Vaughan's soft hand was on his neck, his grip light but controlling. He pulled Duke in and at the last second before their lips could touch, Vaughan averted his head and grazed Duke's cheek with his own beard stubbled one, pausing to place a gentle, lingering kiss there. His lips were as silky and smooth as satin. Still keeping the contact around his neck, Vaughan pulled back just enough to leave a ghost of hot breath over Duke's mouth to get to the other side. He kissed him there too, but this time he lingered even longer. Whispering a warm, "Thank you," against his ear.

A breathy, "You're welcome," was all Duke could muster.

No sooner did Vaughan step back and put some much-needed space between them, than Quick's abrupt knock sounded right before he came through the door. "I'm not interrupting anything am I?"

Duke quickly got behind his desk and sat down, hoping to avoid anyone noticing the considerable bulge in his pants. "No, Quick. I was just giving Vaughan his gift."

"Uh-huh. Well I'm gonna head on home now. Vaughan, I'll see you when you get there."

Vaughan didn't take his eyes off Duke, even when he responded to his father. "Sure thing."

Quick gave Duke a conspiratorial wink which he had no clue to the meaning of before he closed the door. Looking back at Vaughan's sexiness wasn't an option, so Duke pushed around a few files on his desk.

"Why don't you come over to my father's place tonight? We're gonna watch a movie or something. Just chill out."

"I don't want to impose on you and your dad's time, kid." Duke moved around some more files until the dead silence in the room finally made him look up. He didn't like the look on

Vaughan's face. It wasn't an angry one, but a look that clearly displayed irritation and annoyance. Duke tried to recall what he'd just said. "Your dad's been waiting a long while to have this time to spend with you. I just want to give y'all some space. I'll probably hang out tomorrow. Who knows?"

Vaughan buttoned his suit jacket and turned to leave. Before he got to the door, his back went ramrod straight, and he turned and strode back over to Duke, walking around his desk, bending until their faces were inches apart. His eyes were like fire, blazing a searing path over Duke's face. "I'm not a fuckin' kid, Duke," Vaughan hissed. His eyes softened for a second. "The sooner you realize that, the happier you'll be."

Duke watched Vaughan walk out the door, leaving that amazing scent to linger in his office. He spun in his chair, leaning back to take a deep breath. What did he mean? The happier I'll be? No. He can't be saying that. Why would he be interested in some old man when he could clearly have anyone he wanted? When Charlie stuck his head in Duke's office door, he had no clue how long he'd been staring into space.

"Boss, you wanted to see me?"

Duke sighed tiredly. "Yeah, Charlie. Come on in and close the door, buddy."

"Everything went fine down at processing this morning. Sorry it took me a while to get back; I had a doctor's appointment and then stopped to pick up my prescriptions. They gave me a hard time down there again."

"You're not having any problems with your insurance are you?" Duke leaned in.

"No. No. They just need to get a newer system."

"Are you okay?"

"Yeah. Cholesterol's a tad high and my knee still locks up every now and then. Side effects of getting old, boss."

"Tell me about it." Duke huffed.

PROMISES

Charlie waved him off, looking at him like he was crazy. "Old, my aching ass. You're in your prime, buddy. Man. I was something else in my early forties. Still could turn a gal on the dance floor like it was no one's business. Your dad and I pulled all the honeys in our day."

Duke smiled while Charlie reminisced. He never minded hearing Charlie's stories about him and their other friends. That's why it was killing Duke to have to do what he was about to.

"I'm glad you called me in here, Boss. I believe it's time to hang up my hat. I've done this job for almost fifty damn years. I come in whenever my old bones can get me out of bed, and you've been real understanding."

"You're family, Charlie."

"No. You're the boss. But you're also your father's son. He was the loyalist, most dedicated man I've ever had the honor of calling a friend. You are a spitting image, Duke. That's why you've humored this old bird as long as you have. But I hear what the guys are saying about me."

"Damn that! I run this place. You can stay as long as you want to, Charlie."

Charlie laughed. "There's the Duke, Sr. I miss so much. Maybe I hung around as long as I did because I miss your father a lot and you remind me so much of him."

Duke stood and came around his desk. Charlie rose and they embraced for a moment. "You're welcome here anytime. You know that."

"Yeah. I do know."

"I'm gonna put together the best damn retirement package you've ever seen. So good, you'll be able to retire in the Caribbean if you want to."

"Alright then. I ain't gon' complain about that." Charlie clapped Duke on his shoulder. He couldn't believe how fate had worked it all out. He didn't have to switch Charlie to light duty.

PROMISES

He'd decided on his own that he was ready to retire. Now Duke needed to contact his insurance company to make sure Charlie kept his coverage and then he'd get his retirement benefits ready. But first... Duke had a retirement party to plan.

Duke sat at a gay-friendly bar a couple blocks from Quick's house, undecided if he was going to accept Vaughan's invitation. He'd felt so much better when he finally left the office, he didn't want to go home and be alone. It was nearing seven, it wouldn't look that pathetic if he popped up, he did all the time before Vaughan came home. Vaughan. Jesus.

It was clear that Duke had hit a nerve when he called Vaughan a kid. He hated how much he loved it when Vaughan got upset, too. It was sexy as shit. He couldn't possibly take all the flirty innuendo seriously. Vaughan was more than ten years younger than Duke. There's no way that could work out. Even worse was that everyone would think he was getting even with Judge if he got a young guy of his own.

Duke groaned and motioned for another Crown and Coke.

"Looks like you're drowning your troubles," the cute bartender said, setting down the fresh drink. The guy looked like he was just barely legal to serve alcohol. "What's a handsome man like you doing sitting here all alone?"

Duke wanted to turn around to see if the guy was talking to someone else. Damn sure couldn't have been talking to him.

"I like your hair," the slim man said, leaning heavily against the bar, his black-outlined baby blue eyes eating up Duke's face and chest. "Your hair looks silver, not gray. Maybe it's the lighting, but it's really hot. Reminds me of Max on that MTV show: Catfish."

Duke frowned. "I have no clue what you're talking about."

The guy laughed, playfully hitting Duke on his forearm. "Probably not, but just know the guy has this silver and black hair that looks out of control and natural. It's the hottest thing I've ever seen."

Duke took another sip. "Well thank you. I think."

"So, is your wife… or dare I presume… husband, coming to meet you soon?" The guy licked his lips and Duke thought he was dreaming. The kid really was coming on to him. Had to be young because that was the cheesiest pick up line he'd heard in a while.

"Um." Duke chuckled. "No. No husband."

"That's a shame. A man as fine as you is thinking of going home alone."

Duke pulled out his wallet and dropped enough to cover his tab and leave a considerable tip. "I can't tell you how flattering this has all been. But I need to get moving."

"You sure?"

Duke looked up into sincere eyes. This is unbelievable. If he was that irresistible, why had Judge chosen another? Refusing to go down that road just then, Duke nodded his head.

"Okay, then. I'm here until two if you change your mind. The name's Sean."

"Thanks, Sean. Catch you later."

"Oh, I hope so, handsome."

Duke left the bar thinking that if he got that scrawny guy in his bed, he'd break him in half. But Vaughan on the other hand… His thoughts trailed to something dirty and primal as he walked to his truck. He was going to accept Vaughan's invite. He wanted to see if Vaughan was just playing with him like that sweet bartender wanted to… for just one night of fun in bed. Or if Vaughan was wanting more. He hoped it was the latter. Duke didn't bed hop.

As soon as he closed his truck door and pulled out his cell to call Quick and tell him he was coming over, it rang in his hands. Damnit. He recognized the number as one from the Fulton County Jail. So much for his plans. Duty calls.

PROMISES

PROMISES

CHAPTER FIVE

Vaughan listened to his dad and Duke's conversation the next morning while he downed a protein shake and carved a grapefruit. He'd urged his dad to put it on speakerphone so he could hear Duke's voice. His dad rolled his eyes but hit the button.

"So the party is Sunday? This Sunday, as in tomorrow?"

"Yep." Duke's voice sounded distorted, like he was driving.

"Why so soon?"

"He's not coming in on Monday. His last day was Friday, and you know Charlie doesn't like too much fussing over him. So I've already hired caterers, a DJ, a cleaning crew, everything. All we have to do is show up. Some people are already at the office putting up minimal but tasteful decorations. Charlie has two friends that said they could definitely make it, then that leaves us... so why wait?"

"I guess you're right."

"Fine. I'm on my way to the Macy's at the mall after I have breakfast."

"The mall." Quick cringed.

"I need to pick up a jacket or something to wear tomorrow. Nothing fits me anymore and I don't want to only wear a collared shirt."

"You need some help?"

PROMISES

"I can manage, Quick. It's just a jacket. I was gonna come by last night but got called out to Fulton for a bond. Vaughan had invited me, so I thought I'd swing by." There was a pause before the background noise died down. "Hey, buddy. How's it been going with Vaughan?"

Vaughan's eyes widened. He gestured to his dad, not wanting to talk out loud. *Say great, say great.* He tried to mouth, but his dad obviously couldn't read lips.

"He's fine. Why?"

"Um. Nothing. Nothing at all. He just seems different now."

Vaughan really started gesturing. "Tell him I'm more mature," he whispered harshly.

His dad covered the speaker. "I'm not about to pimp you, Vaughan."

"Dad. Come on," he begged.

Vaughan watched his dad slap his hand to his forehead, groaning in irritation.

"Quick. Quick are you there?"

"Yeah, I'm here. I heard you, I was just checking the caller ID, thought I heard it beep. But, um. Vaughan—he has changed. He's the man I raised him to be. Smart, mature as hell. Focused, driven."

Vaughan gave his dad a thumbs up and a motion that said keep talking, which made Quick roll his eyes even harder.

"That's cool. I know you and Remy are proud as hell. A lawyer, that's pretty amazing."

"Yep. He showed me the pen you gave him. That was awesome, dude. Nice job. He was ecstatic."

Vaughan frowned at his dad.

Duke laughed and it made Vaughan smile. "I'm glad he liked it. Hey, um. Make sure to tell him he's invited to Charlie's retirement party."

"Sure will."

"Talk to you later, bud."

PROMISES

After the line went dead, Vaughan felt an amazing surge of energy.

"Son. I'm gonna ask you this one more time."

"Don't Dad. I confessed to you years ago that I had a thing for Duke. Always have. Nothing's changed."

"Why don't you want to wait and see if you meet someone in Atlanta? The market ain't bad out here. You could meet a nice young lawyer when you start your new job, anything could happen."

Vaughan just barely refrained from yelling. "I've been to the other side of the world and back and I've still never met a man like Duke. Key word is 'man.' I don't want some young guy that's most likely still in the closet or god knows what types of hang-ups and complexes he might have. Still wanting to party and binge drink all night. I don't have time for that shit." Vaughan frowned. "You keep saying you support me in this, but you keep trying to get me to change my mind."

His father stood and walked over to him. "I just want you to be happy."

"I know. But I won't be until I have Duke."

Quick breathed out slowly and nodded his head. "Okay, then."

Vaughan darted up the stairs.

"Hey. Where you going? I thought you were gonna work out."

"I need a new jacket for the party tomorrow."

He heard Quick's laughter before the reply. "You have more suit jackets than a congressman."

When Vaughan came back down twenty minutes later in a pair of jeans, an untucked beige collared shirt and a camel colored blazer, his dad whistled at him. "Let me guess. You're going to Macy's."

Vaughan winked, tucking his wallet in his back pocket. "Not usually where I shop, but I'm sure I'll find something."

PROMISES

"I'm sure you will," Quick said softly, still nursing his coffee.

Vaughan went over and looked down at him. He was still a magnificent man. Why he chose to stay home night after night and not date was beyond Vaughan's understanding. His father was tall, thick upper body and lean hips, built just like him. His hair was a little gray at the temples, but was still long and full. His tattoos were cool as shit and went up both arms. He could surely pull a hottie. What was his deal? "Why don't me and you go paint the town red tonight, huh? It's the weekend, let's let loose."

His dad looked up at him with an identical charming smile to the one that he saw in the mirror each day. "Really. Just me and you?"

"Just me and you."

"Sounds good." His father clapped his big hands together and rubbed them like he was already set to go. "Father and son on the prowl."

"I'll be back soon. We'll start at a happy hour somewhere and see where the night takes us," he said, almost to the front door.

"You got it." Was the answer he barely heard when he was already half-way out the door.

CHAPTER SIX

Duke hated malls with a passion, but sometimes they were a necessary evil. He went in through the mall entrance and fought the weekend crowds to get to Macy's. He didn't shop much, but he heard that Macy's had a nice selection of men's business and casualwear. Maybe a bottle of cologne would be a good idea, too. Duke was just able to keep himself from smiling. He felt like he was going on his first date. He remembered fussing over his outfits, pulling everything he had out of the closet. His dad had got tired of him trying stuff on and ended up calling his mom over to help him. They were divorced most of his life, but they had stayed good friends.

He always thought he'd be married by his age. Maybe even with a child, who knew. He thought it'd be Judge, for sure. Although they never actually dated, went out in public or whatever, he was fine with that. He thought it simply wasn't Judge's way. Even though *he* wanted those things: date night, sharing a tub of popcorn at the movies, making out together in a dark booth at a jazz club, holding hands on the beach as the sun set. Duke had thought that as long as he had Judge at home, it'd work out. He'd since realized how wrong he was. Judge knew what Duke really wanted, and instead of stringing him along, he dropped him. It had hurt more than he cared to let on, but he was a big boy. Life went on.

PROMISES

Looking around in Macy's gave him a tension headache. There weren't a lot of people in the men's department, but he was never good at picking clothes. A nice lady in a startling white ruffled blouse and a black pleated skirt came up to him. "Can I help you?"

Duke fingered through the shirts on the rack. "Actually, I'm just looking."

"I can help him if he needs it, Cindy. Thank you." A strong voice cut over the young lady. Duke looked up and saw a man in a nice suit standing on the other side of the rack. His Macy's name tag said Mark R. Duke smiled and told him the same thing as Cindy scurried off, doing little to hide her annoyance.

"Really, I'm good. Don't let me waste your time." He kept looking through the shirts and chose a blue and white striped one along with a dark blue blazer.

"That looks pretty good. I can do some measurements if you want." Mark R. looked up and down Duke's body, making him feel exposed.

"I'll just try them on." Duke hoped his fake smile was convincing. He pointed towards the back of the department and asked, "Fitting rooms over there?"

The guy gave him a suggestive smile and tilted his head in the same direction. "I'll be right here if you need anything."

Duke didn't acknowledge that. He kept walking, thinking he might need to try a different store. What was with everyone lately? Was his dick size advertised on his forehead? Was he wearing a sign that said, "I'll bottom so hard for you"? What the fuck?

Duke hung the new shirt and jacket on the hook and began to take off his shirt. He laid it carefully on the bench before removing his undershirt. There was a light tap on his dressing room door.

"Are you fuckin' kiddin' me?" Duke grumbled quietly. "I said I'm good, sir."

PROMISES

A second later the door opened and Duke was about to curse until he saw it was Vaughan. "What the hell?"

"I told your little admirer out there that I'd take it from here," Vaughan said sensually, closing the door behind him.

"What are you doing here?" Duke said breathily.

"I'm stalking you," Vaughan said in an evil cartoon villain voice that made Duke laugh nervously.

"Cute," Duke said, noticing that Vaughan's eyes were roaming all over his chest. "Eyes up here."

Vaughan let loose his own sexy chuckle and looked up to Duke's eyes. With his back against one side of the dressing room, Vaughan brought one hand up and placed it against the wall next to Duke's head. Duke felt like his heart was going to beat out of his chest when Vaughan leaned in to him and ran his nose down his neck. "Does it bother you when I look at you like that, Duke?"

Duke cleared his throat. He wasn't sure he could speak English just then.

"Because I know no other way to look. Especially at you. I haven't seen you with your shirt off since you went to my dad's beach party when I was twenty-two."

"W-what? You remember that?" Duke looked confused.

Vaughan nudged Duke's cheek, speaking against his rough beard. "I remember that and so much more. I also remember you asking me why I wasn't playing volleyball or swimming."

Duke closed his eyes. Vaughan was so close. That alluring fresh scent dominating the small room. He wanted to put his arms around him, but refrained. "I think I remember that."

Vaughan ran his other hand up Duke's chest. "I'll tell you now. I couldn't get up because my dick was hard as fuck. I watched you the whole time, so close to coming I thought I would die. Couldn't take my eyes off you then." Vaughan breathed a puff of air against Duke's mouth. "Still can't take my eyes off you."

"I've got to be dreaming," Duke whispered.

Vaughan smiled, his forehead pressed against Duke's. "Open your eyes."

"I don't want to wake up," Duke replied, completely lost in the feeling.

Duke heard the sound of a belt clicking and the rustling of fabric. He still didn't open his eyes. He felt his hand grabbed and he didn't fight it as Vaughan pushed Duke's hand down the front of his jeans, inside his boxers.

"Oh, fuck," Duke hissed. His eyes rolled behind his closed lids. Vaughan groaned and pressed into his palm. Keeping his own hand over top of his, pressing Duke's hand down. His cock was hot and hard. Duke closed his hand around it, marveling at the length. *Fuckin' perfect.* Vaughan bit him lightly on his neck.

"You feel that, Duke? I'm not a goddamn kid. I'm not playing games. I'm not trying to tease you. I want you. I wanted you then. I want you even more now."

"Jesus. Vaughan, I never knew." Duke was completely winded. "I didn't even know you were gay. I don't know a goddamn thing anymore."

"I *knew* what you wanted. I knew you'd want a man. So I came back to you when I became one. I could've chosen any city in the world. Why do you think I'm here?" Vaughan pressed against Duke's palm again. "Fuck, I've waited so long for this. Don't deny me, Duke. I can make you happy."

Duke was overwhelmed. He couldn't believe any of this. The strikingly beautiful man had been wanting him for years, and was here now, begging him. He still felt he was gonna be the butt of a very bad joke. He needed to get Vaughan out of his space and think for a while. *Shit. What about Quick? He'd never go for this.*

Vaughan slowly removed Duke's hand. "I don't want to pressure you. I just don't want you to say no so quickly. Think about it. Maybe let me take you on a couple dates and then you can decide if you want to see me. Just give me that much."

Duke looked down at Vaughan's cock, mesmerized. As if hearing Duke's thoughts, Vaughan pulled his briefs lower and righted his long cock so just the head was sticking out of the waistband. A clear bead of precome had formed over the slit and Duke licked his lips before he could think not to.

"Mmm. My thoughts exactly, sweetheart. But I always told myself I would be a gentleman with you. So I'm not gonna push you to your knees here in a Macy's dressing room. You are so much more to me than that. I'm gonna court you." Vaughan stroked Duke's cheek with the back of his hand. "Woo you until you agree to be mine."

Vaughan sure as hell talked like a real man. A man that watched a lot of Humphrey Bogart movies, maybe. He was smooth, debonair, and so charming Duke couldn't refuse. It was everything he'd wanted in a partner. To feel cherished and wanted. He hoped it could be real. He wanted to drop to his knees and take that flushed head into his mouth, all the way to the back of his throat, but he was still just clearheaded enough to know he needed to speak to Quick first.

"Let's get out of here, hmm?" Vaughan kissed Duke's cheek. "Find you something nice to wear for tomorrow, and then I think I have just enough time to take you to lunch before I have to get back home."

Duke was still looking at Vaughan's cock when he swallowed hard and nodded his head in agreement.

"But how about just a little taste of what's yours." Vaughan smothered in closer to Duke's body, pressing his cock against his own, trapped achingly in his pants. Vaughan reached down and gathered the clear bead of fluid off the tip of his dick with his thumb, another bead quickly forming as soon as he did.

"Oh my god." Duke moaned.

PROMISES

"Open up, sweetheart," Vaughan purred in that voice that made Duke leak. He wiped the sticky fluid across Duke's bottom lip before pushing his thumb inside. Duke unashamedly sucked on it like he was man dying of thirst. "That's it, baby."

Duke wrapped his arms around Vaughan's waist and held him as tight to him as he dared. With his eyes squeezed shut, he sucked every trace of Vaughan's essence off his thumb before finally releasing the digit. His breathing was erratic and labored again. He wanted and needed so badly he hurt. He heard Vaughan righting himself and buckling his belt. He tried to get himself under control; he couldn't go back out there in his condition.

"Calm down. Breathe," Vaughan whispered. Taking a few deep breaths himself.

When they were both presentable, Vaughan took the clothes he'd never tried on and politely gave them to Mark R., saying they didn't fit. Duke didn't make eye contact with the store clerk as he let Vaughan lead him to another section of the store. The price tags were considerably higher, but he paid little attention as Vaughan carefully put an outfit together for him, his eyes focused on every pattern and color. While Vaughan was purchasing a pair of cufflinks of his own, Duke went over to the fragrance counter and began to look around.

The older man behind the counter told him of the sales they had going on and to let him know if he wanted to smell something. Duke said a quick thank you and began picking up a few of the testers on the counter.

It was as if he felt Vaughan's heat before he pressed into his back, pushing Duke into the counter. Duke didn't look around to see who was watching. He didn't give a fuck. It felt too good to let worry seep in and cloud the moment.

"Can I ask you a personal question?" Vaughan whispered against the side of Duke's neck.

PROMISES

"I don't see why not." Duke licked his bottom lip for the hundredth time since he'd come out of that dressing room, hoping there was still an inkling of some of Vaughan's precome that he may have missed. He knew he was going to be addicted after he got his first real taste. *Damn. I hope Quick is cool with this. For the love of god.*

"Do you top or bottom?"

Duke choked. Damn, that was *very* personal. He should've known Vaughan was thinking of sex, because he sure was. That long, slender cock looked absolutely perfect for him. Duke was a bottom through and through, but a man didn't have to have a damn beer-can-dick in order to get him off. He preferred a nice smooth, easy fit.

"I have a feeling I already know. But humor me. Have I been right all these years? You're a big assed, strong, sexy bottom aren't you?"

Duke smiled shyly. He felt like a guy getting hit on by the most popular kid in school. Vaughan did that sexy chuckle against the back of his neck. "I knew it."

"Yeah. I mostly bottom," Duke admitted, picking up another cologne bottle, hoping he wasn't blushing too hard. "Does that mean you *only* top?" Duke had a lover that primarily topped before. Judge had never, ever bottomed for him. Had downright refused it. Even though Duke thought there was nothing better than a hard cock driving into his ass, he still had a cock of his own, and he liked to use it sometimes.

Vaughan used his pointer finger on Duke's chin to turn his head towards him. When he spoke, his lips danced across the corner of his mouth. Duke wondered if there was anything Vaughan did that wasn't sexy. "No. I don't *only* top. But for you. I'll do anything you want me to do."

"Damnit. Don't say things like that, Vaughan."

"I have to speak the truth. No games, no lies, no teasing. Remember?"

PROMISES

Duke nodded his head, his words evading him again. When the clerk came back over, he glanced at their positioning but kept his face friendly. "Have you decided on something, sir?"

"May I?" Vaughan interjected.

"By all means," Duke said. He was so ready to get out of the store anyway, and after smelling a few bottles, he had no idea what he wanted.

"A gift set of your *Bleu De Chanel, s'il vous plaît*." Vaughan spoke with a perfect French accent.

Duke was very impressed and he hoped he'd played it cool. But if he was being totally honest with himself... he was Vaughan's already.

CHAPTER SEVEN

"What about her?" Vaughan tossed back his fifth shot and pointed out a beautiful redhead to his dad. He'd pointed out about ten very different women and his father shot each one down, barely looking in their directions. "What's with you?"

"Nothing. I just want to enjoy a night out with my son without a lot of distractions."

Vaughan studied at his drinking partner for a while. "Aren't you lonely?"

He got a serious look in return. "Not anymore."

Vaughan understood. He was gonna have to be careful and make sure he didn't dedicate every bit of his time to Duke. Even though he'd missed the man like crazy, his father had been missing him just as much. Vaughan was a smart guy; he could figure the situation out, make everyone happy. Him, his father, and Duke.

"Alright big guy. Let's get the hell out of here. The music is giving me a headache anyway."

"Here. Here," Quick agreed.

He finished the last of his beer and went up to pay the tab. The quaint hole-in-the-wall in the heart of Atlanta was a hidden gem he'd heard about through the grapevine. The food was great, and while the music was good, old school stuff, it was a little louder than what he expected. The crowd was low key and

PROMISES

people were nice, though. He got a lot of interested looks, mostly from women. He simply returned a slight smile and turned away. He was already taken. His father on the other hand... What was his deal? Vaughan would eventually want to build a life with Duke; he couldn't be his father's companion. He needed to find his own, even if it wasn't for anything serious. At the age of forty-nine, he still had some miles left in him. Since his parents were only teens when they'd been forced to marry, his father had missed out on a lot. Vaughan wanted some happiness for him.

"Let's pop Armageddon in the Blu-ray and veg out on the couch," his father suggested happily, throwing his denim jacket on.

Vaughan mock groaned. "Armageddon again! We've watched it a million times." It was their favorite; they could watch that movie a million more times and still be just as engrossed as the first time they watched it.

"You love it. Come on let's go."

Duke made a third attempt to clip on his gold cufflinks. His collared shirt was white with fine tan pinstripes. He left the top button undone and the hem untucked—just as he'd been instructed. The camel colored Ralph Lauren blazer brought out the tan pinstripes and was the exact length of his shirt. It went perfectly with the faded denim jeans and his brown Clarks casual shoes. He looked in his full-length mirror. He hardly recognized himself. He had to admit, he looked pretty good. His usual ensembles consisted primarily of jeans and t-shirts. With the occasional Polo shirt on special occasions.

He put a small glop of mousse in his hand and tamed his silver locks, simply finger combing them back. His freshly cut edges and sideburns didn't hurt the look at all. Putting a couple dabs of Bleu De Chanel on the skin just above his collar, he was set to go.

PROMISES

His condo was only a few miles from his office. He had another bail bond taking his calls—if any came—tonight, so they could all have a great time with no interruptions. His phone buzzed when he got in his truck. He adjusted the temperature before pulling out his cell. His smile was broad when he saw the sender.

He and Vaughan had exchanged numbers at lunch the previous day. They'd kept the conversation light and used it as an opportunity to get to know each other all over again, as two grown men. He hadn't been home for more than an hour after their outing before he got an "I'm thinking of you" text. It wasn't cheesy or childish. It made Duke feel special. It'd been a long time since he'd been made to feel like that. He read the text.

I'm sure you look good enough to eat
VW

Duke shook his head. The kid was gonna kill him. He wanted Vaughan to do so many dirty things to him, it bordered on illegal. Before he pulled out of his parking lot, he typed a quick response.

You did good on the selection. I hope you like it.
D

When nothing else came, Duke pulled out into traffic and was at his office in less than ten minutes. The parking lot wasn't full, but he quickly recognized Judge's truck, especially since Bookem was lying down in the small patch of grass next to the building. He knew Judge would come. He and Charlie had a nice working relationship whenever Judge had floated in to the office. Judge considered Charlie a friend, so there wasn't a reason to suspect he wouldn't be at this party. Was he ready to see Judge again? It'd been a few months since he'd seen him, since Duke had limited their interactions to phone conferences only. He could do it. That part of his life was over, there was no reason to dwell on the what could've beens. Judge had Detective Austin Michaels now, and just maybe, Duke had Vaughan.

PROMISES

Bookem ran over to him as soon as he got out of his truck and aggressively licked his hand while Duke patted the big Dane around his flank. "Good to see you too, Books."

Walking inside, he saw that the place looked great. The decorations looked tastefully done. Charlie had on a suit with a nice button up shirt. His daughter and her family were around him talking, along with a couple of the guys. As soon as they saw him, Charlie waved him over. Duke cut a quick look at Judge, giving him a head nod in acknowledgement. The way Judge looked at him gave Duke an immeasurable surge of satisfaction. It added a little pep to his step. Judge must have thought he looked good because his eyes scanned him up and down, but Duke acted like he wasn't the least bit fazed.

Duke gave Charlie a big hug, asking him if he liked the decorations. Charlie was modest, but the gleam in his eyes told Duke all he needed to know. Charlie was proud and stunned that all of it was for him. Duke kissed Charlie's daughter on her cheek and Clara thanked him for everything he'd done for her father. Duke shook Clara's husband's hand as well.

Ignoring Judge's eyes on his back, he turned and went to the buffet that had been set up by the caterers and checked to see if everything was in order. He'd just popped a carrot stick in his mouth when he heard Judge right behind him.

"Wow. Don't you clean up nice."

Duke spun around. He kept his face impassive as he wiped his hand with one of the "Congratulations you're retired!" beverage napkins. Duke looked at Judge's usual black t-shirt and jeans and smirked back at him. "Thanks."

Judge looked uncomfortable, so Duke broke the strained silence. "So where's Michaels?"

"Work. Of course. He might make it over later."

"Good. I've only had the pleasure of meeting him once. How's everything going at the house? All the renovations done?"

PROMISES

Judge drank out of his red Solo cup before he answered. "Yeah. It's awesome, man. We'd love to have you over."

Duke smiled broadly. "Work's been insane, but I'd love to see what you've done with the place."

"Just like I thought. Good enough to eat."

Duke saw the frown crease Judge's face before Duke turned towards Vaughan's passionate voice. Duke's smile was shy and he knew he was turning a shade of rose, especially when Vaughan shouldered past Judge and stood directly in front of Duke as if his sole purpose for being there was to be near him. He gave Duke another European kiss, on both cheeks, lingering like he'd done before to whisper in his ear. "Two minutes alone with you, please."

Duke cleared his throat and Vaughan stepped to the side. He looked stunning as usual, but Duke expected nothing less. His short hair was moussed and actually parted on the side. It made him look so distinguished, Duke wanted to put his arm around the man's waist and pull him close to his side. Instead, he pointed to Judge. "Vaughan. I don't know if you remember Judge Josephson." Duke pointed to Vaughan. "Judge this is Vaughan Webb, Quick's son. He's recently come to Atlanta after passing the bar to work in the DA's office."

"No shit," Judge deadpanned. "You're a lawyer? You don't look like one."

Vaughan's laugh was dry. "I'm not sure exactly how a lawyer looks."

"You just look a bit young."

Vaughan nodded once, his lips tight like there was a lot he wanted to say to Judge.

Oh boy. This isn't good. Judge and Duke weren't lovers anymore, but Judge had made it clear that Duke would always be a special friend to him. Now Judge was acting like Duke needed protecting.

PROMISES

CHAPTER EIGHT

There was so much Vaughan wanted to say to Judge that he was literally biting his tongue to the point of pain. He didn't like it at all when he'd come in to see Judge looking at Duke like he was a piece of prime rib. The guy had chosen another man over Duke. He didn't get to be greedy and feast his eyes on Vaughan's man too.

Since his father was consumed with congratulating Charlie, Vaughan took the opportunity to make his presence known. Duke had responded visibly to his kiss and he took it as a victory. Now Judge was giving him shit. The big bastard. If Vaughan were still in high school and weighed an extra hundred pounds, he'd invite Judge outside to the parking lot.

"Well, I'm not sure what you think a lawyer should look like, but I assure you; I am one."

"Hottest lawyer I've ever seen," Duke added, and Vaughan thought his chest would burst with pride. If he had been concerned about Duke hiding them, he wasn't anymore. Now he needed some alone time with him. He turned towards Duke and mouthed, "Your office." He left without saying anything else to Judge. He was irrelevant to Vaughan. He actually should be Judge's new best friend, because it was his stupidity that gave Vaughan the opportunity to be with Duke. If he and Duke were still sleeping together, Vaughan would have had to waste precious time trying to convince Duke to leave him. He gave that very little thought as he headed to Duke's office and closed himself inside to wait.

    The party was in full swing with just about everyone that was invited having showed up. The DJ played Charlie's favorites, all Bluegrass Country, and Vaughan was glad for the quietness of Duke's office. He really did appreciate all types of music, but those tunes had him thinking that someone should be sitting in a corner clicking spoons while another strummed a metal tool on a washboard. His mom always told him that he had an old soul; it's why he was so mature. But that music was a little *too* old school, even for him.

    As soon as Duke entered and closed the door behind him, Vaughan crowded into him, pushing him against the door. He buried his nose in Duke's neck, the tip of his tongue snaking out to lick him just under his collar. "Damn. You smell good."

    Duke murmured against his throat. "You do too. You look really nice tonight."

    Vaughan hummed. He rubbed against Duke's strong physique like a feline marking its mate with its scent. He wanted to absorb Duke. How did one manage that? He ran his fingers through the short strands just above Duke's neck. "Damn. I can't believe this is happening."

    Duke huffed an indignant laugh. "*You* can't believe it."

    Vaughan chuckled deeply. "Well, we can be shocked together. Hmm."

    "Will you kiss me?" Duke said on a choppy breath.

    Vaughan pulled back and smiled, gently cupping Duke's jaw. "When was the last time you were properly kissed?"

    Duke ducked his head but Vaughan tilted his chin back up. He needed to see those dark, soulful eyes, needed to see what Duke wanted, what he craved.

PROMISES

"Umm." Duke shrugged casually, but his eyes pleaded dramatically. "Couple years, I guess. Maybe more. Give or take."

"Fuck." Vaughan groaned. How could he make this perfect for Duke? "I really want to devour you right now. But there's a room full of people out there and there'll probably be a knock on your door any minute."

"Sorry. I know. I just—"

"Hey," Vaughan cut Duke off. "I'm gonna give you every damn thing you need and more, if you'll let me. But you've been thinking about the idea of me and you for what? A couple of days now?" Vaughan put both hands on Duke's neck, forcing him to look in his eyes. Wanted him to see his sincerity. He just barely brushed his lips across Duke's. "I've been thinking about this moment for almost fifteen years."

"Jesus Christ." Duke closed his eyes.

"Open," Vaughan ordered, and Duke easily complied. As soon as Duke was focused back on him, Vaughan pressed his lips more firmly against Duke's parted mouth and flicked his tongue against his bottom lip. "You taste so fuckin' good. No amount of fantasizing compares to this right now."

Duke's arms were around his waist holding on to him for dear life. How the fuck was it possible that he'd been hooking up with Judge for the past few years and hadn't been kissed. Vaughan didn't think he could've thought any less of Judge, but he did. Wouldn't kiss Duke, would only fuck him. That motherfucker. Duke adjusted his head to the other side and Vaughan tamped down those thoughts and oh so gently kissed Duke's supple mouth again. "Fuck," Vaughan hissed. "Enough. I can't... fuck. If we don't stop, I'm gonna have a huge damp spot on my pants that will not be easy to lie about. I've wanted this too much... too long, to do it here, like this."

Duke nodded his head in agreement, his eyes still cast downward at Vaughan's lips. He licked them, enjoying the gasp of breath Duke expelled. "I rode here with my dad, so I have to take him home. Can I take you out tomorrow night? A nice dinner, maybe a movie."

Duke smiled. "I'd like that."

After their night out, Vaughan was going to have to apologize for how hard he was going to fuck Duke. With a devious smile, Vaughan gave Duke one more kiss before he stepped back. "Goddamn, you look hot."

Duke blushed and Vaughan thought it was the most adorable thing in the world. He was getting ready to show Duke what it really meant to be in love. Both of them were floating on cloud nine after they left the office. Stolen touches while no one was looking. Discreet winks from across the room had Duke blushing and no one understanding why. Vaughan thought it was hilarious to see his man so flustered and buzzing with excitement. The best part about the rest of that night was that Duke hadn't paid a lick of attention to Judge.

CHAPTER NINE

Duke was thinking of going to Macy's to put together another outfit, but he didn't want to feel silly. He'd dress casual for his date that night. He wasn't gonna behave like some ridiculous kid with a crush and pull everything out of his closet. A pair of jeans and his corduroy blazer. Nothing wrong with that. He was sure all eyes would be on Vaughan anyway. He fixed himself a bologna and cheese sandwich and sat at his desk going over some of his guys' reports. All of them had to detail the sequence of events of every one of their bounty captures. Just in case anything was needed for court or if anyone tried to sue them.

Dana had pepper sprayed the last guy he picked up and the one before that, he'd tased. Duke was going to have to talk with Dana about his use of excessive force. Bounty hunters had very strict guidelines to follow, and unnecessary use of force was a sure way to get your license revoked or worse, get Duke fined.

A fax came in from a fellow bondsman that hired Duke's hunters to pick up his bail skips. Duke and Quick had gone over the contract last week and believed it was something they could handle. The guy was a violent offender and had been let out on a one hundred thousand dollar bond. Duke had a few of his guys doing surveillance on last known whereabouts but they hadn't gotten lucky yet. The bond agent was getting agitated and wanted Duke to pick up the pace, but he would not go out until he knew he could safely get the guy.

The fax confirmed that their bounty had been spotted at a house in The Bluffs off English Avenue. Crime central. Huge, abandoned homes and ransacked stores littered the area, addicts and dealers were in and out of buildings, whether occupied or vacant. It was a bad part of town and Duke knew it. He'd have to take a couple of the guys with him. Hopefully he could get the guy before dark, making it slightly less dangerous, and then of course, he'd be home in time to get ready for his date.

Duke picked up his phone and called Dana first. Although the guy still had a hoarse cough and nasal congestion that were bad enough to be heard through the phone line, he'd insisted that he wasn't letting Duke and Quick go to that neighborhood without him. Quick confirmed he'd be there in an hour. Duke went to his secured room and retrieved his two 9mm and his bulletproof vest. The gold bounty hunter's star suspended around his neck meant nothing to these guys. They'd fight like hell to keep their freedom. He tucked his TASER in the front of his pants; he'd most likely need it, too. Their primary goal was to bring the bounty back for imprisonment, not the morgue. While he waited next to his truck, he shot off a quick text to Vaughan, his heart already fluttering whenever he thought of him.

Got some work to do that came up suddenly, I might be a little late tonight

Duke waited for the response, which was almost instant.

As long as you're not cancelling.

I'll see you tonight. Got something special just for you.

Duke left it at that. *Oh my goodness. What did that mean?* Duke was hot, thinking about what that something special was. Whatever it was, he hoped it involved that long almost pale cock. Damn the man did serious things to his body, and they'd had very little actual physical contact. The way he looked at

PROMISES

Duke, the way he talked to him, the light touches all set him ablaze. He'd have a little conversation with Quick after they turned over their skip.

No sooner had he thought of him, than Quick pulled up in the truck they used to transport their bounties. "Hey, bud."

"Hey, man." Duke gave Quick a fist bump. "How'd you fare this morning, hmm? Looked like you'd put back quite a few last night."

Quick laughed that deep, gruff sound he made when he was genuinely amused. "I did, dude. That was a real nice event. Charlie looked real happy. I don't think I've ever seen the old man dance, but he wasn't half bad out there, twirling his daughter like that."

"Yeah. It was nice."

Quick glanced at him before dropping his bright green eyes to the asphalt. "Vaughan had a great time too. He was practically bouncing off the walls when we got home."

"Was he?" Duke tried to hide his shy smile and his blush.

"Mmm hmm. He was," Quick said teasingly.

Duke turned to face his best friend. "Look, Quick, I need to ask you—"

Before Duke could finish, Dana pulled up in his extremely loud tricked-out Chevy Nova. "Never mind. I'll tell you later."

"You guys ready to get grimy?" Dana chuckled, the act turning into a harsh cough. His usually handsome face was slightly pale and splotchy. His nose was swollen and red, like he'd been blowing it way too much. Duke checked his eyes, which appeared to be a little bloodshot, but that was most likely from lack of rest. He was in a bulletproof vest as well and looked prepared to do battle. They'd picked up enough skippers in The Bluffs that they knew it didn't always go smoothly.

"All right, guys. There may be very little activity going on down there now, so the daylight is our friend, the freaks come out at night." Duke smirked. "I've gotten a solid visual confirmation that our skip is at the address. It's a well-known meth dealing hot spot, so let's try to draw him out instead of us going in."

Quick and Dana both shook their heads in agreement. They didn't speak much on the thirty-minute drive there. All of them knowing they were venturing into dangerous drug and gang territory. Once they turned onto Murphy Ave. they saw a group of shady men posted outside a D&M Liquor store, smoking weed and drinking from brown paper bags. The way they followed their vehicle with their calculating gaze was more than a little unsettling. Most dealers could recognize law enforcement right away, no matter what vehicle they were in.

"We need to make this fast, boss," Dana said, his Sig Sauer resting in his lap. "Word will travel through here in no time."

"I know," Duke assured him. Quick slowed down and turned onto Bluff Street, parking a few houses down from where their skip was supposed to be.

"I say we go knock hard, count to three and bust in. If we sit here too long, we'll become a target," Quick advised, checking his own weapon, removing the safety.

Duke did the same. His guys were right. Eventually, someone would approach them, they had to do their business and get the fuck out of there. "Alright fellas. You know the drill. Quick, me and you in first, Dana, watch our six."

They got out and quickly jogged the half-block to the rundown townhome with boarded-up windows on the lower floor and broken ones on the upper. The front door was practically hanging off the hinges and Duke had a sinking feeling the occupants weren't worried about security. There were people out on porches along the way. Most of them young and gang affiliated, made obvious by the colors they wore. Duke just prayed they stayed out of their way as they did their jobs.

When they'd all bounded up the few steps onto the rickety porch, Quick was fast to beat on the splintered door and yell their identification. Duke counted down: "Three, two, one!" Quick reared back and kicked the door as hard as could with his large, steel toe boot, and the door flew into the house with them charging in right along with it.

"Bail recovery agents! We are armed!" Duke yelled, his voice deep and intimidating.

The first level was rank and musty. The ratty furniture in what should've been the living room looked like it'd been eaten by rodents. The small television was ancient and had several beer and liquor bottles on it, same as the crates along the walls. There was no one in sight. Dana yanked one of the boards off the missing window to allow in some light, and to also enable them to see if anyone was approaching.

There was the sound of hurried footsteps upstairs and Duke and Quick ran towards the stairs, taking them two at a time. "Bounty recovery agents! Aaron Williams! Aaron Williams, come out with your hands raised! We are armed!" Duke shouted; his weapon aimed in front of him. The large townhome had another level above the second floor. Duke looked over the bannister and Dana gave him a thumbs up. Quick cleared another room, coming out kicking debris and rubble out of his way. People were inside the dwelling, but the agents didn't know where. It was possible they'd gone up to the third level, but Duke and Quick continued to clear all the rooms on the second floor.

The bathroom was empty, but the cosmetics that lay strewn across the rusty countertop had Duke's antennas up. There were possibly women inside, too. Quick kicked open another door, this time into a bedroom, and a woman came flying out at them, armed with a baseball bat. Her piercing scream was loud enough to be heard down the block. Fuck! Duke aimed his weapons at her but she kept coming.

"Guys run!" she screamed to the house's other occupants.

Duke brought his arm up to block the first swing, the blow catching him so hard on his forearm he would swear he heard the bone crack. He grabbed the bat on the second swing and tried to yank it from her grip. She was heavyset and strong. She may have been high as well, because she didn't go down when Quick yanked her by her knotty hair and pulled her away from him. Duke yanked at the bat again and this time she lost her grip. Quick had her in a headlock, barking at her to get down on the ground.

    Duke was grasping his forearm, grimacing in pain when he looked up and saw angry, three full-grown men emerge from the back room. The one he immediately recognized as their bounty raised a shotgun and Duke hollered for Quick to get down. They both dove into one of the empty bedrooms and fired back. The men would have to come past the room to get to the stairs, so Duke and Quick scrambled to their feet, ducking on each side of the door as bullets riddled the walls around them. The sound of glass shattering had Duke diving into action. He had left Dana downstairs and he couldn't leave him to fend for himself. Duke stuck his arm out the door and fired a couple rounds, the sound of the woman's cry assured him he'd hit someone. He'd hoped it hadn't been her. "I just want Aaron Williams!" Duke yelled. A man charged by the door and Quick ran after him while Duke provided him cover fire.

    "Police are in route!" Dana yelled. "We got company! Hostiles coming up the sidewalk fast!"

    Fuck! Shit! We got to get the fuck out of here! Duke thought. *Fuck the bounty, I should've never agreed to this.*

    Looking down the dank hallway, he saw the crazy women lying on the floor; her body crouched over a bleeding man. It wasn't his bounty. He'd shot someone else. Duke walked carefully towards her, his weapon still aimed. "Ma'am. Step away from him and let me see your hands!"

    She probably couldn't hear his demands over her own wailing. The guy she lay over looked like he'd taken a bullet to his stomach and was quickly bleeding out. Couldn't have been older than twenty-five. As Duke drew closer, he could see the guy's eyelids twitching. *Fuck!* Where the hell had –

Duke hadn't even finished that thought when he was slammed from behind. His weapon was knocked from his grip as he took another hard shot to his ribs. He yelled out, trying to turn and reach for his other weapon. He was spun around and an angry blow glanced his cheek, but the next one hit him square on his temple, knocking him to the ground. He was confused and dazed. He rolled to his side, hoping to quench some of the pain and was hit hard in the back, with either an object or a boot, he wasn't sure. Gritting his teeth and trying to eat the pain, he ambled to his feet, grabbing his attacker around his mid-section, trying to hold off any more blows, at least until his guys got up there to help him.

Duke heard more gunshots, didn't know if he was confusing the lights flashing across his vision with muzzle flashes. The police couldn't have gotten there that fast, it had to be his guys taking fire from elsewhere. *Shit!* More hits came down on his back and Duke hollered out in agony. He finally reached for and gripped his other 9mm, but it was knocked loose by another blow to his side. Hits were coming from all directions. Duke registered that someone else was hitting him, not just Aaron. Screaming. Wailing. Cursing. It was the crazy woman. She had that damn bat. Duke was focused on trying to keep Aaron in his sights. *He* was the cold-blooded killer; they'd deal with the lady later.

Duke was using any energy he had left to fight off his assailants, his fists swinging and flying as fast as his racing heart. He hoped he was giving half as good as he was getting. He felt the pain in his fist, knew he'd landed a couple shots, but Aaron was big and probably doped up. Duke wondered if the guy even felt his punches. Something struck him hard across the back of his head and more bright flashes of white appeared before his eyes a split second before the pain registered. It was

PROMISES

like nothing he'd felt before. His head felt like it'd been split wide open. He crashed to the ground, hitting the wood floor face-first, the wind knocked out of him. He tried to take in air but it tasted poisonous, the thick, moldy, crack-infused oxygen acrid and bitter on his tongue. Nausea was fast approaching. Duke curled in on himself. Gagged and spit out blood. *Oh, fuck.*

He could hear the woman's banshee cries like she had a bullhorn pressed directly against his ear. She was yelling at someone to run… to go. Duke was on his belly. There were loud footsteps around him but he couldn't see faces. He wasn't capable of lifting his head, but through squinted eyes he could see the shiny chrome of his weapon on the floor against the wall. He felt if he could just get to it everything would be all right. Sirens wailed. Shots were still being fired. Someone was firing a shotgun or else Duke's head was so sensitive, every sound was amplified. He pushed off with one knee, but something hard and unforgiving landed across his lower back, followed by another blow and another and another. His last thoughts before he blacked out were of his guys. He hoped they'd at least made it out. Then he welcomed the darkness. Anything to stop the pain.

PROMISES

CHAPTER TEN

Duke wasn't sure where he was or who he was with, but he knew he'd never been as scared in his entire life. He could hear voices, sort of. Faraway sounds, like he was in a tunnel or underwater. His eyes fluttered open but he quickly shut them. The light was blinding and his head felt like someone was driving a corkscrew threw the back of his skull. What the fuck is happening? He was confused. He wanted to try to conjure up memories of his last activities, but it seemed that doing so made his head hurt worse. He realized a few seconds later that he was in an ambulance.

He could hear snatches of the conversation.

"Caucasian male, 45 years old... Unconscious at the scene... Blunt force trauma... Vital signs... Heart rate 112. ETA three minutes." Duke's eyes fluttered again. The pain was so severe he wished someone would knock him out again. No sooner had he drifted away than his body was jostled hard and he groaned aloud, his head noting its disapproval of that sound. Next thing he knew, he was moving fast, away from the daylight and into an artificially lit corridor. The smell hit him fast. Antiseptics and chemicals. He was obviously in a hospital, but Duke just wanted to go home and sleep for days. He hoped he got a good doctor who would quickly take pity on him and drug him back to oblivion.

PROMISES

"Duke! Duke! We're here! Hang in there, man!"

Duke's eyes danced around him. Quick. Quick was there, close by. He sounded afraid. Duke sighed softly in relief, only meeting slight resistance when he tried to take in more air. At least his best friend was fine. He wondered how bad off he was. When he was wheeled into the room, it immediately came alive with people: nurses, white coats; sounds overloaded his senses, beeping and whirring of machines, what felt like thousands of hands touching him at once. He was trying to breathe through the pain but he couldn't. Just wasn't able to take in enough air. He was so confused and dizzy. What was happening to him? It felt almost like an out of body experience.

"BP and oxygen level are dropping."

"We need a CT, stat. Alert the trauma surgeon and prep an OR."

OR? OR? As in surgery?

"Sir. Sir. Can you hear me?"

Fuck yes! Stop yelling. Duke groaned. He didn't think he could muster much else. "P-pain."

"I know. Hold on. We're gonna take care of you. I'm Dr. Robertson, the trauma surgeon. We got a lot going on trying to catalogue all your injuries. It appears you have some internal injuries that we need to asses first. I'll get you something for the pain as fast as I can."

"My guys," Duke croaked.

"You got a couple of men outside talking to the police. Don't try to talk anymore, sir."

That wouldn't be a problem. Duke felt a sharp pinch in the crook of his arm; it was only seconds before he began to float. Mmm, that's much better. He didn't feel the pain as much as he felt the pressure on his chest. Like someone was sitting on him. He felt his bed moving, his eyes would barely open, but he could see the ceiling moving, too. Where were they taking him? He couldn't talk, was too drowsy to form a complete thought. Was he going to surgery already? Wait! Wait! Duke closed his eyes. He couldn't let negative thoughts in if he was indeed about to go under the knife for the first time in his more than forty years of life. He inhaled a very shallow breath and thought of something that made him happy. Ahhh, my honey. He thought of Vaughan.

When Duke woke again, it was pitch dark. In and outside. Memories immediately flooded him. He was in the hospital because a skip and a crazy meth-head junkie bitch had beat the shit out of him. He had no clue how long he'd been asleep or even if it was still the same day. He was sure he was still in the hospital because of the smell, the sounds, and of course the terribly uncomfortable bed. Trying to move, he realized that he had limited mobility. There were wires and cords everywhere. Had he had surgery already? He lifted his right arm to his face and winced when something rock solid connected with his sensitive cheek. He squinted in the darkness, using his other hand to feel around. With his dry lips open in shock, his breathing was even shallower; he realized he had a cast on his right arm. He hoped that was the extent of his injuries but had a sinking feeling it was just the beginning of a long list of ailments.

Duke must have fallen asleep again because the next thing he remembered was the doctor waking him. "Sir. Mr. Morgan. Can you open your eyes for me?"

Duke fought hard enough to finally pry his eyelids open. He was so exhausted, like he'd run a marathon he hadn't trained for.

"Good. I'm Dr. Chauncey. I've been your treating physician since you came out of surgery this morning. You're in the nephrology unit."

This morning. So it's the same day? Neph… neph what? Duke grimaced when a jolt of pain shot up his spine to the back of his skull. "You still experiencing a lot of pain? Can you tell me your pain level on a scale of one through ten, ten being the most severe?" Dr. Chauncey said all this while looking in his eyes with a bright light on the end of his pen.

Duke finished processing what the doctor said and he finally managed a garbled, "Eight."

"Okay. I'll make sure the nurse starts a PCA soon. I wanted to talk to you about the injuries you sustained today."

The doctor's face looked like he'd rather be anywhere but there about to say what he had to. "Mr. Morgan, you came into the ER this morning with multiple contusions to your face and body. Quite a few superficial wounds and a badly fractured radius that we casted pretty quickly." The doctor paused and pulled up a stool. He sat gingerly and looked Duke in his eye when he spoke. "You also suffered two cracked ribs which caused concern that fragments may have broken off and caused internal bleeding. There is some internal injury and we repaired as much as we could in hopes we can take a closer look when the swelling goes down. However, the CT scan showed considerable damage to your kidneys from a beating you sustained during your attempted apprehension. It appears that both kidneys are badly damaged and you've been diagnosed with a grade five kidney injury."

"What's this mean, doc? I need surgery? Dialysis or some shit?" Duke murmured. His throat felt like sharp blades were slicing down it.

The doctor looked extremely uncomfortable. "Um. No. As of this morning your kidneys have not been able to do their job, which is filtering contaminants and expelling them through your urine. Which you've produced very little of since you've been here. I'm afraid you are in acute kidney failure."

"Fuck," Duke said solemnly. That was bad.

PROMISES

"One of the kidneys is completely inoperable, the other is in pretty bad shape and can't be repaired enough that it could function as your sole kidney."

"What are you saying, doc? Spit it out honestly. Am I going to die?"

"Unfortunately, because your kidneys were damaged by blunt force trauma, it limits a lot of what most kidney failure candidates are eligible for as far as alternative treatments because they either have one working kidney or their condition was not immediate onset. Soon, you'll be in chronic kidney failure, at which time we typically start a patient on hemodialysis treatments until a donor becomes available. But… but because of the other internal injuries you suffered, you won't be deemed a suitable candidate for dialysis. If you did try it, your life expectancy would be considerably shorter than typical. But you'd stay on the machine that will do the job your kidneys can't until...."

"Until I die," Duke whispered.

"Well. Until you choose not to receive dialysis anymore and are taken off the machines… and then… yes… soon after… you'll die. Or you stay on it until your name comes up on the donor list."

"Donor list?"

The doctor looked hesitant. "Um. Yes, sir. I've already started running the necessary additional test to submit your name, but unfortunately, some patients wait as long as ten years to become eligible. In the interim, if you did start dialysis, your entire life would have to change. You couldn't do much physical activity at all or especially work as a—"

"Wait. You telling me I couldn't be a bounty hunter anymore either!" Duke was panicking. There was no other word to describe it. His life was done. On a machine for years, living as a damn near vegetable. He couldn't do it. He'd rather die.

"All this from a few kicks to my back." Duke grumbled.

PROMISES

"Sir according to the police report. You blacked out during the beating, but you were hit more than just a few times and it was bat and a pipe. The kicks are what probably broke your ribs. The kidneys are pretty well protected by your back muscles, but the type of force with which you were hit can definitely injure them beyond repair."

"If I don't do the dialysis." Duke gulped a breath, his eyes stinging with moisture. "How long would I have?"

"I'm sorry to say… Only weeks. You are already stage five. You would however, be made comfortable during that time."

Duke turned his head as a tear rolled down the side of his face into his hairline. He wasn't ready to go.

"Sir. Do you have any family members that could be possible donors?"

"No. My parents are deceased and I'm an only child. My only living relative is my aunt and she's in a nursing home."

"I'm going to continue to do workups with your blood and look over your chart. If I come up with anything, I'll let you know. I'm also going to get a third opinion." The doctor stood up but Duke didn't have any words. If he spoke right now he'd start bawling. "You have friends in the family waiting room, would you like me to go ahead and speak to them?"

Duke knew it was the easy way out, but he didn't think he could look Quick in the eye and tell him he was about to die. Oh god, Vaughan. Duke closed his eyes and prayed silently.

CHAPTER ELEVEN

Vaughan had run to the bathroom, his father hot on his heels as he shouldered into the first stall and emptied everything in his stomach. Duke was dying. Had literally been beat to death. No fucking way! God could not be so cruel. He'd done everything right in his life so he could be the man worthy of Duke's love and when he was right there, their chance was being taken away.

"It's not fair! It's not fair!" Vaughan snapped, backing out of the stall, facing his father who looked just as helpless as him.

"I know, son. I know. It's not fair. But life happens and there's not a damn thing we can do about it."

"I can't lose him now!" Vaughan screamed.

His dad pulled him into his big arms and held him tight. Held him until he didn't feel like ramming his head into the bathroom wall. He needed to get his shit together. Vaughan stood taller and angrily wiped the tears from his cheeks.

"Dad, just give me a minute, okay?"

Quick rubbed his shoulder. "You sure?"

"Yes."

"Okay. I'm gonna go see Duke now." He squeezed him tight. "You pull yourself together, Vaughan. Duke needs us to be strong."

Vaughan's sob startled him. "I know. I understand. Just… just give me some time alone."

PROMISES

As soon as he was alone, Vaughan thought he might be able to compose himself, but when he thought of going on without Duke, he slid down the wall and cradled his head in his hands, letting the tears flow freely. Damn, when was the last time he'd cried? Now he couldn't stop. His love was dying, a part of him drifting right along with him. Vaughan felt so helpless and out of control. His life was all about scheduling and planning. This was not a part of any of his plans. It was after eleven at night. He was supposed to be buried so deep inside Duke right now that he'd never find his way out. He had planned a candlelit dinner. A horse and carriage ride through downtown Atlanta and then, then he was going to make love to him until dawn. But now…

Vaughan gulped, his forehead creasing as his hostility and anger grew. He would not lose Duke. He refused. He'd cut out both his kidneys and give them to… fuck! Vaughan pulled out his phone and got online while sitting right there in the men's room.

After twenty minutes, he climbed off the floor. Vaughan hurried to the sink, quickly washing his hands and face, tucking his shirt back in. If he was doing what he was thinking of doing, he couldn't look like an insane person. Vaughan power stepped all the way to the front desk. "I need to speak with Dr. Chauncey in the Nephrology Unit, it's a life or death emergency."

The help associate looked to be in her eighties but her eye was keen. Her nametag said Ginger Colmbs, Volunteer. She looked Vaughan up and down—even peeked behind him—before slowly picking up the receiver. He heard her mumble a few words into the phone before hanging up. She looked back at him and asked for his name. Vaughan paused. *Why does she need that?* As if she read his mind she added, "I need to sign you in. Dr. Chauncey is an attending surgeon here. I also need ID please."

"Michael Palmer," Vaughan said, and patted his shirt pockets, back pockets, and inside his blazer in a show of looking for his wallet. "Oh, no. Damnit. I left my wallet at home in my rush to get here."

She was looking annoyed, but thank goodness, she typed a few keys on her computer and printed out a name badge for him. She pointed to a vast waiting area located at the front of the hospital next to the gift shop. "You can wait there for him. He'll be down as soon as he can."

Vaughan ran his hand through his hair and huffed a scared breath. His heart was beating a mile a minute in his chest. Was he still hurting like hell? Was he scared shitless over what he was about to do? Or was he terrified his plan might not work? All of the above.

Vaughan was standing in front of the gift shop looking at a teddy bear with his arms wrapped around an "It's a Boy" balloon. He'd jumped almost to the roof when he heard his name called. *Jeez. Calm down, V. You got this.* Vaughan walked up to the doctor, looking him in his eyes as he did. The man's eyes lit with recognition when he got closer. Damn.

"I know that's not your name so you can take that off. I remember from upstairs. You're one of Mr. Morgan's visitors," the man said coolly.

Vaughan pulled off the nametag and crumbled it up. "I wanted to remain anonymous, Dr. Chauncey."

"Anonymous for what?"

"I want to donate one of my kidneys to Mr. Morgan… one hundred percent anonymously. He can't know."

Dr. Chauncey frowned. "I know you're not family because I already asked Mr. Morgan about that. So why can't he know?"

"I looked this up. There are anonymous donations made all the time… right?"

"Well—"

Vaughan didn't let him finish. "If the patient is willing to participate in a kidney transplant procedure the hospital is not legally obligated to tell the patient the donor's identity."

PROMISES

"Did a quick Google search, did ya?" Dr. Chauncey smirked and Vaughan almost grabbed the man by his throat. Did he think it was a goddamn game? A man's—his man's—life was at stake and the clock was ticking.

"Yes, I did. Regardless, I'm an educated man. Not in the degree of medicine but I'm a lawyer. I know my rights on this. I can donate my kidney if I want, and since I'm a living donor, I can also specify where it goes. I bet if I went over to another hospital and told them I was there to donate a perfectly good, working organ, they'd have a needle in my arm in ten seconds flat, testing my blood. Are you going to deny your patient a chance at a normal life?" Vaughan's voice was rising and people were slowing down as they passed by them. Dr. Chauncey looked around before turning back to Vaughan with a stern expression.

"Lower your voice. And I didn't say I was denying anything."

"So you'll do it!" Vaughan grabbed Dr. Chauncey's biceps through his mid-thigh white lab coat.

"Wait. I didn't say that either. There are an extensive number of tests that need to be done to determine compatibility, sir."

"My name is Vaughan Webb, doctor."

"Mr. Webb, the testing can take weeks. But most living donors can't specify who they donate to because of blood type matching."

"I'm O doctor. My blood type is O," Vaughan said confidently. His blood matched with any and everyone's, but most of all... Duke's.

Dr. Chauncey arched a brow and Vaughan knew he had the guy; so like the lawyer he was, he kept driving his point. "I also know you don't have to be one hundred percent compatible in other areas. I have the cash to do this right now, damn going through insurance bureaucracy. You can save his life, doctor.

PROMISES

You can also speed up the process using your patient's need right now. I saw that more hospitals are using the one-day donor evaluation method to make it easier on the donor. Please. I'm begging you. Let me do this." Vaughan was terrified but his voice was strong. "Start the testing immediately, please, doctor."

Dr. Chauncey pinched the bridge of his nose. "First of all, this isn't Johns Hopkins; it's going to take more than one day for your eval. Our transplant team is slightly smaller. Second, are you sure you're O?"

"Are you sure of your blood type, doctor?" Vaughan's composure was waning.

"Follow me." Dr. Chauncey turned and started walking towards the elevators; Vaughan stopped him.

"I can't go back up there. Someone could see me with you."

Dr. Chauncey turned; his long narrow face was twisted. "Are you sure you need to be anonymous?"

"Du… Mr. Morgan is an extremely proud man. He'd never accept it, especially from me. That's the god's honest truth."

"Are you an enemy that's going to hold it over his head the rest of his life?"

"I'm the man that loves him… now *that* really is the god's honest truth," Vaughan said softly.

Dr. Chauncey's brows rose almost into his hairline. Finally, the man got it. There were no more guessing games. Just being involved romantically with the recipient didn't disqualify him to donate… that's the first thing he'd Googled.

"Let's go to the ER. We can start there." Dr. Chauncey made a left down a long hallway.

Vaughan wanted to jump on the man's back and kiss his cheek, but didn't think that would go well on the psych evaluation he was going to have to undergo. Instead he choose humor to settle, hopefully, both of their nerves. "If I were Mr. Morgan's enemy… wouldn't the ultimate revenge be to sit by and let him die… not save his life? I don't think revenge works the way I'm doing it."

Dr. Chauncey didn't turn to look at Vaughan, but he could see the corner of his mouth twitching as they continued to walk. *Yeah, doctor. You asked a dumbass question back there.*

CHAPTER TWELVE

"You know you didn't do this. This isn't your fault, Quick. Don't do this to me, man," Duke whispered through a clogged throat. His emotions were riding him harder than a cowboy on a rank bull. He was in immense pain. His head throbbed, so did his body. He'd lost track of how many bruises mapped his back and torso. Everything ached, but he'd rather feel the pain caused by the beating than the pain in his heart. He hadn't pushed for his morphine drip in several hours, mostly because he didn't want to be drowsy when Vaughan showed up. *He is going to show up, right?*

"Duke, all hell broke loose in that fuckin' house. I thought we could get that sonofabitch and be outta there. I went downstairs to check the perimeter. Next thing I know Dana and me are crouched behind the wall holding off shooters outside and every time I tried to get back upsta—" Quick's voice hitched before he could continue. "I tried to get upstairs, Duke. I swear. Dana was yelling and cursing, then he was hit in the shoulder. We could hear them fighting you. Those goddamn bastards." Quick pounded hard on the wall with the side of his fist. Cursing everyone in existence.

Moisture was building behind Duke's closed eyelids and his heart was beating so hard he just knew that a nurse would come in any minute and call a cardiac arrest code. When Duke finally opened his eyes, Quick's back was to him as he stood at the window, most likely looking at nothing.

"I'm gonna find that motherfucking bitch and I'm gonna kill her slowly. Aaron Williams better thank god his ass is already back in jail," Quick ground out through clenched teeth.

Duke knew Quick was angry, he'd be too if the situation were reversed, but the emotion wasn't helping anything. The woman that had apparently beat him along with his bounty was still on the run as far as they knew. Duke had killed her son. She held him in her arms as he bled out. She'd snapped and gone crazy on him. He didn't want to think about any of that. He literally had weeks to live. "Quick, where's Vaughan?" Duke finally said.

Quick's eyes were red and moist when he turned around. He sat down gently in one of the two chairs in Duke's room, clasping his hands in his lap. He didn't look at him when he finally answered. "He's gonna be up here real soon. I'm sure. He just asked for a little time. He's um… he's um…."

"Find him, please. Make sure he's okay," Duke pleaded, his voice emotion-filled. "It's late, Quick. Get him to go home and rest, then he can come back tomorrow."

Quick stood up, patted him gently on his thigh under the scratchy hospital blanket, and walked hesitantly to the door. "Duke. I know about Vaughan's feelings for you. I have for a long time." Quick's head was down and his voice quivered but Duke understood every word, each one stabbing him in his chest. "I would've been damn proud to have you as a son-in-law, Duke. I uh… I just wanted you to know that."

Duke turned his head as Quick walked out the door. He couldn't respond. He could hardly breathe. *Son-in-law. Jesus.* Quick had known. His best friend would've been okay with him dating his son. Vaughan had obviously been very serious about his feelings for Duke if he told his father. So many would'ves and could'ves played in the back of his mind as he reflected on

PROMISES

his life. Would they have been good together? Would he and Vaughan have gone the distance? Would Vaughan have loved him the way he'd always dreamed of being loved, cared for, and cherished? Duke reached for the button to push for his pain meds. He just wanted to sleep and not think. If this would've happened a couple months earlier, pre Vaughan, then he would've been okay with dying but now… now… he begged to live. Begged for a shot at love.

"I'm fine to do more, let's continue," Vaughan urged eagerly. He'd been in the lab for the better part of four hours. Dr. Chancy had left to go cover his rounds a while ago and Vaughan hadn't heard from him since. Vaughan hadn't filled out so much damn paperwork since he'd applied for law school. They wanted to know everything about him from his blood type to his cock size. Okay, that was a stretch but they probed into every aspect of his life. Good thing was he felt like he was passing with flying colors, like every other test in his life.

The blood type compatibility, tissue typing, antibody screening, urinalysis, and much more had already been collected to test. Now he was hassling the technicians on getting someone to do his X-rays that night.

"Sir. I understand you're anxious, but there's no way to do *all* the testing tonight. It's just not possible, not to mention it's after one in the morning." The overworked lab technician sighed as Vaughan refused to accept no for an answer. She'd been the one dealing with him the most, and when her two associates had left for the evening, then it was all down to her.

"Hospitals don't close. What if someone came into the ER right now and needed an X-ray? Are you saying they couldn't get it?"

The lady pushed her stray brown curls behind her ear; the rest of her bun looking like it'd been cuter when she left home twelve hours ago. Her eyes were a pretty gray color, almost bluish. Vaughan turned on his charming smile, hoping it wasn't falling short since he wasn't only physically exhausted but mentally as well. The ladies usually fell for his boyish charm.

"I believe the one tech that's on duty tonight is pretty busy. Dr. Chauncey said we'd do the preliminaries this evening and you could make an appointment tomorrow to finish up. You're pretty lucky. Most donors have to take at least two to three days out of their schedule just to complete all the testing."

"No. No." Vaughan shook his head. There's no way he could go home without having an appointment for the surgery. He wouldn't rest until he was one hundred percent sure that Duke was going to survive.

"Yes."

Vaughan turned around to the definitive order in Dr. Chauncey's voice. "That's it for tonight, Mr. Webb. I emailed the doctor for the psych eval, but he probably won't respond until tomorrow… or actually later today when he gets in." Dr. Chauncey put his hand up to stop Vaughan's ongoing protests, continuing what he was saying. "He knows this is a critical case and we can get you in real soon, but I don't think it'll be today."

Vaughan dropped his head in his hands, fending off more tears. Crying wasn't going to solve a goddamn thing. Everything was going to be all right, he was seeing to that, but he'd have to be patient. Why he'd thought donating a kidney would be easy and quick was obviously….

"I just checked on Mr. Morgan."

Vaughan's head shot up and next thing he knew he was up out of his seat, moving across the lab area to stand in front of the doctor. "How is he? Is he… is he…?"

"He's fine. His other injuries are not going to be a factor in performing the surgery laparoscopically. He's a relatively healthy man. No heart conditions, history of diabetes. I've submitted him to the donor board for review. I should have an answer for you in the next couple days. That's really the best I can do, Mr. Webb. I'll remind you that this isn't Johns Hopkins. We can't do everything in twenty-four hours. We're just not staffed that way."

Well get me the fucking Nightingale and transport our asses over there then. Vaughan ground his teeth. That wasn't necessarily bad news. He hated the sound of "a couple days," but at least the doc was talking about Duke surviving the surgery, like he was sure it was going to happen. His tests must be looking good, then. He figured he'd cut them some slack. He needed to get his affairs in order anyway. As if the doctor sensed him calming down, he added, "Rushing can cause oversights, Mr. Webb."

"Can you call me Vaughan, please?"

"Vaughan. We want Mr. Morgan to have a fighting chance and I'm glad you're adamant about helping him, but I feel this decision was made hastily. So talking with Dr. Townsend, our psychiatrist, will really be the deciding factor. Our candidates need to be willing to donate, not feel obligated to donate."

"I don't feel obligated at all. It's not like he asked me and now I feel like I can't say no. Doing it anonymously should take that thought off the table. Right?"

Dr. Chauncey opened the door to the lab and motioned for Vaughan to walk through it. "Dr. Townsend will call you soon. In the meantime, read over those pamphlets and the material I gave you earlier. There's some pre-donation recommendations you should know about and also what you'll need in preparation for surgery."

"Surgery!"

Oh no. Vaughan recognized his father's voice before he even turned around. How the hell did he find him down in the ER? Vaughan quickly shook Dr. Chauncey's hand and thanked him for his help, trying to quickly usher him away before turning to face his father.

PROMISES

Quick had been texting him for hours. All he responses were that he was walking the grounds, so obviously his dad had been looking for him.

"Vaughan David Webb." His growl still caused goosebumps on his arms, even as an adult. "What the hell do you think you're doing?"

Vaughan tucked some of the papers back inside the large folder where he had accumulated all the information about a living donor surgery, and began walking towards the front of the hospital to get to the main elevators, his father's heavy boot steps fast on his heels. "I'm gonna save him, Dad, and there's not a force on this earth that can stop me."

Vaughan's bicep was grabbed in an unforgivable grip as his father yanked him around to face him. "You sure about that?" Those magnetic green eyes were radiating authority. Quick was a hulking man, standing even taller than him, his face a contorted mask of hurt and ferocity. That look used to freeze Vaughan in his tracks, but now, it made him jut his chin out and puff up his chest. He'd meant it. Nothing would stop him from saving Duke, hell, from at least trying. Did his father really think he'd sit on his ass and wait for Duke's funeral?

"You had to know I'd do this. I know you thought about it too."

"My blood isn't compatible or some shit like that." His father shook his head.

"Why is it okay for you to consider donating but not me? I'm the one in love with him, have been for years. I'm doing it, that's all there is to it, Dad." Vaughan kept walking. It was late and there was no one in the quiet halls. Each door they passed was dark, all the departments closed.

"I won't lose my best friend and risk losing my son." The elder Mr. Webb continued to protest as Vaughan took long determined strides, his father having no problem keeping up.

PROMISES

"It's a simple procedure. I've done some research and Dr. Chauncey went over it, too. It's not as invasive as you think. A few punctures for the instruments, a small incision right above the pubic bone to remove the organ, there's minimal pain and the hospital stay is a day or two at most. Then I'll be back to work in two to four weeks. Simple"

"I don't care about the procedures. No, Vaughan. You are not doing this! You are my son! Once I tell Duke, he will forbid you to do this. He'd never let you put yourself—"

Vaughan spun on his heel, his anger simmering hotly below the surface. He'd never disrespected his father a day in his life and didn't want to start, but he had to let him know that it wasn't debatable. He stood almost eye-to-eye with the only man he'd loved longer than Duke. If anyone walked by right then, they'd probably call security because it looked like two big ass motherfuckers were squaring off to do some damage to each other. Vaughan controlled his tone, but the rough timbre of his baritone sounded scary even to him. "You must be under the impression that I'm asking for permission." Vaughan stepped even closer, his eyes boring into his father's. "I'm doing this Dad, whether you like it or not. I don't need your permission; I don't even need your blessing. But Duke and I have a shot at something real, and I'm not ready to let it go. I can't. Don't you get that, or have you been alone that long?" Vaughan cringed at that last statement. He saw the pain in his father's eyes and immediately wanted to take it back. Vaughan swallowed and kept going. "I know you're scared. I know you don't want to lose Duke."

"I don't want to lose either of you!" he yelled in response.

"And you won't have to as long as you stand down. If you tell Duke, then you're right. He'd refuse the surgery. Even if there's only a zero point five percent mortality risk." Vaughan cast his eyes down, his voice a mere whisper now. "I don't even think he'd allow that small amount."

"He has a right to know."

"And I'll tell him myself."

"After."

"Yes. After. When I feel it's time." Vaughan pointed at his chest. "That's my decision, not yours."

"This is crazy." His dad ran his hand over his messy hair. "I can't believe this."

Vaughan gripped Quick's shoulders and pulled him into him. He felt his dad shake in his arms but he held him as tightly as he had earlier. "I'm gonna save him, Dad. Please. You gotta let me save him. I'm a healthy man. There's no reason I can't survive it." They stayed in the embrace for a while before Vaughan finally pulled back. His heart broke for his dad. He could understand how much it was to digest. Hearing his friend was dying, then his son opting to donate an organ, it's the biggest challenge they'd ever faced. But Vaughan was a man. He needed to accept that.

"Swear you won't tell him. Promise me."

He didn't say a word.

Vaughan frowned, his blood felt like ice water in his veins. He was trying to control himself, but if his dad messed this up, he wasn't sure what he'd do. "If you tell him, if you mess this up. I'll never forgive you." Vaughan turned and walked away. It was harsh, but reality. It may have been an exaggeration. But if Duke died, he'd definitely get as far away from Atlanta as he could. So where was that? Australia, Indonesia. There was no telling when he'd forgive his father or want to see him again.

CHAPTER THIRTEEN

Duke tried to turn to his other side and must have cried out at the pain that move caused, because he immediately felt a gentle hand on his cheek, a soothing deep murmur next to his ear. "Easy, sweetheart."

Vaughan.

Duke tried to open his eyes, the lids heavy from the medication the doctor had pushed when he last checked on him. Insisting that Duke not lie there in excruciating pain. He knew it was his man... Oh goodness... he knew it was Vaughan. He couldn't refer to him as his man; they wouldn't have that. Never make it there. He felt moisture run down the side of his face but his eyes were still closed. "Vaughan," he barely managed. His voice sounded horrible, like he had throat cancer along with all his other ailments.

"Yes. I'm here." Softer purring and caresses to his face and his hair. The back of his head was very tender from the bruises and the concussion, but he'd welcome any of Vaughan's touches. He could smell him; he was so close to him.

"What time is it?" Duke croaked.

"Very early. Like almost four."

"Jesus," Duke huffed. "You need to rest."

"I need to be right here," Vaughan argued gently. Duke could feel Vaughan's body heat; feel his weight next to him. It felt like he was sitting on the side of his bed, leaning over him, careful not to put too much weight on him. Duke slowly lifted the arm that didn't have a cast on it and laid his hand on Vaughan's thigh, or so he presumed since his eyes remained shut. Gazing into those intense eyes would be his undoing. After a few seconds of silence or maybe he'd drifted off again, he felt Vaughan's soft lips on his cheek, his eyelids, grazing over his temple. A warm gentle breath ghosted over Duke's forehead as Vaughan moved to the other side, placing the most comforting, delicate kisses he'd ever felt in his life. Would ever feel. Duke felt his chest tighten painfully and he fought to control his emotions. His body shook and he knew Vaughan felt it because he responded quickly. "It's okay, sweetheart. Calm down, Duke. I'm right here with you. I'll always be here."

Duke sighed tiredly. He needed more rest. Every time he thought of how fucking unfair everything was, he'd feel this tremendous weight on him, like a boulder pressing him into the uncomfortable bed he was confined to. Duke was exhausted again but he thought he might have been dreaming when he heard Vaughan's beautiful voice assuring him that he was going to be okay. Vaughan swore he'd make everything okay. Oh, how he wished he could. It had to be a dream. Right? There was nothing anyone could do for him. He was going to die right here.

~~~~

When Duke woke again it was a lot brighter in his room, he could see the light through his lids. He smelled food and antiseptics. When he finally managed to open both eyes, he saw there was a lunch tray sitting on his table along with a couple bottles of water and what looked like a can of ginger ale. He knew he had to be hungry, he hadn't eaten in quite a while, but the thought of food made him nauseous. Duke managed to push the button on his bed railing and raise his head. He must have had a visitor or two because there was a "Get Well" balloon tied to a slender vase of carnations and sitting on the windowsill was

PROMISES

a plant with small white lilies emerging through the green leaves. There was white bow around the bottom of the pot. He could see there was a card but didn't know who it was from.

His body was tight; muscles ached in every part of him. His arm throbbed and the constant thud in the back of his head had magnified exponentially. It must be time for more medication or something. He glanced up at the clock in his room and gasped. It was after noon. Had he been asleep that long? When did Vaughan leave? His memory was cloudy, had to be all the pain meds. Hey, maybe that was a pretty good idea. Stay doped up until it was time for him to check out. Sleep through his final days, because honestly, who wanted to watch them? He was just about to push his morphine drip when he heard a light tap on the door and it was simultaneously pushed open.

Duke turned and looked into dark red-rimmed eyes. He knew he'd be here eventually but he wasn't prepared for his visit yet. Not him.

"Quick called me yesterday." The deep voice radiated around the room as Judge's large presence filled the space. He came to the side of the bed and placed his large palm on Duke's shoulder. He watched Judge's bottom lip quiver slightly before he opened his mouth to speak again. "Goddamn you, Duke."

Duke blew out a weary sigh. He turned his palm upwards, silently asking for Judge's hand. It took a second but Judge finally put his hand in Duke's and gave it a firm squeeze before dropping his forehead to their joined hands. They didn't speak at all. What could be said? They'd been lovers at one time. Friends for even longer. Although their relationship never extended past work and an occasional hook up whenever Judge was in town, Duke had missed him terribly. He was glad that his friend had found love; regardless that it wasn't with him. Judge was happy, would be long after he was gone. He wanted that for his friend. They stayed that way until the nurse came in and took Duke's vitals for the umpteenth time.

PROMISES

"Good afternoon Mr. Morgan. It appeared you slept better last night. I came in a few times and you never woke while I checked your vitals."

Duke nodded his head. If she calls that sleeping good, then okay. Judge was standing over by the window, trying to stay out of the way while the nurse did what she had to do. Duke remembered her from yesterday. She must work the morning shift. *Kathy,* he thought. *Yes, her name is Kathy.* Her scrubs were bright pink and blue and her honey-blonde hair was pulled back neatly and pinned up with a shiny butterfly clip. She was pretty and sweet, as were most of the nurses he'd encountered the last couple days.

She finished with her notes and pulled Duke's tray closer to him. "It'll make you feel better if you eat a little, Mr. Morgan. This is chicken soup and in this container is Jell-O."

"I'm not hungry."

"You need to keep your strength up, Mr. Morgan." She smiled sadly.

Duke was wondering what the point was. Keep up his strength. Why? He wasn't doing dialysis for years on end. He was accepting his fate. He refused to live miserably for the next four or five years, not working the job he'd done since he was a teen, and being a burden to his few friends, while he waited on a too-long list for a kidney that might never come. No way.

"Just a few sips of soup, please," Nurse Kathy said softly.

"No thank you," Duke grumbled, turning away from her, barely controlling the cry of pain that escaped without permission.

"He'll eat it," Judge growled. "Leave it."

Nurse Kathy's eyes widened slightly when Judge walked back over to Duke. Judge was a large and intimidating man, especially when he wore black from head to toe. Kathy was probably afraid for Duke but she released the tray and quickly left the room.

PROMISES

Judge didn't say a word as he lifted the lid off the bowl and unwrapped the spoon from the napkin. He used the buttons on the remote control and inclined Duke until he winced. He couldn't sit up too far without his ribs angrily protesting. Judge dropped the guardrail and somehow gingerly sat his large frame beside him. Judge picked up the bowl—his massive hands making it appear small—dipped the spoon into the broth and slowly put it to Duke's lips. He knew it wasn't an option not to open his mouth. He parted his dry lips and Judge gently eased the spoon in and let the lukewarm broth settle on his tongue before sliding soothingly down his parched throat. It tasted like comfort. It was bland and cooling quickly but the way it was being delivered made it perfect. Judge dipped the spoon again, repeating the same gesture. When Duke opened again, Judge smiled slightly, giving him an appreciative wink. Thank god for his friends. He wasn't going to die alone. Before he knew it, he'd eaten all the soup and the Jell-O, fed to him by his friend. Judge took the cloth napkin and wet it with warm tap water to clean Duke's mouth and chin of the few drops that got away.

Judge pushed the tray away and put the bed's rail back in place. "Don't starve yourself Duke. This is hard enough without… without…." Judge turned away from him. Duke could see the tension and strain in Judge's back.

"I'm sorry," Duke whispered.

Judge turned back around, his onyx-colored eyes were glossy as they locked in on Duke's own. He picked up Duke's hand and kissed his palm before placing it back down. Judge's voice was rough and husky. "I gotta go, Duke."

"I know," Duke said, just as quietly.

"I'll be back real soon."

"Judge." Duke mustered the strength to say what had to be said. "Nothing changed regarding the business."

"Duke." Judge sighed. Shaking his head miserably. "Not now."

PROMISES

"After we called it quits. I never changed anything with my lawyer. You and Quick will own my businesses. You are joint owners, fifty-fifty."

Judge leaned in and kissed Duke's forehead, his lips lingering against the damp skin there. Duke hadn't realized his was sweating because he had chill bumps all over. He shivered in Judge's presence, remembering what it felt like to be touched and handled by him. Judge placed his thick palm on Duke's bruised cheek, careful not to hurt him. "Rest. I'll be back soon." Judge left, not commenting on Duke's confession. Judge and Quick were the first ones there when Duke started his business. They loved and bleed for his company, leaving it to them was the best and most logical thing for him to do.

CHAPTER FOURTEEN

"Thank you so much Mr. Roland. I really appreciate it. I will be in the hospital for a couple days and then post-op recovery time is estimated to be three to four weeks... Yes, sir... I can still provide some assistance with cases... No, sir... I can research case law and submit information via email... Thank you, sir. Yes, this was unexpected, but I'm just thankful that my job will still be here after all this is done. Yes, sir. Thank you again. I'll be in touch." Vaughan hung up the phone. He felt another gust of relief. He hadn't even officially started the job yet and already he was taking medical leave. He told his boss a version of the truth. That he was donating a kidney, but to a family member on his mother's side. There was no reason for him to disclose exactly what his situation was. He'd save his man's life and get to work as soon as he could.

He was sitting at his father's desk, using his computer to handle his business before he had to be at the hospital to meet the shrink. He'd gotten in today at two on a cancellation. Dr. Chauncey called and informed him that the board had met at eleven that morning and accepted Duke as a candidate. As soon as Vaughan finished the last leg of his testing, he'd get a date to check in to the hospital. He was starting to breathe easier. It was looking like this was going to happen. He wished he could tell Duke that everything was going to be okay, but he wouldn't risk telling him and Duke declining the surgery because of it. As long as he didn't know, Duke would thank god for answering his prayer and have the surgery.

He was still wondering what excuse he'd give Duke for why he wouldn't be there by his side before he went in for the transplant. He was still debating that. Vaughan wasn't used to lying or even omitting the truth. He believed a man should be about his word. A real man didn't have to lie. Now, he saw the shades of gray regarding his long-held rule. Duke wasn't a fool, but they would have to pull this off or else he'd lose the love of his life and his father would lose his best friend.

He'd had a long talk with his father that morning. They'd woken early since Vaughan had affairs to get in order and Quick was running Duke's business. After showing his father more research, he believed he'd put him at ease. Checking his watch, he saw he had forty minutes before his appointment; being late wouldn't look good. He wore a black and gray stripped business suit, wanting to appear professional. Duke would think he was working when he stopped by after his appointment. Grabbing the folder which he was referring to as his "donor documents," and his wallet, he headed out the front door.

~~~

The appointment took well over two hours. It was more like an interrogation than a conversation. The doctor asked him a lot of questions that were very similar to each other. Do you believe in god? Do you believe in heaven? Do you have a god complex? Do you believe man makes his own fate or do you believe in a higher power? Vaughan knew the right answers, the wrong answers, and the answers they wanted to hear, so the latter was what he gave them.

"Well, I believe this concludes our session. Do you have any questions for me Mr. Webb?"

"Did I pass? Am I well-balanced enough to donate a kidney?"

PROMISES

The doctor looked up from his notes, a slight crinkle appearing next to his left eye when he smirked. "There's no pass or fail."

Vaughan stood and re-buttoned his Donna Karan suit jacket. The psychologist's office was set up just like any other shrink's, regardless that it was in the hospital. The lighting was dim and the couch and chaise lounge were positioned so the doctor could face him from his burgundy wingback chair. Gazing out the window, his stomach begin to whirl with anticipation. "You know what I mean. You know exactly what I'm asking."

"You're more than capable. It's truly commendable what you're doing." The doctor flipped a couple pages in a manila folder and looked back up at him. "I understand you're doing an anonymous donation."

"Yes, I am. I don't want the recipient to feel he owes me anything afterward. I want us to have the exact same relationship *after* the surgery that we had before it."

"Of course." The doctor stood and smoothed down his black and gray sweater vest. "Do you know what happens now, Mr. Webb? Did Dr. Chauncey explain the steps following our appointment?"

"Yes, sir. If you give me a sane bill of health, I should be contacted with a surgery date."

"Exactly."

Vaughan smiled. Truly smiled for the first time since the whole ordeal began. He graciously shook the doctor's hand and headed to the bank of elevators that would take him to see Duke. While he watched the lighted numbers descend, his stomach growled angrily. Shit. When was the last time he'd eaten? Was it completely fucked that he couldn't remember? Checking his watch, he saw it was only a half past three. A quick stop in the cafeteria wouldn't hurt. While he waited in line to pay for his southwest chicken salad he called his father to inform him that he believed the psych eval went very well and he believed all was going to be okay. Quick was at the jail for a bond so he couldn't talk long but he actually whooped out loud and that just amped Vaughan's mood up to the nth degree. He made quick work of his salad, missing Duke and needing to see him.

He walked past the nurse's station on Duke's floor and got more than a few appreciative glances, but came to an abrupt halt when he heard his name called. He spun around and saw Dr. Chauncey waving him back the way he'd come. The doctor turned before he reached him and led Vaughan into a private family waiting room.

"Dr. Chauncey. Good afternoon. I just finished with Dr. Skool; I think it went well. How soon should—"

Dr. Chauncey raised his thin hand, cutting off Vaughan's anxious babbling. "I know. The transplant coordinator already sent me the email. The psychologist has signed off, so I wanted to tell you that if you had your affairs in—"

"Oh, yes. Yes! I do! Everything is lined up with the billing office and my job, and my father will be doing all my post-op care. We're ready to go!" Vaughan cut in, his head and heart pounding with anticipation.

"Calm down." Dr. Chauncey smiled. "If you have a coronary, I won't be able to operate on you."

This was a good sign. Had to be. The doctor was joking with him.

"I have an opening on Friday at six a.m. Can you be here?"

Vaughan wanted to drop to his knees. *Oh thank you, god. Thank you, thank you.* Tears welled up in his eyes and he just barely contained himself from wailing. It was fate. He and Duke were supposed to be together. He knew it right at that moment. Duke could've been severely injured in a way that couldn't be repaired. But the good lord was giving them a chance. Vaughan nodded his head and finally spoke in a hushed murmur, "Yes. Friday is fine."

PROMISES

Dr. Chauncey looked on him with so much compassion. He simply patted his shoulder and informed him that the surgery date was set.

"Doctor. You're still going to keep my name out of this, right?"

Dr. Chauncey looked at Vaughan like he had snot oozing out his nose. He appeared disgusted. *Oh no.*

"Vaughan you are my patient now. I would never violate your rights. You have asked to remain anonymous and I have to respect and honor that. Besides, it's my experience that patients dying of kidney failure rarely insist on the details of where the kidney is coming from."

"Yeah. But even if Duke's on the kidney donation list, his name wouldn't come up now if there was a kidney available."

"Just let me handle everything, okay?"

Vaughan took a breath. That sounded freakin' perfect to him. Yes. He'd let the good doctor handle it all.

PROMISES

CHAPTER FIFTEEN

Duke gritted his teeth at the pain in his back. Was that the kidney pain? He wanted to peer down at the collection bag hanging on the side of his bed, but he had a feeling that would probably hurt like a bitch to accomplish and he wouldn't like what he saw. It would probably contain little to no urine or be full of blood. The stitches in his head were starting to itch like crazy, and the knot on the back of his head was pulsing a steady beat like an out of tune bass drum. He reached his right hand up to rub at the wound on his left cheek and ended up banging his cast on the bedrail. Fuckin' fuck! He was trying harder and harder not to push that morphine button. He hated the way he felt when he did and he wanted to be alert if Vaughan came by.

He picked up the remote with his good hand – that hand had an IV in it – but at least it wasn't covered with rock hard plaster. Maybe finding something half-decent on television would turn his mind off. His conscious thoughts were a persistent loop of unanswered questions that he flat out didn't want the answer to, but lying there ignorant wasn't making him feel better. What would dying feel like? Would he eventually be so bad off that he couldn't have company? When would Vaughan stop coming to see him? Would he stay until the end? Would he even know his loved ones were there? Fuck. Stop already!

PROMISES

A light tapping on his door cut off his internal war. He didn't say anything as the door was slightly pushed open and somehow – instinctually— he knew who it was. Knew it was Vaughan. Could smell him before his body even made it all the way into the room. Duke closed his eyes and let the wonderful scent take him someplace that wasn't a hospital room. After a few moments he felt the bed dip beside his left thigh, then a gentle caress along his check.

"Hey, sweetheart."

Duke slowly opened his tired eyes. Vaughan was truly a sight. If he'd ever needed something beautiful to look at during all the ugliness he was experiencing… it was that moment. He was in a perfectly tailored suit; he knew it, because he was just able to make out the glittering gold cufflink inside the cuff of the crisp white shirt. He looked so polished and put together. Duke wanted to yank that pristine pink and gray striped tie until Vaughan was completely on top of him. He sighed silently. That would never happen. He'd never feel Vaughan on top of him, inside him, pounding the anxiety of a hard day away.

"Duke?"

The sweet sound made him realize he'd closed his eyes again.

"Duke." Vaughan looked at him with so much admiration that it caused his chest to hurt even more.

"I'm okay," Duke finally croaked. His mouth felt horrible, like he'd eaten a sheep. Dry and parched. "I'm better now that I'm seeing you."

"Good."

I wouldn't say good. "Were you at work? How's your new job?"

"It's a job." Vaughan skated over the question, immediately changing the subject. "Has the doctor been in today?"

"Um." Duke cleared his throat again and saw Vaughan reach for the cup of water that sat by his bed. He placed the straw to his lips and Duke didn't know how he felt about that. But that damn cast did make it hard for him to maneuver the small cup. Still, he didn't want to appear helpless in front of Vaughan. From what he understood, Vaughan had looked up to him. Admired and lusted after him. Now Duke was nothing more than a useless lump of man lying in a hospital bed with failing kidneys, waiting to die a quick but agonizing death. He took a small sip only so he could speak a little better and waited for Vaughan to put the cup back. "No. Not that I remember. I think he may have come in this morning."

The look on Vaughan's face was a mix of fear and anxiousness, but Duke couldn't be exactly sure because it was gone in an instant. Before he could question it, there was another knock on his door. He was hoping it wasn't another visitor, because there were things he needed to talk to Vaughan about. He was going to tell him that he would've given him a chance. That he would've let him woo him… and fuck him good. He probably would've let that last point hang in the air unsaid, but he wanted Vaughan to know before he left this earth that they would've had something wonderful, but Vaughan needed to go on with his life. He didn't want him coming to the hospital anymore. Duke was a done deal.

"Hey, Duke. How you feeling today?"

Oh great. It was his doctor. He sure sounded extra cheerful. Well at least someone's life was going well. "Good afternoon, Dr. Chauncey."

"Duke, I have wonderful news!" Dr. Chauncey smiled.

Duke tried to sit up a little higher, again wincing at the pain in his back. Vaughan put his hand on his arm. His face was completely impassive, but Duke's heart was pounding. Good news? What could it possibly be? Surely his kidneys hadn't healed on their own.

"Are you okay, Duke? Did you push your morphine drip to—?"

PROMISES

"Doctor, just spit it out. I'm fine. What's the news?" Duke almost growled.

"We have a donor. You go in for surgery Friday."

Duke's mouth dropped open. He turned and looked at Vaughan and he wore the exact same expression before finally, a slight smile curved his lips.

"Oh, my god. Are you serious?" Vaughan gasped.

The doctor looked at Vaughan for a split second before turning back to Duke. "I wouldn't joke about that. I've scoured every database in the country, Duke. We have a perfectly healthy, compatible kidney for you."

"Jesus Christ," Vaughan breathed. "He's gonna live?"

Duke didn't know who to look at. He felt like he might be dreaming, but he hadn't taken too much morphine, so he couldn't be hallucinating. "Dr. Chauncey. Are you telling me that my name came up already?"

"What I'm telling you Duke is that there's a kidney available and it's yours if you want it. What do you say?" Dr. Chauncey's expression and words were stern but kind.

"Fuck," Duke whispered. "Yes."

"Good, very good." His doctor smiled. Duke thought he saw him throw a quick wink at Vaughan but he could've been wrong. "Friday it is." Dr. Chauncey walked out, leaving Duke completely awestruck.

Dr. Chauncey was right. Duke had inquired how and why, but he didn't press the issue. The good doctor had said it easily. There was a kidney available, do you want it or do you wanna play twenty questions? Dr. Chauncey almost made it sound like he'd done something underhanded and the less Duke knew the better.

Vaughan had played his part, though. The shocked and flabbergasted look. He should get an Academy Award© for best

PROMISES

clueless performance in a potential lover's hospital room. He squeezed Duke's hand, kissing each knuckle. But the moisture building up in the corners of his eyes was completely genuine. He was so happy the doctor didn't wait to give Duke the good news, because he looked like he really needed the lift. It was like seeing him had put Duke in a worse mood. He hoped that wasn't the case.

"You must have been praying hard for a miracle. I sure was." Vaughan leaned down and kissed Duke's forehead. "This is amazing!"

"It's fuckin' unreal. How the hell? I'm sure there are people in front of me who have been—"

"Hey," Vaughan whispered, cutting Duke off. "Your prayers have been answered. Don't question it... just say thank you."

Duke smiled. "Yeah. But who do I thank god for sending? Is the donor dead? If so, how I can thank her family? Is she alive? How do I thank her?"

Him. Thank him.

PROMISES

CHAPTER SIXTEEN

"Are you nervous?"

"Hell, no," Duke replied to Quick. As soon as Vaughan left, he'd called Judge, Charlie, and Quick to tell them the amazing news. Duke hadn't smiled, or laughed in days, but after telling his friends, it damn near sounded like a house party instead of a hospital room. "I'm just ready to get out of this fuckin' place and live life, man."

"Fuck yeah!" Judge's deep voice was deafening in the small room, so no one was surprised when the charge nurse came in with her hands on her ample hips and a thunderous scowl on her round face.

Duke laughed hard. Way too hard for his still very sore ribs. But fuck it. He'd heal and he'd live. Fuck it all! Charlie placed a gentle hand on Duke's shoulder, urging him to calm down.

"Hey there now, boy. Ease up. Don't want you to have to postpone the surgery because you done injured something else," Charlie said, a playful gruffness to his tone.

"I think that's our cue, fellas. We better head out before this nice lady loses her religion behind us roughnecks." Quick smirked, throwing the nurse a wink that made her frown smooth out and her plump cheeks turn a rosy pink.

Good ole Quick. Always smooth.

PROMISES

"I'll bring my stuff over to your place in the morning, Duke, and head over here after," Charlie informed him. Duke nodded. Charlie had immediately volunteered to stay with Duke while he recovered. Even though the doctor said the surgery was not as invasive as in the past, there would still be a recovery period, not to mention Duke still had only one useful arm, fractured ribs and a slowly healing concussion. He'd secretly hoped that Vaughan would volunteer for that position, but he knew that it was way too early to hope for that. They hadn't even had a date yet. Besides, Vaughan also had a new job to excel at. The beautiful man might find a healthy young stud working around all those police officers and hotshot attorneys.

As his guys cleared out of the room, Duke's last thoughts weighed him down. Vaughan hadn't come back like he'd promised. Quick told him Vaughan was working on a very big case, while still trying to visit Duke. He'd felt like shit. He hadn't exactly welcomed Vaughan when he'd first shown up earlier. He'd been ready to tell Vaughan to stay away until Dr. Chauncey delivered the great news. His cell phone rang beside his bed and Duke had no clue how long he'd sat there lost in thought.

Vaughan's name showed up on the caller ID and Duke's heart fluttered. He juggled the phone with his bad arm before he got it under control enough to answer. "Hey," he said quietly.

"Hey yourself. How you doing, handsome?"

Oh, god. Vaughan's voice was like a soothing balm. It was late in the evening and Vaughan had thought about him. Thought enough to call him. "I'm doing, ya know. Your dad just left a little while ago."

"I know. He told me he was heading over to see you. He hasn't sounded so happy in ages. But. Enough about him. I need to talk about you. I'm so anxious for this to be past us so we can get back on track," Vaughan declared softly.

PROMISES

Duke cleared his suddenly dry throat. "Back on track?" Jesus. Was Vaughan still considering them? Damn, he hoped so. The man could make him fly like nothing else, and all he'd done was say a few romantic lines, and briefly brush his lips with his.

"Yes." Vaughan's voice was dark and deep. "You still owe me a date, handsome, and I fully intend to collect."

Duke smiled. "Well, I like to pay what I owe."

Vaughan let loose a sadistic chuckle that had Duke's balls tingling. "Oh, you will pay. Over. And over. And over, honey."

Duke had to take a few calming breaths. Getting an erection with a catheter was never pleasurable. Yeah. Mornings sucked. "Jesus, Vaughan."

"Mmm. Okay." Vaughan's laugh lost its seductive edge. "I'll behave... for now."

Duke sighed, wishing Vaughan had been able to stay longer today, but he said he had to get back to the office. He hoped he'd get to see his gorgeous face before they wheeled him into the OR in the morning. He felt like such an old man. The whole mess had happened because he was working hard and ended up taking on three people by himself. Some may consider him brave, but he felt foolish.

"Why are you so quiet?" Vaughan spoke up.

"Just thinking."

"About?"

Truthfully. "You. Me. Us. The Surgery. Life."

"That's a lot."

"Yes, and it's complicated."

"Hopefully, I'm the easy part." Vaughan's grin could almost be heard.

"Actually you're the most complex. I want to understand you... but." Duke tried unsuccessfully to say what he meant. But anytime he was faced with Vaughan, he couldn't understand what the man wanted with him? Duke was much older, set in his ways, needy and under-loved, starved for affection and on top of all that… he was laid up. What the hell was Vaughan thinking?

"But… you still don't get why I want you, huh?"

"I'm sorry. I'm not trying to be cynical here."

"Well, you're not doing a very good job. You're amazing, Duke. I've watched you for years."

Duke snorted. *Amazing? How?*

"You said I could have a chance. You said – when you thought you were dying – that you would've given me a chance. But now that you're gonna live—"

"*Might* live."

"*Gonna* live," Vaughan said sternly. "Are you rethinking this… us?"

"Vaughan."

"For the love god, Duke. I'm doing every—" Vaughan stopped midsentence.

"Doing what?" Duke prompted when Vaughan paused. "What are you doing?"

"Praying every minute that you haven't changed your mind." Vaughan's voice had gone to that sweet, low timbre that Duke loved. That he couldn't refuse.

"I haven't." *Baby. How can I?* "I'll give you as much time as you need." *Just don't hurt me, Vaughan.*

"That's what I needed to hear." Vaughan laughed before sobering quickly. "Sweetheart, I'm gonna come by and see you pretty early and then I have a flight to catch at nine. My job is sending me on assignment already. Can you believe that?"

Duke frowned. Vaughan sounded weird. Unsure. *Assignment*. "Where are you going?"

"Um. Miami. They want me to go with the lead attorney to interview a witness that left the jurisdiction. It shouldn't take more than a few days, and then I'll be right back by your side. I promise. My dad said he'd keep me posted, since I'm sure you'll be concentrating on recovering."

PROMISES

"Of course. I'm glad your job is entrusting you with so much responsibility already." Duke's gut twisted. He wanted to see Vaughan's face before and after his surgery, but he guessed that wasn't going to be possible. The man had to work, right? But wasn't this more important? He had to stop this. This needy shit. That's what ran Judge off. Vaughan couldn't hold his hand every minute. Duke was scared, though. He'd admit it to himself, if no one else.

"Yeah. I was pretty shocked. Anyway. Don't worry about that. It's late. Focus on getting as much rest as you can and I'll be there bright and early to give you a kiss before you go in for surgery."

"That sounds like something to look forward to." Duke smiled, trying hard to sound convincing.

"Night, handsome."

"Goodnight, Vaughan."

PROMISES

CHAPTER SEVENTEEN

Vaughan pressed the end button, cradling the phone to his chest. His eyes burned with tears. He hated lying, detested it. His father always told him that a real man doesn't have to lie, cheat, or steal. Vaughan may not be a thief or a cheat but he was definitely a liar. Would Duke ever trust him once he found out the truth? He turned back to his small duffle bag and silently prayed that Duke would. It was the right thing to do. He could feel it. If Duke had any inclination that it was him, he had no doubt he'd cancel the surgery. Vaughan wouldn't take that risk. He'd lie and break any other commandment on the list if it meant giving them a chance. He finished packing by dropping his leather toiletry bag on top of his change of clothes, along with his transplant folders.

He had to be checked in to the unit at six a.m. That meant he'd have to go to Duke's room at 0'dark thirty and then go to his own room so he could be prepped on time. He was going to have to juggle quite a bit over the next couple weeks, but he could do. He would do it.

"You all packed and ready?"

"Yes, sir," he answered his father. Quick's face was a mask of uncertainty and worry. "I told you. I'm going to be fine, Dad. Have faith. This is not as complex as you may think."

PROMISES

Quick waved one large hand at him. "I know. I read up on it, son. I just… well, you know. I'm a parent before I'm anything. I'm gonna worry."

Vaughan took a deep breath and went over to face him. "Thank you for trusting me."

"You've never given me a reason not to, Vaughan. I just hope you know what you're doing."

"I've never been so sure of anything before." Vaughan hugged his dad for a long time. "I love him. I love him too much not to try."

"I just hope you don't get hurt in all this."

"I won't. I promise."

"You can't promise that, son. Never make a promise you can't keep," Quick told him for the millionth time in his life.

Vaughan patted his dad on the back. "I know."

Vaughan couldn't eat or drink anything, so they sat together on the back porch and looked out over the lush lawn, the dewdrops glistening as the moonlight hit the blades of grass. It was peaceful and quiet until his dad's work phone rung.

"Goddamnit, not now," Quick barked, pulling out the large phone.

"Go on. I understand."

"I wanted to have this time with you," his father said, pulling on his long hair. "But since Charlie's retired and with Dana and Duke hurt we haven't had the time to hire more guys. So it's just me running the bail bonds and Judge running the PI office."

"It's okay. Duke's gotta have a business to come back to. I'll see you in the morning. I'll go to see Duke first, around five, and then I'll check in."

"I'll be here to drive you to the hospital. You don't want to leave your car in the lot anyway."

"Sure thing." Vaughan gave him another quick hug and headed back inside. "Be safe."

PROMISES

"It's just a bond. I'll be back in a couple hours. You go on and sleep."

But sleep never came.

Vaughan stifled his yawn right before he tapped on Duke's door. He wished he would've gotten at least an hour of sleep, but all he did was toss and turn. His mind wouldn't shut off. He thought of everything under sun that could and couldn't happen. After a while, he simply concentrated on what his and Duke's first date was going to be like. At least that made him smile. If he couldn't sleep, he'd think happy thoughts.

Surprisingly, Duke was awake. He was sitting up for the most part—as far as he could— watching the early-morning news.

"Why are watching that crap? It's always bad news." Vaughan entered with a smile on his face. He was wearing a pair of tan slacks and a cream fleece pullover. Classic traveling clothes for an attorney, right? Had to play the part. The small duffle on his shoulder adding to the traveling illusion.

"I'm in the bad news business, Vaughan," Duke answered with his own smile. Thank goodness. He was glad Duke was in relatively good spirits.

Vaughan stopped and looked at Duke. He was clean-shaven and a pleasant soap and water scent wafted off of him. He looked good. He looked fresh and ready. "You look good, babe. Ready to knock 'em dead." Vaughan almost rolled his eyes at his own stupid comment. Damn, Duke wasn't getting ready to play a football game for Pete's sake; he was having life-saving surgery. It had to be his nerves getting the best of him. Coupled with the lack of sleep. It might be best if Vaughan just sat and visited… keeping his mouth shut.

PROMISES

"I brushed my teeth real good," Duke said softly, his beautiful eyes staring right at Vaughan's mouth.

Vaughan walked close to Duke's bed and dropped his bag off his shoulder. His own smile was wide and genuine. He'd said he'd kiss Duke before his surgery and obviously the man hadn't forgotten. Seemed like he'd been looking forward to it because he was prepped and ready. Vaughan laughed. "That's good to know, but it wouldn't have mattered." Vaughan dropped the guardrail on the left side, his eyes never leaving Duke's. Propping his hip on the bed, careful not to sit too close, Vaughan leaned in and Duke closed his eyes right before their lips met.

Vaughan could taste the minty toothpaste along with the subtle taste that Vaughan recognized immediately as all Duke. He felt Duke's left hand gently graze his cheek before traveling over to his mouth. Vaughan pulled back just a hair and let Duke trace his bottom lip with the pad of his thumb.

"You have the most beautiful mouth I've ever seen," Duke whispered.

Vaughan leaned back in. It was the sign he'd been looking for. Duke looked at him with so much awe and wonder, Vaughan knew right then that they were going to make it. Not only through the surgery, but also as a couple. Duke was finally looking at him the same way Vaughan had looked at him since he was sixteen. Like he was head over heels in love. Vaughan pressed his lips to Duke's cheek, his temple, his eyes, his forehead, before making his way right back to his supple mouth.

"You taste like heaven," Vaughan murmured into Duke's mouth. Kissing and gently licking his way inside. Light, gentle nips of his teeth against Duke's lips had Vaughan's cock rising rapidly. He took his time, exploring his man until he couldn't stop the moans from escaping his parted lips.

"Oh, god. I don't want you to… but stop. You gotta stop." Duke's eyes were closed tight, tiny beads of sweat popping up around his hairline.

PROMISES

Vaughan got worried. *Shit.* He didn't mean to hurt Duke and his expression must've conveyed that because Duke quickly reassured him.

"Don't get me wrong." Duke rubbed Vaughan's arm, braced by his head. "It felt so damn good. Better than anything I've felt in a very long time. Too good… if you get my meaning." Duke glanced down at the small bulge in the blanket and Vaughan nodded his understanding. Duke didn't want to get full on wood. That probably would've been very uncomfortable.

"I can easily get carried away with you, sweetheart." Vaughan released a calming breath as he pulled back from their intimate position. "But, if I'm anything, I'm patient. I can wait a little while longer." Vaughan stood and raised the rail on the bed. As soon as he did, his father came through the door with Dr. Chauncey following close behind.

"Son. You better get going; you don't want to be late." His father glared at him, then at his watch.

Damn. It was already six o'clock. He felt like he'd just got there. How long were he and Duke snuggling? Dr. Chauncey gave him a quick exasperated look before turning his attention to Duke.

"Everything still a go, Doc?"

Dr. Chauncey nodded once while looking over Duke's chart. "We're still going. Your blood pressure is a little higher than I'd like but not enough to have to postpone."

Everyone in the room breathed a sigh of relief. Dr. Chauncey laughed, snapping the folder shut. "The nurse will be in to get you soon. Not much longer now. The surgery should take about three and a half to four hours since I'm going to also try to do some more repairs on your own kidney that will remain in place. The goal is to restore at least a half of its functionality."

"Do you think everything will go okay?" Vaughan asked.

PROMISES

"I'm very confident it will." Patting Duke's shoulder one final time, Dr. Chauncey said, "I'll see you in there, Duke," and left the room.

Vaughan had to get to his room. He didn't want to cause delays. And it looked like Dr. Chauncey was telling him with his eyes to move his ass.

Quick was over by the window, giving them their last few seconds alone. Vaughan bent and kissed Duke's forehead. He wanted so much more, but in due time. "I'll be back as soon as I can. I'll be thinking about you the entire time, even if you don't see my face, sweetheart. Please know that I'm right there with you. I'm closer than you think, okay?"

Duke gave him a tight smile and Vaughan squeezed Duke's good hand before he hurried out the door, not wanting Duke to decode his message. He was partway down the hall when he heard his name called. Vaughan turned just in time to collide with his father's broad chest. He couldn't control the silent tears that fell. He wanted to tell Duke so badly, but that was as close as he could get to the truth. He was there with him, not far away at all.

"It's alright, son. You're both going to be in each other's arms in no time." His father's soothing voice eased his tension. He had to calm himself. He didn't want his own blood pressure to skyrocket. Quick helped him get settled in his room while Dr. Chauncey went over a few last remarks, but Vaughan knew what was going to happen, he'd had an extensive and informative, albeit short, evaluation. He just wanted it done. He was chewing on his jaw, a nervous habit he's had since he was a kid—when his father put his hand on shoulder. "I'm so damn proud of you, Vaughan."

Vaughan wasn't expecting that. Those intense eyes shone with adoration and Vaughan had to reign in his emotions again. "You have become a damn good man. Strong and confident."

PROMISES

"Like you," Vaughan interjected. "Just like I was raised to be."

Quick smiled that crooked grin and Vaughan felt his heart lighten. He and his man were going to pull through this surgery and they were going to be a family.

"Dad. Go back to Duke. I want him to be with someone before they take him." The nurse was putting in Vaughan's IV while he spoke. His dad looked so unsure, but kissed him on his cheek and whispered a choked, "I love you," before he left his room.

"Try to relax, Mr. Webb. The orderlies will be in to get you soon." A blue paper-like, disposable surgical cap was placed over his head to complete his prep. The nurse smiled that classic reassuring nurse's smile and left him in a semi-dark room. His lack of sleep had to be the reason he'd dozed off, because next thing he knew he was moving. Felt more like floating. He fought the sleep, prying open his heavy eyelids. The lights above him flew past as he was wheeled down a chilly hallway. His teeth clattered loudly and his hands shook beneath the scratchy hospital blanket. He was nervous, no doubt. He could use a familiar face right now but things were moving in a blur. He could hear voices but none that he recognized. A slight bang registered as doors swung open into a room marked "AUTHORIZED PERSONNEL ONLY" and bright lights and a strong antiseptic stench assaulted him. People flittered around in pastel-colored scrubs, with masks covering half of their faces, all of them with their own task to complete.

His stretcher came to an abrupt stop and Vaughan's eyes were wide as saucers as he tried to take in everything around him. He said a quick prayer that he and Duke would both pull through. It was short and to the point. He wanted to raise his head but it felt heavy. He wanted to see everything happening around him, but the staff went on as if he wasn't even there. He half-expected Duke to be right beside him, but he knew it didn't work that way. Duke was in the next operating room over, or nearby, at least. His chest moved up and down rapidly and he tried desperately to calm himself. One wrong or bad alert from one of the many machines he was attached to and it could all be stopped. He felt the blood pressure cuff inflate again, squeezing his bicep. The nurse beside him called out some numbers that Vaughan didn't understand. There was so much shit in the room, so much technical equipment that it made Vaughan dizzy. He didn't dwell on his environment any longer when he saw a man's face appear over his. He was older, if the crinkles next to his smoky gray eyes were any indication

"Vaughan. I'm Dr. Waynes. I'm the anesthesiologist. I'm going to place this mask over your face and I want you to take a few deep breaths and count down from one hundred. Can you do that?"

Vaughan nodded, but the mask was already being placed over his face. He wanted to follow exact directions because he couldn't shake the sinking feeling that something would go wrong. Dr. Waynes looked over at a monitor near the head of Vaughan's bed as he began to count in his head. *One hundred, ninety-nine, ninety-eight.* Dr. Chauncey's eyes were staring down at him, his mouth and head completely covered. Dr. Chauncey was speaking to him but he barely was able to make it out while he counted. He had to follow directions. *Ninety-seven, ninety-six, ninety—*

CHAPTER EIGHTEEN

"Duke. Duke. Duke."

Duke frowned. Someone was calling him from very far away. He tried to focus his attention on hearing what Quick was saying, because that's who he'd been talking to earlier. He thought. No. This person's voice was not as deep as his friend's. Duke fought through the grogginess, clawing his way back to reality. As he came closer and closer to the surface, his body began to ache in various places.

"Don't try to move, Duke. Open your eyes."

Who the hell is that? Duke's eyelids fluttered as memories floated back to his consciousness. Surgery. Kidney.

"That's it, Duke. Open your eyes."

Duke forced his eyelids to move. It was hard, or at least it felt hard. God. Why was he feeling like this? Like he had a boulder sitting on his stomach. He soon realized that not only was he sore as hell, he was scared, too. Did the surgery work? Was his body feeling like this because it was rejecting the kidney? He'd read about that. Damnit. He was still going to die.

"Duke. Are you awake?"

He felt hands, then something tugging at his hospital gown and then the obvious feel of a stethoscope pressing on his chest before a female voice began rattling off his vitals.

"Duke."

PROMISES

"Shh. What?" Duke finally croaked, annoyed and damn if that didn't hurt. His throat was a fiery mess. Burned and ached all at the same time.

A quiet chuckle reached him. "What... what, is that I want you to wake up so I can tell you how great the surgery went and you have one very good functioning kidney and the other is not in as bad a shape as it was. You're going to be all right, Duke. And no I won't 'Shh.' I like to brag after an operation."

Duke realized that it was Dr. Chauncey talking and when he finally dragged his eyelids open and kept them that way, he felt a small smile grace his lips in spite of his pain. He was going to live. Oh, god. Vaughan. He was going to have a shot at the hottest guy on the planet. But first he had to get out of the bed. "Sore," he managed on a harsh groan.

"You're going to be for a while. But the laparoscopy went fine and I didn't have any complications. Your throat will be fine in a couple days. It's sore from the breathing tube. Although you still have some other injuries that need time to heal, I want you up and walking this evening.

"What the hell." Duke grimaced. "I'm hurting all over, Doc."

He watched Dr. Chauncey make some more notes in his folder while the nurse read off information from the monitors and typed in some of the doctor's orders. Including a slow two- to five-minute walk after he was removed from the post-op wing and back up to a room.

"I want to go home. I'll do all my exercises like I'm supposed to, Doc. I promise. And I have someone there to help me." Every word tore at his sore throat, but Duke had to let them know he needed out of that place fast, before he lost his chance at something wonderful. Vaughan wouldn't wait forever. But as Duke thought about it more, it became clear that he would. Actually, from the sound of it... Vaughan had waited for him. Waited for some time.

PROMISES

"A couple days, Duke. Give me a couple days to make sure everything is working properly and then you're welcome to go home and recover."

"Can I see my friend, please?" Duke asked.

"He's still in the waiting room." It was great that Dr. Chauncey knew who he was talking about. He was so lucky to get that doctor. He'd saved his life. Stopped at nothing to get Duke a kidney. How would he ever repay him? Or his donor? "Quick can come up after we get you back in your room, but he knows the surgery was a success."

Duke thought he'd said okay and thank you, but he didn't remember. He'd already begun feeling the effects of the pain medicine the nurse gave him. He was exhausted. Then he was asleep.

When he stirred again it was because strong hands were on his shoulders and his friend's voice was stern and uncompromising in the small room. "He's still resting. How the hell do you expect someone to take a stroll when he's just had major surgery? This is absurd. Get the doctor in here, now."

If Duke could've managed to smile, he would have. It appeared it was time for him to wake and walk, but his friend disagreed. Duke's body actually did too, but his mind was stronger, and so was his will. If he wanted out of there soon he'd do anything they asked.

"You rang, Mr. Webb?"

Duke still hadn't opened his eyes because he didn't necessarily want to. They were actually pretty entertaining. Now Dr. Chauncey was in the room. His calm doctor-tone immediately bringing Quick's rant to a screeching halt. He heard his friend clear his throat before speaking again. "This guy is trying to wake Duke up for a damn walk. Is this right? He's not well enough to walk yet."

"How do you know?" Dr. Chauncey said easily, sounding quite amused.

PROMISES

Quick stuttered. "B-because he... he... he just can't. He's tired. Look at him."

Damn. How bad did he look? Thank goodness Vaughan was out of town. Hopefully he'd look better by the time he made it back, and most of all... he hoped he'd be at home.

"Quick. Standing and moving prevents a lot of post-op complications. The most critical is the pooling of secretions in the lungs while under anesthesia. Staying static and still is extremely dangerous. Lungs can develop bacterial growth if he doesn't move around; change positions, breathe deeply. Then, of course, we want to prevent blood clots, upset intestines—I can go on if you're not satisfied with my reasoning so far. Duke is strong, he'd appreciate it, trust me. So will his back. I'm just gonna do a dangle for now. Just let his legs hang over the side of the bed and maybe have him take a couple steps around the room first. He can rest and take some more pain meds right after. Then I want him back up again first thing in the morning."

Duke had opened his eyes and was watching his friend. Quick didn't know that Duke was awake since Quick was watching the doctor so intently. Although Quick was nodding his head in understanding, his gaze seemed to be focused on the doctor's mouth. Duke frowned. His friend looked intrigued, as his large chest rose and fell rapidly, like he was out of breath. Then he saw it, the look of lust that crossed over Quick's handsome face right before the doctor turned back to Duke. What the hell? Oh yes, Duke definitely had to get out of this damn hospital bed sooner rather than later. He and his friend had so much to discuss.

"I'm okay, Quick. I can do a... What did you say, Doc...? Dangle? Sure, I can dangle and manage a few steps," Duke said, his voice still gravelly, even after his few sips of water.

By the time Duke shuffled the few feet from his bed to his hospital door, he had a thick sheen of sweat on his forehead and plenty of moisture dripping down his sore back. His tender ribs

PROMISES

protested with every step, but he pressed on. His casted arm was resting on his best friend's muscular forearm, while the bulky male orderly had his good arm wrapped over his, keeping Duke steady. He'd only managed three steps, barely gotten out his door—not even making it to the nurse's station—before he stopped. Winded and in pain, his stomach heaved with nauseous exertion. Shit, he was going to puke right in the middle of the hallway.

"Duke. Buddy, you okay?" Quick's nervous tone made him want to reassure his friend, but he couldn't at the moment. Opening his mouth would surely cause the water and broth he'd consumed to spray out in front of him. He gave a tight shake of his head and Quick hurriedly demanded that the orderly turn around and take him back to his room.

"This was good, Mr. Morgan. Some people don't make it two steps away from the bed." The big guy turned them slowly and got Duke back in his room. But damn if Duke didn't want to cry as soon as he was back in the bed. It seemed that his mind must've been so focused on staying upright and not embarrassing the hell out of himself that he hadn't registered the extent of his pain until he was lying back down. The orderly made sure to push his morphine drip before he made some notes—probably of Duke's progress—on the computer. He shut everything down and told Duke that another guy would be there in the morning.

"Get some rest, buddy. I see Vaughan has called about ten times. Let me give him an update and I'll come back tonight for a bit. I think Judge said he'd be in tomorrow, he's busy as shit in the office trying to keep up with the new contracts."

Duke liked the sound of that. His businesses was still thriving. Thank the lord he wouldn't be in the poor house after all was said and done. "No problem," Duke forced through gritted teeth. He thought about Vaughan, liking that he'd been calling and checking on him. He wanted to send a message but didn't want to make Quick uncomfortable. So he used a generic, "Tell him I look forward to talking to him soon."

"I will, man. Get some rest," Quick said, and left him alone. Although it was only a little after five, Duke knew he was ready to go to sleep—probably for the night.

CHAPTER NINETEEN

"Dad, how is he? Is he in a lot of pain? Did he ask about me?" Vaughan fired off the questions as soon as his father entered his room. Dr. Chauncey had already told him how everything went and that Duke was doing well after post-op. That was after Vaughan got his own glowing report. He had tenderness in his abdomen but nothing too terrible. He had hurt worse when he was bumped by a drunk cab driver in Paris. The driver hadn't been going that fast, but Vaughan still was hit hard enough to roll up on the hood before crashing back down onto the asphalt, breaking his clavicle.

Quick put up his hands, stopping Vaughan's string of questions. His father leaned down and pecked him on the forehead before asking, "How are you doing, son?"

"I'm fine. I just walked down the waiting room and back a little while ago. Dr. Chauncey said Duke was up too. How'd he do with his walk? I know his ribs had to be screaming."

His father sighed and sat down in the one chair in the room. "Yeah, he was hurting, but you know Duke. He's built Ford tough. He kept going until he looked pale as a ghost and about to pass out before I demanded that it was enough. He's a stubborn jackass is what he is. He'd probably have walked home if it meant getting closer to you."

PROMISES

Vaughan's eyes widened. It was the first time his dad had referenced Duke's feelings for him and he jumped on it. Sitting up a little too quickly had him wincing, but he wanted to know. "Did you and he talk about me? What did he say?"

Quick rolled his eyes, pulling out a folded newspaper from in his jacket, an amusing glint in his eye as he unfolded and started to read it, completely ignoring his son. Quick crossed his booted foot over his knee and whistled tunelessly, like he hadn't a care.

"Dad, come on," Vaughan practically whined. He knew he sounded like a moody child but he didn't care. Duke had talked to his father about him and he wanted... no he needed to know... what he'd said.

"What?" Quick feigned ignorance.

"Oh, forget it. I'll find out myself." Vaughan eased back down to a comfortable position and picked up his cell phone, but a big hand stopped him from dialing.

"Okay, okay. Just hang up. Duke is asleep anyway." Quick rubbed his temples and dropped his paper on the small table next to his chair. "He's head over heels, son."

Vaughan's smile was bright enough to keep his room lit if the power went out. "Seriously," he whispered.

"He's been my friend for a long time. I know him. He's in love, or maybe smitten to death."

"Smitten?" Vaughan frowned.

Quick waved his hand. "You know what I mean. I don't know what the term is these days when you're hot for someone, okay." He sighed, looking up at his son. "Duke had it bad for Judge, but the way he looks when he's talking about you... I never saw it when he talked about Judge. I think he was looking for companionship with Judge, knowing he wouldn't get the flower, dinners, and love thing from him. He was willing to accept that because he didn't want to live a lonely life, ya know.

Judge was there and was comfortable, but long-term he wasn't able to give Duke what he wanted."

"No. He could give it to some hot, young, Atlanta detective, though." Vaughan seethed. He'd never understand how anyone could turn Duke away. Judge would always be on his shit list for that, no matter how stand up the guy's friends believed him to be.

"Judge is a damn good man. He was always up front and honest with Duke. Judge found what he wanted in life and now, so has Duke. So fate worked its magic like always and you'll all be with who you're supposed to be with."

"I guess," Vaughan said tiredly, yawning widely. His earlier exercise was starting to catch up with him and he felt an overwhelming sense of exhaustion right before he closed his eyes, still staring at his father. He later remembered thinking before he drifted to sleep, Who are you fated to be with, Dad?

Vaughan eased up the couple steps in front of his dad's house and Quick carefully propped him against the wrought iron rail while he fumbled with his keys. Vaughan breathed a sigh of fresh air right before he went inside. It was great to be home. He'd been holed up in that hospital for three very long days. It would've only been two but he hadn't been able to produce a bowel movement by the second day, so Dr. Chauncey, being the overly cautious doctor he was, insisted that Vaughan stay one more day, and made sure that he was at least passing gas. It was all so personal and nasty, but that was the medical profession. A little embarrassment was a small price to pay to have Duke in his arms for the rest of their lives.

Duke had gone home the day before since he was doing so well. Charlie and his daughter were helping care for Duke while Quick took care of Vaughan. Duke was under the impression that Quick was busy handling the office. Duke didn't know

PROMISES

Judge had taken a couple bounties and asked a couple of his guys from the PI office to come over and assist Quick, which made him more available to care for his very own post-op patient. Vaughan thanked the heavens that it was all going to be over very soon. As soon as Duke confessed his undying love for him, Vaughan would tell him the truth, and not a moment before.

"I'm gonna help you upstairs, then I can fix you a bowl of soup. I made some homemade chicken noodle. You used to love my soup when you were sick as a kid. Do you remember?" Quick smiled at him as he led him up the small flight of stairs to the second floor.

"Of course I do. I loved your soup whether I was sick or not. I think I even faked it a few times to get it." Vaughan chuckled wearily. He was tired and sore, he'd willingly admit that much. He knew what to expect. He'd do his exercises and stay mobile so he'd heal properly. By his next checkup, Dr. Chauncey would be amazed. However, at the moment he needed a hot shower, food, and rest… after he talked to Duke.

They'd talked every day, a couple times a day, and always right before they went to bed. It was so strange talking to Duke like he was in another state, all while he was right down the hall. He'd come out of his hospital room on the second day for his evening walk on the ward and had almost run into Duke doing the same thing. Moving so abruptly and ducking behind the wall had caused Vaughan a little pain, but it was worth it to keep his secret until the right time. As if his father knew what Vaughan was thinking, he got a big bath sheet from the linen closet and placed it in the bathroom attached to the large guest room. He put Vaughan's pills on the nightstand and his bag under the bed for the time being. Lastly, Quick retrieved Vaughan's phone and placed it on the bed next to his pillow. With a quick smile, he left so his son could clean himself up. He'd needed help the first couple days, but he could manage alone for the most part.

PROMISES

He unbuttoned his shirt and eased it off his stiff shoulders. Damnit, hospital beds suck ass. He knew a lot of his back pain and the tightness in his shoulders would dissipate now that he had a comfortable bed to sleep in. He pushed at the slack waistband of his very low-slung sweats, careful not to touch the bandages that covered his incisions. Three small gauze pads were taped over the half-inch incisions where the laparoscopes were inserted and one medium-length bandage was over the slightly larger two-inch incision where his kidney had been removed from his body and placed in his lover's. Vaughan lightly brushed his hand over the bandage. His head swam, and his heart beat with a strong, thumping pulse. He was so in love, he'd given away his kidney. A throb began behind his left eye anytime he thought that Duke would reject him. But that wasn't possible. He banished those thoughts to the very back of his mind. There was no way. Vaughan could already feel how deeply Duke felt for him, just based on their conversations each night before bedtime. He hated the lies he had to tell in the beginning of their conversations, and any time Duke asked how his work assignment was going. Vaughan always quickly changed the subject. But each time the call came to end, there were words left floating out there, unsaid, before they each hung up. Even now, he ached to hear the man's rough, deep voice... Oh god... To taste him again. Vaughan's cock began to rise but he ignored it. His next orgasm would be given to Duke.

"How's the case going?" Duke asked Vaughan as he lay in bed watching the football game on mute.

"Work, work, work. All day. So much that I don't want to talk about it. I'd rather talk about you, babe," Vaughan answered sensually.

Damn why did the man have to drip sex? Duke wanted to fly down to Miami and burst through Vaughan's hotel room door and writhe all over him, bathing himself in that delicious scent that lingered on Vaughan's smooth skin and close his eyes while Vaughan talked about everything and nothing, as long as he used that damn voice.

"Alright," Duke said back. "No more work talk. How about... When are you coming home talk?" Duke had asked him the first day after his surgery but Vaughan didn't know. Maybe he did now.

"Soon, sweetheart. Maybe a week and half, two at most."

Fuck! Two long weeks. Well, maybe it was for the best because Duke needed to heal. Wasn't like he could do anything anyway, but at least he and Vaughan could talk face-to-face if he was home. Eat together. Watch television, movies, fucking hell... Netflix. He didn't care, as long as the man he was quickly falling for was close to him. Two damn weeks. Duke groaned before he could think better of it. There was a brief pause before he heard Vaughan let out a ragged breath.

"Don't make that sound again, Duke," Vaughan whispered seductively. "Next time I hear that sound from you, I want to be buried deep inside you. I want you to repeat that sound over and over again while I make love to you."

"Oh, fuck," Duke groaned, squeezing the base of his rock hard cock. It'd been that way ever since he'd picked up the receiver and heard Vaughan's voice. His stomach muscles clenched involuntarily and the hiss that escaped him was far from sexy. His body was showing him that it wasn't close to ready for that type of activity yet. Duke placed his hand over the small incision right above his pubic bone. The scratchy cast rubbing his sensitive skin as he did.

"Calm down. Don't hurt yourself," Vaughan said softly. "Due time, honey."

"I can't fuckin' wait," Duke murmured.

"You can and you will," Vaughan scolded, asserting his dominance, and Duke wanted to moan his submission.

PROMISES

Yes, I will wait. Because you told me to.

Duke hadn't felt like this in so long. His body vibrated all over from Vaughn's words. He felt like he was back in college, learning his body; figuring out what it craved. He'd found out fast that he wanted a man to dominate him, control the sex, and ride him hard into submission. He wasn't a masochist. He didn't want to be flogged or whipped, but damn if he didn't get off on a man that could make him leak with well-worded orders. Judge never found that appealing about him. He wanted another alpha in the bed with him, fighting him for control. That wasn't Duke. He was strong, masculine, and all alpha… just not inside the bedroom. Duke might have moaned again at the thought of Vaughan finding that quality about him hot.

"Duke. You alright, son?" Charlie tapped on his door as he spoke through it.

Shit. How loud had Duke moaned? "I'm good, Charlie. Was just settling back down into bed," he answered quickly, feeling slightly embarrassed, especially when Vaughan started to laugh teasingly in his ear.

"Need some help?"

"No!" The thought of Charlie coming in and seeing Duke's erection sticking straight up like a rocket was mortifying. Duke calmed down before Charlie, thinking Duke was upset, came in anyway. "No, I'm good. I'm gonna get some sleep. Night."

"Good night. See you in the morning."

"Night," Duke said, and listened as his friend walked slowly down the hall to Duke's second bedroom.

"He still staying with you?" Vaughan asked after a while.

"Yes."

"That's good."

"I'm thinking of sending him home at the end of the week though."

"I'd hate to think of you there alone, especially if you need help or something."

PROMISES

"I'm getting stronger every day. I feel good. I'm moving more during the day. I'm pissing good—" Duke stopped, cringing with mortification that he'd just said that last part. That wasn't attractive at all. It made him sound geriatric.

"That's great, sweetheart. I can't wait to get back home so I can see for myself that you're okay." Vaughan's voice dropped a couple octaves. "Need to see you so bad."

"Me too." Duke's shaking voice betraying his faked composure.

"Soon, okay? I promise," Vaughan assured him softly.

"Promise." Duke didn't care how needy or desperate he sounded right then. He needed Vaughan like he'd needed a kidney. Needed him to survive. Already, he was hooked. If Vaughan did him like Judge did, just found someone else and left suddenly, he wasn't sure if living was going to be such a great idea anymore. It would suck balls, that for sure. "Vaughan, just don't—"

"Duke, baby. I can hear it in your voice. I won't hurt you. That, I can promise easily. I'll show you when I get back, okay. That if you'll have me. I'm in this for the long haul."

Duke smiled, relieved and reassured. It would do for the moment. But after they hung up, he thought some more about the differences between them. Those thoughts always came back to taunt him. How much younger Vaughan was. How smart and talented he was. How culturally diverse he was.

All Duke knew was how to run a bail bonds and private investigations business. He hadn't traveled the world or studied at the best schools in the country like Vaughan. He didn't dress like a supermodel, hell; he could barely shop for one decent outfit. He wasn't as suave and debonair as Vaughan either, but for some reason the man wanted him, so he had to have some faith. He was just an ordinary working man, but Vaughan saw something that obviously no other man had seen. Duke certainly

PROMISES

couldn't see whatever it was that Vaughan did in him. He hoped he could hold on to a man as wonderful and beautiful as Vaughan. He fell asleep wishing there was something to guarantee him Vaughan was serious and his heart was safe with him.

CHAPTER TWENTY

It had only been a week and two days. Vaughan was still down in Miami for work. Duke missed him so much, but at least he was healing and would be able to see Vaughan when he came back. He'd had his checkup the day before and Dr. Chauncey was happy with his progress. His incisions were healing, still red and puckered, but no sign of infection or rejection to be found. It was such a relief to move around more freely. He did fifteen minutes of light exercise twice a day, eager to get stronger, but careful not to overdo it. Vaughan had made him swear he wasn't doing too much. He wouldn't be dishonest. He kept his physical therapy to only what the doctors recommended.

He wanted to call Vaughan and tell him that he was in his office today for the first time in weeks, but he knew Vaughan would be busy in the middle of the day. He'd have to tell him that night when he called. He sat at his desk, looking out over the street as people moved about, their schedules busy. Quick had been in that morning but wasn't there when Duke made it in. He was hoping to speak with Quick; get the details on the few bounties he'd had to give away. Luckily, they still did bonds, so the business was fine for the time being.

When Duke thought about taking another bounty his heart clenched and his stomach rolled. The nightmares didn't help him feel ready for it, either. Charlie kept asking him to see a psychiatrist, telling him that it was possible Duke might have some PTSD from his experience in that crack house. Duke would wait a while, but if they got worse, he fully intended to take the old man's advice. He'd never steer Duke wrong.

He'd been sitting there for a couple hours when his side started to ache too much to ignore. Ribs took forfreakingever to heal. That's where ninety percent of Duke's pain came from. He had some in his back, but mostly it was those damn ribs. He knew his entire midsection been beaten mercilessly and there was still some internal bruising… All very painful… But he'd heal. He just had to be patient.

Duke shut down his computer and was about to stand when his phone rang on his hip. He picked up and saw Judge's name up on the display. He hadn't seen the big guy since he'd been discharged, but he knew how busy he was and Duke appreciated that Judge had ensured that his businesses stayed operational in his absence. Judge was a good friend to him. "Hey, man. What's up?" Duke answered.

"Hey. You home?" Judge asked in that gruff voice that used to make Duke squirm. But weirdly… Not anymore.

"No. I'm at the office. Just stopped by to one: get out of the damn house, two: check in with Quick, but he wasn't here."

"No. I guess not."

"What do you mean?" Duke said, flicking off the light in his office and locking the door behind him.

"Austin was at the hospital interviewing a witness that's a patient on the fifth floor. Anyway, he called and told me Quick was there with his son in the Nephrology unit."

Duke was shaking his head in disbelief as Judge spoke. That wasn't possible because Quick had a bond he was working on at the courthouse and Vaughan was in Miami. Judge's boyfriend must be mistaken. Duke finally broke into Judge's side of the conversation. "He must've mistaken them." Even the words sounded stupid to Duke's own ears. How could he mistake Quick? And he damn sure couldn't mistake Vaughan.

"No one can mistake Quick's big ass, with that long fuckin' hair and tattoos, man."

Very true. "Well, how would Austin know who Vaughan is?" Maybe Quick was there with someone else.

"I showed Austin the pictures I took at Charlie's retirement party and Austin specifically pointed out Vaughan asking who he was and I told him that he was Quick's son, recently back from school. And Austin never forgets a face."

"This isn't possible," Duke whispered to himself. Why would Vaughan lie? Or maybe he just got home and was checking on... Hell, Duke couldn't come up with anything right then. Vaughan was at work. In Miami. Judge was still talking and Duke had to stop his internal monologue and listen.

"You know, man. I was skeptical when I saw him all over you at Charlie's party. I really thought you were trying to get back at me or something... for... you know... and him being younger."

Duke scrunched his entire face up at the absurdity. 'Getting back at him.' Is he fuckin' serious? "Why the hell would you think some bullshit like that?"

"Chill. Chill. I know. It was dumb, okay. But it seemed weird for Quick's son to be all over you, dude. You have to admit. But man. Anyone that would donate a kidney to someone else... That's real dedication, man. The kid is all right in my book. Why didn't you tell me it was him?"

"WHAT!" Duke screamed, immediately clutching his side in pain. He hadn't realized that he'd been walking without thinking and was already back in his truck. He turned over the ignition since he was sweating from the heat that had filled the cab in the last couple hours. If he was going to think clearly, he had to cool off and breathe. His ears rang and his heart felt like it would beat right out of his chest and fall onto the floorboards.

PROMISES

"You don't know," Judge said timidly.

"WAIT! WAIT A FUCKIN' MINUTE!"

"Duke, whoa. Calm down, please. I thought you knew."

Duke could hear Judge cussing and swearing under his breath.

"Are you telling me that Vaughan is the donor?" Duke's voice was so tinged with emotion and pain that he hoped his words were comprehensible. "Are you sure?"

Judge was saying something, but his voice was muffled like he had his palm over the mouth of the receiver and Duke assumed he was talking to his lover. Trying to clarify some of the information. Then Duke heard, "Just give me the phone," and the next voice he heard was deep and melodic.

"Hi, Duke. It's Austin. I'm glad you're okay, man. Judge was real upset when he thought you wouldn't make it."

Duke wanted to tell Austin to get to the damn point, but he listened, trying control his breathing.

"Anyway. Judge told you why I was at the hospital. My witness gets dialysis at the hospital five days a week and I was there talking to him when I saw Quick and his son standing at the nurse's desk with a couple doctors. I was gonna head over and introduce myself but I thought I'd let them finish flirting with the ladies, because the nurses were going on and on. I mean really gushing over them both. But when the doctor turned and told Vaughan that everyone on that floor loves a living donor and how brave and generous everyone believes them to be, Vaughan was actually blushing. So I knew it was him and not Quick. Especially since his walk was slow and measured when he left, like he'd... like he'd had surgery."

Okay, Duke thought. That was a lot of good evidence, but still not concrete. Austin's next words shattered that delusion. "The doctor also walked with them to the elevators and as they passed me, the doctor said Vaughan was healing well and would see him in a couple weeks. So I put two and two together and figured; how much of coincidence could this really be? I told Judge, since he'd been skeptical of the guy's intentions. No one would donate a kidney to just anyone... not unless there was some serious love there."

Shit. Shit. Shit. How is this possible? Vaughan was the anonymous donor. No one had told him. Why? What the hell kind of friend was Quick? What the hell kind of man was Vaughan? Why did he lie? Why was he still lying? Duke needed answers now, right now. He thanked Austin tiredly and was getting ready to hang up when he heard Judge again.

"Oh man. Me and my big fuckin' mouth. Don't go crazy, Duke. I'm sure he has his reasons for not telling you... yet," Judge added hurriedly, but Duke wasn't in the mood. He only had two people in the world that he needed to talk to right now. Actually three.

Duke was still sitting in his truck in his parking lot. Thinking. His head pounding, sweat pouring down his temples into his collar. His body ached dully, but he was fueled by adrenaline. Surely he'd feel it all when his body calmed down. He finally looked back at his phone and pulled up his internet browser. He retrieved the phone number he needed and pressed the send button.

"Fulton County District Attorney's office. This is Madeline, how can I help you?"

Duke took a calming breath before speaking. "Attorney Vaughan Webb's office, please."

"Sure, one moment."

Duke sighed. He was sure there was an explanation for everything. "Hello, this is Sarah. How can I help you?"

Duke frowned in confusion, thinking the next voice he'd hear would be Vaughan's. "Um. I'm holding for Mr. Webb, please."

"I'm sorry but Mr. Webb isn't here. I'm his assistant, is there something I can help you with?"

PROMISES

Of course he's not there. He's in Miami. "Is there a better time to call and reach him?"

The woman hummed first before responding. "Actually, Mr. Webb won't be available for a few weeks. I'm his assistant, but he wasn't able to start on his scheduled date. He's out on medical leave."

"Excuse me?" Duke asked incredulously. Medical leave.

"Yes. His start date was postponed at the last minute. Was his name given in regards to a specific case the firm is handling, because it must be a mix up. I can transfer you to the duty attorney and you can let him know what case you're inquiring about—"

Duke stopped her midsentence. He'd heard all he needed. "No. That's fine. I'm sorry to have disturbed you."

"Are you sure? I can transfer you."

"No. Thank you."

"Have a good day."

Duke hung up. Fuck me. Vaughan had saved his life. Only thing he didn't understand was the secrecy. The lies. Well that all stopped now.

CHAPTER TWENTY-ONE

Vaughan did one final lap around his father's spacious backyard before he decided to take a break. Dr. Chauncey said he was doing great and should keep up his light exercise regime, so that's what he was doing. A casual walk around the yard, breathing deeply and filling his lungs with fresh air while taking in the tranquil landscape. There was even a small fountain installed near the deck, and Vaughan's thoughts went to Duke and how much he'd love to lie in one of the plush lounge chairs with his man between his legs, resting his head on his chest. Both of them gracing each other with lazy kisses while they looked up at the dark sky and listened to nature. He pushed for one more lap, desperately needing his body back in shape.

"Vaughan, that's enough for today. You walked this morning, too. Don't want to strain yourself, son," his father called to him, closing the backdoor.

Vaughan was sweating. The Atlanta heat in the fall was bad, but the evenings were cooling off, which would be perfect for his upcoming dates with Duke. Man, did he have it bad. Maybe Vaughan really did have an old soul, because most of his friends were partiers, drinkers… tramps. But Vaughan always knew how he wanted to live his adult life, and that was peacefully and comfortably with Duke. He wanted to walk on the waterfront with him, maybe take some boat rides on the harbor. Vaughan loved the water.

"Dad, I'm gonna take a shower. Are you going back to work?"

"Nope. I'm all clear for this evening. How about a movie tonight?"

"Heck, yeah. Sounds good, old man."

"What do you want for dinner?"

Vaughan paused on his slow walk up the stairs. He was so tired from his extra laps, his stomach was cramping painfully from the workout. "Something light. Maybe a grilled chicken salad or something."

"I gotta go out and get some more lettuce then." Quick was already picking up his wallet and phone, ignoring Vaughan's objections to him having to make a special trip. "It's all good. I need to get a few other things anyway. Be back in a bit."

Vaughan shook his head at his dad. The man was truly amazing. He was so glad he came back to Atlanta, not only to be with Duke, but Quick, too. They had always been close, but over the seven-and-a-half years of schooling Vaughan had to complete, they'd missed a lot of time together. His father had been taking such good care of him, he felt spoiled again. Helping him with everything from changing his sheets, to doing his laundry and cooking for him.

After he finished his shower he felt a little better, but was still bone tired. He wiped at the foggy mirror, looking at the red scars on his abdomen. He decided to let them air dry before putting on fresh bandages. He pulled on a loose pair of cotton pajama pants but left the matching button up shirt open. He made his way back downstairs, his hair still damp. He was going to get his blanket and lay it out on the couch in preparation for their movie night. He was fixing his cover when he heard the doorbell chime. He wasn't expecting anyone and his father never got unexpected visitors, so he figured the old man forgot his key again, or he had too many bags in his hands to open the door.

Vaughan stood up straight, his incisions pulling a little. He winced, buttoning his shirt as he made his way to the door. "You forget your key again you—" Vaughan stopped immediately, his teasing grin falling like a rock to the ground as he opened the door and saw the man he loved standing there looking angry and in pain.

"Duke. Jesus Christ. What are you doing out of bed?" Vaughan asked nervously, pulling his shirt, making sure all the buttons were fastened securely. Duke's sharp eyes followed the gesture before moving back up to his face. He wished he knew what Duke was thinking, because his usually kind brown eyes were shooting daggers at him. "Come inside before you hurt yourself."

Vaughan walked back inside carefully, hoping Duke would follow, but wouldn't notice anything. Like how slow Vaughan was moving. He had to turn his back on Duke or the guy would see the exhaustion in his eyes, just like Vaughan could see it in his. His lover looked so tired, and Vaughan ached to wrap him in his arms and take care of him. Not to mention how much he'd missed him while they were both recovering. Duke had on a pair of track pants and a plain white t-shirt like he'd not planned on going out. His salt-and-pepper-colored hair was longer than usual and free of product, blown in whatever direction the wind had taken it.

Duke was at his dad's house. How the hell did Vaughan explain that he was there and not in Miami? Um. Did he take the red-eye last night? Or did his flight get in a little while ago and he was just getting ready to call Duke after he'd unpacked and showered? Ugh. More fuckin' lies. But he had to think of something, he was a lawyer for crying out loud. Maybe he could stall or divert.

PROMISES

Vaughan acted like it was critical to get them something to drink, so he kept going towards the kitchen, needing to come up with a plan quickly, preferably one that involved the fewest lies. "Let me get you something to drink, sweetheart. Please sit down; you look exhausted. I'm going to get us some—"

"Stop," Duke growled, and Vaughan paused mid-stride, but he didn't turn around. He knew Duke was too smart for this to go on. Especially the way Vaughan was acting. If everything was normal, Vaughan would be all over Duke right now, not scurrying away.

Vaughan stopped at the breakfast bar, his back still to Duke. Something was wrong. Duke wouldn't be there otherwise. "Duke, you should be in bed. What are you doing out? Where's Charlie?"

There was no response, but Vaughan could feel the heat and anger radiating from his man, especially since he was standing close enough for Vaughan to feel the hot breath ghosting across his still-moist skin on the back of his neck. His body burned with the need to touch Duke. His mind warring with him to come clean now. Oh god, but how? It was too soon. "My dad said you were doing better. Have you had a doctor's appointment yet?"

"Turn around," Duke finally demanded on a harsh breath.

When Vaughan turned after several long seconds, he was face-to-face with his love. Duke's eyelids were hanging low, and there were dark smudges beneath his eyes. Vaughan almost reached out and smoothed the deep frown that ran down the center of Duke's forehead. The skin around his eyes had crinkled with laugh lines over the years but the creases there now weren't from amusement. Duke was thinking hard. The next words that left Duke's mouth had Vaughan stunned and eager to go back in time and forget his idea to be the anonymous donor.

"I thought you said you were an honest man and you didn't play games."

PROMISES

Vaughan turned his head just slightly. Did Duke know it all or did he simply find out that Vaughan wasn't in Miami? He wasn't sure. *Fuckin', fuck, fuck!* He never would've came up with that idea, but how else could he recover? Duke would want to see him when he'd been released. He wouldn't understand why Vaughan couldn't come over if he only lived a few minutes away. Even if he could blame it on a new job. No one worked twenty-four hours a day. Not even attorneys. "I don't play games, sweetheart."

Duke nodded his head once, his casted hand going up to his temple, scratching it like he didn't understand something. "You conveniently left off the honesty part."

"Duke. I'm not a liar. I swear," Vaughan whispered painfully. "But I'll do and say just about anything to protect the—"

"The what?" Duke said, inching in closer when Vaughan didn't finish.

No. Not yet. It's not time to tell him, yet. "To protect those I care about," Vaughan amended.

"So you care about me?"

"Of course I do. You already know that," Vaughan argued. He was deliberately not mentioning Miami. He wouldn't unless he had to.

"I don't know shit. I thought I did. I thought I knew how you felt. I thought I knew how I felt. I thought I was destined to be alone. I thought I had to have favor with god to be given a second chance at life. I thought I was going to be loved… finally."

"Duke." Vaughan sighed, but stopped abruptly when Duke's hands reached for the top button of his shirt. "Don't."

"Don't you dare try to stop me," Duke cut in, unhooking the second button from the top of Vaughan's shirt, those dark chocolate pools boring into his skull.

PROMISES

So Duke knew. How the hell? No one knew but the Doc and Vaughan knew he took his confidentiality oath seriously. His father—of course he'd never betray him. Other than that, no one. Not even his mom knew he was less one kidney. So how the hell? "How?"

Duke's eyes stayed on Vaughan as he undid another button, slowly and carefully, like Vaughan had C4 strapped to his chest.

"Sweetheart. Who told you?"

Duke ignored his questions and undid the button right above Vaughan's navel, his eyes still on him. Vaughan was too scared to break the contact. Too scared to look down and see that his three incisions were already visible. Duke's eyes remained locked on him. He desperately tried to convey his love for the man through his stare. Hopefully now that Duke knew the truth, he wouldn't think Vaughan was deceptive, he'd think he was a man in love.

"Was it my father?"

Duke unfastened the last button and Vaughan's shirt was open. He could feel the cool air on his still-tender wounds. Neither one of them looked away but he saw and felt the quickening of Duke's breathing. Dropping his heavy, casted hand, Duke used the other one to gently push back the sides of Vaughan's shirt, his hot palm resting on his hip.

"Look," Vaughan whispered, so gently. "Look at how much you mean to me." Vaughan's eyes didn't drop as he spoke; he kept his gaze fixed on Duke as he watched his love's sexy dark brown eyes trail down his sparsely haired chest to his abdomen. Duke gasped, his eyes filling with moisture. Vaughan felt hesitant but nimble fingers trail across the tiny incisions, but as Duke got to the larger one over near his pubic bone, where the kidney had actually been removed from his body, his hand began to shake. The skin around his incisions looked raw and irritated because he'd had his staples removed earlier that day, but he hoped his man could handle it. Duke's face was smooth and even, his expression revealing very little, almost as if he were in shock. A lone, quiet tear fell down Duke's scruffy cheek, the drop of moisture landing heavily on the floor between them.

"Don't cry, sweetheart."

"What have you done?" Duke uttered on a groan, continuing to stare at the incisions like they'd disappear and prove Vaughan really didn't love him as much as he was claiming.

"I did the only thing that I knew in my heart was right, because sitting back and watching you die just wasn't an option."

Duke's hand tightened on Vaughan's hip and a surge of lust and attraction ran through him so fast that Vaughan jerked in the hold. Duke winced but Vaughan was quick to reassure him. "I'm not hurting. I'm always affected that way when you touch me."

Duke was silent as he continued to stare.

"Who told you, Duke?"

Duke looked back into Vaughan's eyes, his mouth a tight line.

Vaughan was getting a little agitated. "Why aren't you answering my questions?"

"Because you're asking the wrong questions," Duke responded quickly. "The questions you're asking should be directed at you... not me. You should ask yourself: Why didn't I tell him? How could I lie to him?"

"I've asked myself that plenty of times and the answer is always the same, baby. I didn't tell you because I couldn't risk you refusing. Although the risk of mortality is miniscule for live donors, you wouldn't have allowed me to take it. I was going to tell you, I swear it. But I didn't want you to feel obligated to me." Vaughan's own emotions were barreling to the surface as he continued to plead his case. He was so nervous that Duke would turn on his heels and leave, claiming Vaughan wasn't trustworthy, regardless of him lying only in the course of saving his life. And isn't that what Vaughan wanted in the first place? For Duke to decide what their relationship would be solely on his feelings for him, not because he'd saved his life? "I wanted you to love me for me. Not because I gave you a kidney."

"Damnit, Vaughan. This is so hard for me to understand. That—"

"That anyone could love you so much," Vaughan interjected. He gripped Duke's chin, tilting his head back up. He took a chance and leaned down to lightly brush Duke's lips with his. The heady sensation of touching Duke, being intimate with him made Vaughan dizzy. "Or, you can't understand that I love you that much."

"Both," Duke whispered. His head was still angled as if wanting more contact with Vaughan's mouth, so he happily obliged. He kissed him deeply, his tongue tapping lightly before bursting through the barrier, exploring his man again. Getting familiar again. Duke's good hand came up and gripped the side of Vaughan's neck, rubbing his thumb back and forth over his rapidly beating pulse. Duke moaned and angled to the other side, his own tongue on its quest for exploration. Vaughan let Duke explore for a while as he leaned back and gave Duke the entire span of his long throat. Oh, how beautifully he did it. Duke nuzzled into him, lightly kissing and licking his way across his Adam's apple. Vaughan gripped Duke's cheek, forcing him to stay at an especially sensitive spot on his throat and was getting ready to take it up a notch when he heard a deep, growly throat clearing.

CHAPTER TWENTY-TWO

Duke separated his mouth from Vaughan's neck, albeit begrudgingly. The gorgeous man smelled so fucking good and tasted like the finest wine, which was crazy since he was so young. But as he got to know Vaughan and spent more time talking with him, he was noticing how much of a man he truly was. Mature and strong. Fearless had been added to Duke's long list of Vaughan's admirable qualities. And the man loved him. Loved him enough to put his own life on the line to save him. Seeing those scars, exactly like his own, had completely undone him. Despite his suspicions, he wasn't prepared to actually see the physical proof. How the hell would Duke even consider walking away? He'd wanted reassurance and he guessed he'd gotten it. This beautiful man intended to be with Duke forever.

"I guess the cat's out the bag," Quick said drily, as he strolled past, looking at his son's open shirt, his surgical wounds on full display. Quick's thickly corded forearms were loaded up with packed grocery bags as he made his way through the rest of the house.

Duke let go of Vaughan, but the man held on to him, still looking into his eyes, his hand still caressing Duke's cheek. He had a bone to pick with his best friend. He wasn't letting him off the hook as easily as he did Vaughan. He pulled Vaughan's hand away and kissed a couple of his knuckles before dropping it and turning to follow Quick into the kitchen. "You asshole!" Duke thundered as soon as he turned the corner and saw his friend casually posted-up against the counter drinking a bottle of water.

"Here we go," Quick mumbled under his breath.

"Seriously." Duke gaped. "How the hell could you allow him to do something like this? It was dangerous and foolish, Roman. What if something had happened to him? You would've lost your best friend and your son, but you would've hated me. Probably wouldn't have attended my funeral if Vaughan had died on that table. I can't believe you let him do it!"

Quick's green eyes flashed with anger before he took a breath to try and reel it in. "Have you fuckin' met my son? Huh? What the fuck makes you think he asked for permission? He's a grown man, Duke! He made a decision and that was it. No matter how much I disliked it, especially the part about being anonymous; I had no say! All I could do was pray for both of your lives, so that's what I did." Quick finished his piece and turned back to putting away the groceries.

Duke pushed his knuckles into his eye sockets. "He made the decision with his heart, not his logical mind."

"That's why nothing on this earth would've changed it. Not me, his momma, you, or any other thing on this planet. He's in love, Duke." Quick turned back, and Duke noticed his pal was looking over his shoulder, meaning Vaughan had to be standing there behind him. "He would've gave you both his fuckin' kidneys."

Jesus. He was in love with his best friend's son. This was like a story out of a bad episode of *To Catch a Predator*. Duke had to shut down that thought. He hadn't fallen for Vaughan when he was a teenager. Had never looked at him sexually for even a second. But before him stood a man who knew what he wanted and kept his own counsel. He was a good man for Duke. Quick must've seen a look on Duke's face because his friend came over and guided him to one of the chairs at the small table in Quick's eat-in kitchen. Duke looked out the bay window over the luxurious backyard he'd help his friend design.

"You remember what I said to you in the hospital before we got the bad news?"

Duke blinked. *Remember… Remember what? Oh shit. Quick said he would've been proud to have Duke as a son-in-law.* A coffee mug with piping hot tea was placed in front of him and he looked up to see Quick watching him, waiting for an answer. "Yeah, buddy. I remember."

"I wasn't blowing smoke, Duke. You're my man, fifty-grand and all. We've been through so much together. Now here's another. We beat this thing, man. All of us together. Let go of the anger and be happy. Be happy with my boy because he deserves it. He went through hell, Duke when he found out about you getting hurt so bad. It took him a while to calm himself down, but when he did, that brilliant mind of his went into solution mode. That's what he does."

"I'm lucky," Duke whispered, sipping his tea.

"Well," Quick drawled. "You're dating my son now, and this is my first time getting to interrogate his boyfriend."

Vaughan groaned from in the doorway, having been silent while Duke and Quick hashed it out. Now he was looking mortified. Duke laughed, but Quick had a deadly serious expression on his face. He watched his best friend sit down in the seat across from him and clasp his large hands together. "So Mr. Morgan. What are your future plans? Where do you see yourself in… say, ten to fifteen years? Long-term goals if you would."

Duke tried desperately not to laugh but it was ridiculously hard. "Um. Since I'm headed towards fifty soon, I'm thinking of retiring around that time, then applying for Medicare. I figure having a lawyer boyfriend will be helpful filling out those long ass forms."

PROMISES

Vaughan spit his water across the room as he exploded with laughter, but Duke held his in and so did Quick. He watched as his friend took another drink of his water; nodding his head like Duke had given a great answer.

"What about employment? Do you got a job, boy?" Quick said, pulling up his old drill sergeant tone.

Duke stayed composed. *Boy, huh?* "Yeah. I got a job. A pretty thriving business. I'm thinking of firing a couple employees soon, though." Duke grinned evilly.

"Okay, enough about employment." Quick feigned nervousness. He knew damn well that Duke would never fire him. Quick and Judge both were practically co-owners.

"What are your intentions with my son, Mr. Morgan?"

Duke shrugged nonchalantly. "I don't know yet."

"You don't know!" Quick barked. "Damn. I thought you were gonna say you were getting ready to propose right before I came in."

"Propose." Duke choked on his tea.

"Heck yeah. Damn, Duke. What the hell does my son have to do, man… give you a fuckin' kidney?"

Duke dropped his head into his hands as Quick and Vaughan had a good laugh at his expense. "So how long have you two been working on that joke, huh?"

"It's all mine. I thought of it a few days ago," Quick said humorously. "Was a pretty good one, wasn't it?"

"Whatever," Duke muttered. "You gonna be here all week with that act?"

"Now. On to more important shit. One: What the hell are you doing out of bed? Two: How did you find out?" Quick demanded as he rattled around pots and pans, looking for a specific one. When he found his griddle, he placed it over two of the gas range's burners and turned on the flame, placing some raw chicken breasts on it.

PROMISES

Vaughan stood behind Duke, rubbing his shoulders. He hadn't realized they'd slumped with fatigue until his boyfriend put his hands on them. Boyfriend. *Wow, that was fast.* He wanted to bask in the attention, but it felt bizarre with his friend in the same room. He tapped on Vaughan's hand and he lowered his head, kissing Duke gently on the cheek as he did. "Babe. It's a little weird doing this with your dad in the room, don't you think?"

"No."

"Yes." Quick jumped right in, flipping the chicken breast, his back still to them.

"I told you," Duke confirmed.

Vaughan went to his father and clapped him a couple times on his shoulder. "He's not uncomfortable. Are you, Dad?"

"Little bit," Quick deadpanned.

Duke laughed. That was Quick's sense of humor at its finest and Duke loved it. Always had. It wasn't slapstick or ironic comedy, simply that impassive, matter-of-fact, dry wit. They were best friends, and now they were… they were… they were something special. He was Quick's best friend and hopefully one day, his son-in-law. They were a modern family to say the least.

"Judge told me," Duke finally confessed.

Vaughan and Quick exchanged confused looks before looking back to him to elaborate. "Judge's boyfriend, Austin, saw you at the hospital when you went in for your check-up earlier. He's a detective. From what I heard, a pretty good one. He easily put two and two, ya know."

"Damn," Vaughan whispered.

"Well thank goodness. I was sick of the ducking and dodging anyway. Flittering around lying and covering up your tracks, boy," Quick grumbled, pointing at his son. "Next time, Vaughan, you'll handle your own skeletons. I'm a grown ass man."

PROMISES

Duke and Vaughan both huffed and stood up to leave Quick to his one-man rant. He did make a mental note to have a good, long conversation about his friend's sexual orientation soon, because he had a feeling that it may have altered a bit. Duke hadn't forgotten that look in Quick's eye when he argued with the doc.

"Duke come in here and get comfortable on the couch. We were gonna watch a movie while we eat dinner," Vaughan said, taking his palm in his.

"Well, I don't want to intrude. That's gonna be important to me. You and your dad need time together. He's missed you something terrible and I don't want—"

Vaughan placed his index finger over Duke's lips to silence him and he immediately obeyed. Vaughan groaned and inched in closer, his shirt now half buttoned back up. Duke couldn't help but drop his eyes to Vaughan's soft, pinkish lips. "What about what I need? About what I want?"

"I'll do anything you want," Duke whispered, and his immediate compliance didn't have a damn thing to do with his recently discovered intel on the origin of his new kidney. He'd felt like that from the moment Vaughan turned up the heat on them.

"Good." Vaughan grinned. "Stay and eat. Relax. Then come to bed with me."

Duke grimaced, looking over his shoulder. "Not in your father's house. Not cool at all. Besides. My medicine is home. I can bypass a pain pill but I can't skip my immunosuppressants."

"I'm sure Dad wouldn't mind picking them up for you."

"I'm not sleeping with you here, with your old man only a few feet away. I respect my friend too much to do that."

Vaughan wrapped his arms gently around Duke's waist, careful not to apply too much pressure on his ribs. He leaned in and kissed Duke first, before pressing their foreheads together. "Don't worry, sweetheart. I'm not gonna make love to you tonight. Not until we're both feeling better and healed. I couldn't take that sweet ass like I'd want to, so I'm gonna wait patiently like I've been doing. Right now, you being alive is enough for me. Plenty."

"Okay." Duke blushed. He was actually flushed like a schoolgirl.

CHAPTER TWENTY - THREE

Vaughan watched the deep rouge color creep up Duke's face, his ears turning bright red under Vaughan's attention. *Perfect*. It did amazing things to Vaughan's heart and his ego. He wished he could take his man right away, but Duke already looked tired as hell and if his grimacing was any indication, he was in significant pain, too. He'd take care of his love. He could do nothing else.

"Sit, sweetheart. I'm going to get you one of my pain pills, okay, then we'll get your other stuff."

"Yeah. It's been a long day."

"I can't believe you came over here. I don't think you should be exerting yourself like this." Vaughan went over to the credenza and shook a Vicodin into his palm and took it back over to the couch. Duke quickly took the pill with Vaughan's glass of water and sat back.

"I had to see for myself. I had to look at you." Duke didn't bother mentioning he'd called Vaughan's job too. There was no need.

Vaughan sat next to him, releasing his own weary sigh as he did. "I'm sorry. I just… I couldn't risk you saying no. And after the conversation you just had with my 'old man' as you so eloquently put it, it appears I made the right decision. You would've denied me."

PROMISES

Duke's eyes were getting heavy. "I don't know. Maybe. I can't say for sure. I wasn't scared of dying; I was just disappointed as hell. Before you came, I might've been able to make my peace with it. But since I'd got a brief taste of you, I felt like dying before I really got a chance to be loved by you was pretty shitty."

Vaughan made to turn and kiss Duke, but yelped at the pull on his incision. Duke's eyes flew open and he sat up too fast, releasing his own cry of pain. They both looked at each other and chuckled. *This is going to be interesting.*

"Freakin' dumb and dumber over here. You two are gonna be the death of me. Tell me. Who's going to donate me a new heart when you both give me a goddamn heart attack?" Quick barked, a deep frown on his face. He placed the tray on the coffee table and Duke's mouth watered at the delicious-looking salads. "From the sounds of it, there'll be no movie tonight. I'll go get Duke's other meds from his place and we can watch the flick tomorrow." Vaughan put Duke's plate on one of the TV trays and pulled it close to him before taking his own and placing it on his lap. He ate quietly because Quick was updating Duke on the business. When he came back in with his homemade banana pudding, Vaughan had to control his eagerness. Oh, how he loved it when his dad made that for him. Obviously it had been a special treat that he'd wanted to surprise him with, but he was glad he'd shared it with Duke.

"I'm gonna go and get the room ready. Come up in a few minutes, okay?"

"Sure." Duke smiled slightly, then turning to gauge his friend's reaction.

Quick paid them little attention as he put the dishes in the sink for the morning, locked up the house, and closed all the shades. Vaughan winked at Duke right before he disappeared up the stairs.

"You going to the office tomorrow?" Quick asked after everything was done.

"Hadn't planned on it."

"Good."

"Excuse me?"

Quick gave him a stern look. "You heard me... Good. I need you to get better, man. Stay here and rest. Make sure my son doesn't overdo it on the exercising again. You watch him and he can watch you. I know it's the blind leading the blind, but I have work to get done now that I'm not playing you two monkeys' game anymore."

"Okaaay," Duke drawled. "I'll leave you to it."

"Are you going upstairs to sleep with my son now?"

"Oh, god. Come on, Roman. You know I'm not—"

Quick put up his hands in surrender. "I'm just fuckin' with you. Go on up and rest, dude. I'll run over and get your stuff and be back in a few." Before Quick could get out the door he added, "I got an early bond hearing tomorrow, then I'm going to the office. I'll see y'all tomorrow night. I'll call before I walk in the door though," Quick said mockingly.

"Rome," Duke griped tiredly.

"Okay. Okay, I'm done for real now."

"Good," Duke mumbled, walking towards the landing for the stairs.

"Son, a man's coming up to your room," Quick bellowed loud enough to wake the dead. Duke rolled his eyes so hard he thought he'd never see his irises again.

"Oh happy day, Father," Vaughan crooned from somewhere upstairs. His voice way too sexy and deep to pull off a fair maiden's tone. "A gentlemen caller of my very own."

"You two are idiots," Duke murmured, taking each step carefully.

"Night." Quick laughed. "Hey! Remember, these walls are thin. Just to let you know."

"Then keep your porn on mute and jerk off quietly, I need to sleep," Duke bitched back right before he reached the top of the stairs. But he heard his best friend's grumbled "Fucker," before he got down the hall.

CHAPTER TWENTY-FOUR

He chanted over and over in his mind. *I'm gonna sleep with Duke, I'm gonna sleep with Duke.* Despite the fact that he couldn't fuck him yet, it was still going to be heady lying with him. Touching him, smelling him, caressing. Those weren't off limits.

Vaughan had just finished brushing his teeth after he fluffed up the sheets on the bed, too tired and achy to change them. Since his father had done it for him the night before and Vaughan hadn't beat off in ages, he felt it was good enough.

He'd heard his dad announce Duke's arrival so tactlessly and he had to respond in kind. When Duke turned the corner into the guest room Vaughan's heart skipped a beat, the lyrics to Etta James' *At Last* annoyingly filled his mind, and he had to blink hard to banish them. He'd play it cool even though he wanted to pounce on the man like an animal would its mate. Vaughan was almost there, within reach of claiming what he'd waited so long for. They needed another couple weeks to heal completely, so he'd take the time to get to know Duke better.

"You look so tired, babe. Why don't you take a quick shower and come join me." Vaughan tilted his head towards the queen-sized bed in the center of the room. He loved the way Duke nodded his head once and headed towards the bathroom to follow his suggestion, a slight pinkish tone gracing his strong cheeks. *So damn handsome.* Vaughan pulled back the covers and climbed beneath the cool cotton sheets. He sighed heavily and sank bank into the pillows on his side of the bed. He was so excited and drained at the same time. It had been a pretty long day and he hadn't realized how much he'd needed relaxation until he stopped moving.

When the shower turned off a few minutes later, Vaughan's stomach fluttered and his cock twitched happily. It was obvious Duke had gotten the same post-op instructions as him, that showers were to be limited. Maybe turning on the television would derail his mind from the direction it was headed, as he thought about Duke next to him half-naked and smelling like his soap. Ah. *The Late Show.* That's about as nonsexual as he could get at that hour.

"You don't watch the news," Duke said, coming out the bathroom, a billow of steam following him like he deserved to make a dramatic, sexy entrance. He had a long, soft white bath sheet wrapped around his lower half, tucked low enough that Vaughan could see Duke's scar. *Duke's scars. Jesus Christ... my other kidney is in there.* How did Vaughan not prepare himself for that? He swung his legs over the side of the bed and sat up, staring at Duke as he rummaged through the top drawer of the one large chests Vaughan had in the room. His man pulled a pair of pajama pants out, but before he removed the towel and put them on, he turned and noticed Vaughan staring intently at him.

"What's wrong?" Duke frowned, looking concerned. His eyes followed Vaughan's line of sight and it was like a lightbulb flicked on in his head. "I must've worn the same expression a few hours ago."

Vaughan thought he was going to lose it. He'd come so close to losing the man in front of him. A man that had been his focus through the grueling college and law school years. All the exams, studying, traveling, loneliness and aching, so much stress he'd endured – all so he could be a man worthy of the one standing so close to him now. Vaughan brought both hands up and delicately placed them on Duke's hipbones. His eyes heavy but focused, he took in all of the splendor before him. All the magfuckingnificence that was Duke Morgan. Badass bounty hunter and brilliant businessman. Strong, solid chest, fine definition around his abs. Not as much as before, but once Duke got back to his daily routine and exercise regimen, all that would change. Vaughan could already tell that Duke had started to work his arms again because the one that wasn't casted look bulky and solid. The V that formed at the bottom of his abdomen was something out of a *Men's Health* photo shoot. And to stoke the hot flames blazing within Vaughan, Duke had the nerve to have fuzzy black hair spread across those thick pecks and down past his belly button. But oh god, as it did… the hairs there were a beautiful, enticing blend of silver and black. Even the small bald areas where Duke's incisions were didn't detract from his beauty. Vaughan thought he'd come right there just looking at him.

"Jesus, kid," Duke groaned, squirming under Vaughan's scrutiny.

Kid, hmm? Vaughan didn't like that. He stood slowly, lifting one hand and brushing his knuckles across Duke's coarse cheek, up to the scar that had recently lost its stiches above his right eyebrow. Damn, if the scars and bruises weren't a fuckin' turn on now, too. Now that Duke was going to live. Even the cast was hot. It told Vaughan that it took a house full of crazy cracked-up psychos to take his man down and they still hadn't succeeded.

But, being called "kid" wasn't gonna fly. Why'd he stay away so long if he was going to come back only to still be considered a young'un? Vaughan drove his fingers up into Duke's long hair and gave a slight pull at the length on top, not enough to hurt, but enough to make Duke anticipate the hurt. Hurt he'd inflict later. He leaned in and took a long whiff, his nose against Duke's damp neck, inhaling until his lungs would no longer expand. Did that a few times while Duke waited patiently. Tuning his lips against Duke's ear he spoke as calmly but as intimidatingly as he could, ensuring his lover got the picture.

"Listen to me, sweetheart. I'm your man. Do you understand me? I'm not a kid. I'm not a boy. I'm the man who's going to love you more than anyone ever has. And as soon as we're healed up—" Vaughan gently blew his hot breath inside Duke's ear, licking his fleshy lobe, only to blow again. Duke moaned prettily, though it was deep and growly. "I'm gonna go ahead and apologize now."

"Apologize for?" Duke gritted out.

Vaughan took his hand, still clutching that thick, wavy hair and tugged it to the side so he could claim Duke's mouth at exactly the angle he desired. When he finally came up for air, both of them panting into each other's mouth, Vaughan played his trump card. "Apologize because as soon as we're healed. I'm going to show you the man I am. I'm going to fuck you so hard your ass is gonna curve to my dick. And you'll love me back because I'm the only *man* that can make your body fly."

"Oh my fuckin' god, Vaughan," Duke cried, holding his stiff cock through the terrycloth fabric still covering his lower half. "You can't say shit like that."

Vaughan kissed Duke again, needing more. Would he ever have enough of Duke? He was skeptical at best. "You taste so fuckin' good. Like life and experience." Vaughan licked at Duke's lips and a languid smile appeared on his face; Vaughan couldn't stop his own radiant smile.

"Come on. Bedtime," Vaughan said, suddenly. He had to cool them down, or else his father would be banging on the door barking at them to stop trying to kill each other.

"That sounds good." Duke still held the pajama pants as he turned back to the bathroom, looking over his shoulder as

PROMISES

Vaughan watched Duke strip off the towel and gingerly step into the pants, making sure the waistband didn't ride up to irritate his incision. But not before giving Vaughan a good look at his furry ass. His mouth watered. He'd slick all that hair down around that dark hole with his saliva real soon.

Duke climbed into the other side of the bed, seemingly careful not to cross over the invisible line running down the center of it. *Oh no. Can't be none of that.* Vaughan sat up and placed a pillow on Duke's right side so he could prop his casted arm up while he slept on his back. Vaughan turned on his side and eased closer until his leg was intertwined with Duke's, one arm resting on top of his pillow, the other on Duke's chest. Stroking him calmly, easing him to sleep. He wasn't only there to fuck Duke the way he needed it, he was there to be his partner, and that meant taking care of every need. And just then his man needed rest.

PROMISES

CHAPTER TWENTY-FIVE

Duke tried to pry himself from his nightmare, his chest heaving because in his dream he'd been running for his life. Why did he keep having the same damn dream over and over? Who was he running from? Then everything went still and tranquil. A large warm hand was caressing him from his throat down to his navel, so patient and careful. The sweetest, gentlest touch he'd ever felt. Like he was being cherished. He needed to open his eyes all the way, but what if he was still dreaming. Finally, he was completely free of the dream, breathing normally; he didn't want to wake and ruin it.

"Easy, sweetheart. It was just a dream," a sensual voice said next to his throat.

Duke wanted to bury himself under Vaughan's delicious morning growl and stay there until he was forced away. It comforted him like nothing ever had. Waking up drenched in sweat, his voice hoarse from yelling out had been a frequent occurrence in recent weeks; starting right before he left the hospital. He was afraid that he may have to take Charlie's advice. The old man had run into Duke's bedroom one too many times looking as frightened as Duke felt before he reluctantly insisted Charlie go home. Nightmares had never killed anyone. He'd figure it out on his own.

"Do you get them a lot, babe?"

PROMISES

Duke was wide-awake, but he kept his eyes closed, wanting to soak up every moment of comfort, every inch of contact that Vaughan was giving him. He was so close; Duke could feel the warmth wisping over his sensitive neck with each word he spoke. He moaned slightly when Vaughan stroked his chest, not bothered by the sweat that clung to him. "I'm fine."

"I know you are," Vaughan quipped back. "But I didn't ask how you were."

"I have them almost nightly, but at least they're not getting worse. I don't think I was yelling." *Oh no, was I?*

"No. You weren't yelling but you were breathing hard and grunting."

Great. "Your dad probably thought we were going at it." Duke rolled his eyes. "Well… The grunting is better than how I used to wake up. Honestly. This was the best I've slept in months."

Duke finally opened his eyes fully and turned to look at Vaughan, and the sight took his breath away. *Holy shit.* Duke was speechless. How was it possible for someone to wake up looking like Vaughan did right then? Duke was discreetly trying make sure he didn't have a drool trail on his chin while Vaughan laid there looking, like the song says: *I woke up like this… flawless.* All that sexily tousled honey-brown hair somehow looked as if it'd been styled that way. Smooth, olive skin that went for miles down Vaughan's entire body glowed beautifully in the morning light. Shit, who could possibly wake up to the sight of him every morning and still be a functioning, working citizen? All Duke wanted to do was turn towards that gorgeous man and let himself be had, all day, into the evening, and then all night. He'd never leave their bed.

A man like him didn't get so lucky. He was just an aging roughneck with no social or cultural skills. His life was common and boring. If he wasn't at Quick's eating nachos and watching a game, then his fantastic nights consisted of beer and catching up on his favorite shows on DVR – *Ice Road Truckers*, *Deadliest Catch*, *Arrow*, *Person of Interest*—basically anything that showcased badasses; he liked it.

Fact was Duke knew nothing of dating and romance. He always liked the idea of it but had never gotten a chance to experience it. It looked like that was about to change because Vaughan was the Grand Poohbah of romance. He had no doubt he would be more than happy to teach Duke how to tap into his inner Casanova.

"What are you thinking about so hard, handsome?"

Duke chuckled lightly. "You."

"Me."

"Yep."

"What about me?"

"I'm thinking how I don't want to get out this bed with you still in it."

"Then don't," Vaughan almost growled, turning and sidling closer. "Stay right here with me. Close to me. Touching me. Kissing me."

Duke closed his eyes when Vaughan's lips touched his collarbone, then the bottom of his jaw, his soft lips making their way to his mouth. But Vaughan lingered around the edge of Duke's lips, the corner of his mouth twitching persistently as his man continued to blow and talk against his skin. "I wouldn't mind you staying right here with me, keeping me company. We can have breakfast. Do our therapy together. Talk. Exercise. Then I usually take a pill after exercising."

"Me too," Duke agreed.

Vaughan turned stunning, bright eyes on him. "Yeah. Then we can shower and take a long nap… naked."

Duke groaned. "I'm gonna die of blue balls."

"You're so weak," Vaughan said playfully, tugging on patches of hair across Duke's chest. "I've waited for you far longer than you've waited for me, love."

PROMISES

"I never said I had patience." Duke folded his hand over Vaughan's to stop him from yanking on more hair. "I'm glad it's a quality *you* possess. But don't expect me to have it."

Vaughan's laugh was sinful. "Sure thing, babe. Come on, then. Let's rise and shine."

Duke pushed at his insistent erection.

"That's not what I meant by rise."

Duke scowled at Vaughn. "It doesn't seem to listen to me anymore when you're around."

Vaughan reached his hand out and Duke let himself be pulled to a sitting position. He let the covers pool between his legs while he waited for his cock to get under control. Which didn't take long because aches and pains began to make themselves known everywhere. His incisions were pulling. His back was sore from having to sleep on it constantly and his arm itched like it had herpes. The cast was driving him insane, and unfortunately, he didn't have the dissembled wire hanger that he'd been using to scratch beneath the hard plaster. Duke sat on the edge of the bed watching Vaughan rummage through the dresser for more clothes. After a minute, Vaughan threw him a soft pair of sweats and a tank top, but Duke was busy clawing at his skin above the cast, digging his finger in as deep as it could go.

"You itching, honey?" Vaughan smirked at him.

"This is shitty, Vaughan. You ever had an itch you couldn't scratch?"

Vaughan gave him an "Are you for real?" stare.

"Never mind," Duke mumbled, still assaulting his skin.

Vaughan kneeled in front of him, gently prying Duke's finger from under his cast. "Trust me, okay?"

That was all he said before he disappeared into the bathroom. Duke hadn't gone back to scratching, but was close, when Vaughan emerged with a hair dryer. He watched him plug it in and then sit next to Duke, placing the heavy, casted arm on

PROMISES

his lap. He powered on the device and set it to cool air. Vaughan lifted his arm and begin to blow the cool air inside the very small opening at the edge of his cast. The air somehow reached the area that burned regularly from itching. Duke watched Vaughan focus on his task. Watched how intently he took care of him. The blow dryer was actually working. Immediately cooling Duke's skin. So much that it wasn't itching.

Three more weeks and this dang thing will be gone.

"Your skin is very sensitive and delicate under there right now, sweetheart. Scratching it like that, or with objects you shove between the cast and your skin, can cause open sores and abrasions to get infected beneath it. Blowing cool air on it helps a lot, but I have some other tricks, too. Just tell me when it starts to become too much and you need to scratch."

Duke leaned in and placed a kiss on Vaughan's cheek. He lingered there while Vaughan continued to work on making him comfortable. "You are amazing," Duke confessed.

Vaughan smiled almost shyly and cut off the dryer. "Better?" he asked.

"Yes," Duke whispered. He was so close to Vaughan's mouth that his body vibrated. He wanted a kiss. He understood they couldn't do more but he'd take anything... really, anything. "Vaughan."

PROMISES

CHAPTER TWENTY-SIX

Duke's moan was evidence of how much he needed Vaughan. There was no denying it. Duke was aching for affection. God knew how long it'd been since the man had felt appreciated and valued, but Vaughan would make sure he never felt the need again. He'd love Duke for as long as he could.

Duke's plea against his lips as he whispered painfully for Vaughan to do something had him almost throwing them back onto the bed—surgery be damned—and healing Duke from the inside out. "Shh. I'm gonna give you everything you've ever needed, Duke. I promise you. But please don't ask me to make love to you right now." Vaughan squeezed his eyes shut, holding onto Duke's hand like he'd wither away if he weren't anchored. "I don't know if I have the strength to deny you."

Vaughan didn't open his eyes until he felt Duke's final kiss on his jaw before the bed dipped and Duke was closing himself into the bathroom. *Thank you, lord.* It'd be damn hard to explain to Dr. Chauncey that they both needed an emergency visit because they'd both needed to fuck and have kinky, rough sex. Claiming, violent, possessive sex.

Vaughan yelled through the door when he heard the water running, "I have toothbrushes under the sink."

"Got it," Duke called back.

PROMISES

Vaughan pulled out his notepad and his new thermometer from the nightstand drawer so he could go back to being a responsible post-op living donor. They both still had things they needed to do now that their surgery was complete to ensure Duke and he were both healing properly. That meant keeping a food journal, along with weighing themselves and taking their temperature every day. Tracking those things would help the doctor determine if Duke's body was rejecting the kidney or if infection was present in either one of them.

Duke had put on the clothes Vaughan gave him, and he felt proud that he was wearing his clothes. Trying not to stare, Vaughan asked Duke, "Do you have your journal with you?"

It took a second for Duke to catch on, but after a few moments his eyebrows rose higher. "Oh, shit. How the hell could I forget about that? I can't even remember what I ate yesterday."

Vaughan opened the notepad to a clean page. "Well, you had a salad here and banana pudding. Just list that and we'll do better keeping track today. But for the time being, here." Vaughan handed Duke the thermometer. Without amusement or disdain, Duke popped it in his mouth and picked up Vaughan's brush off the dresser and began brushing back his wayward locks. When Duke removed the thermometer he looked at it.

"I'm good."

When he handed the thermometer back, Vaughan saw it was ninety-eight point eight.

"Is this what you're going to do while I'm here?"

"Excuse me?" Vaughan stood, buttoning up the rest of his lounge shirt over his own tank top.

"I don't want a babysitter. I'm capable of managing my own journal." Duke's eyes were hard and penetrating. "I don't want to burden you. You don't have to be responsible for not only saving me but also for my post-op care. You'll be tired of me before we've had one date."

PROMISES

Vaughan snorted lightly. He stood and carefully wrapped his arms around Duke's waist and leaned in until their foreheads were pressed together. "I would never try to babysit you, micromanage you, or make you feel like you're incapable. I was just letting you know that I have everything you need to spend the day with me. I'm sorry. Forgive me for making you feel like that."

Duke was staring at him like he had two heads.

"Baby. I really am sorry. I won't do that again. I swear. I'll leave the stuff in the bathroom, the thermometer, gauze, pain reliever, and you just use when you want." Vaughan rubbed one hand up and down Duke's arm and stroked his cheek with the other. "Okay?"

"Sure." Duke broke apart after kissing Vaughan's forehead. "I didn't mean to be snappy. I don't know what's gotten into me."

"Let's go eat. I'm starving. I might start eating you if I don't get some food soon."

"I'm delicious and meaty," Duke teased, easing the tension that had drifted in like a storm cloud, settling over them.

Making their way downstairs, Vaughan realized that his father said he'd be leaving early for work, so they were there alone. He smelled coffee and bacon as soon as his feet hit the landing. When they entered the kitchen, Vaughan went straight for the coffee, fixing them both a cup while Duke pulled out two plates. The food was warming in the oven and Vaughan was so grateful for his dad's thoughtfulness. The eggs and bacon rejuvenated both of them. Duke read the paper his friend had left on the table while Vaughan answered emails on his laptop. It was oddly domesticated. Comfortable.

"What's the weather today, babe?"

Duke flipped back to the front page. "Um. High eighties."

"Nice." Vaughan closed his laptop and took another sip of his coffee. "You want another cup of Joe before we go for a walk?"

"Yeah." Duke thrust his empty cup across the table. "That last cup was really good."

"I added cinnamon." Vaughan winked.

"You spoil me." Duke shook his head, a grin spreading across his face.

"It's just a spice, honey. I haven't begun to spoil you."

Duke held Vaughan's hand loosely while they walked around his best friend's spacious backyard. They kept the pace comfortable and easy. They weren't up to brisk walking yet, but probably after their next checkup they'd be cleared to get on a treadmill or stationary bike and increase the pace and elevation.

Duke had been so surprised at how easily Vaughan had apologized for upsetting him that morning. People, not to mention potential lovers, never apologized to him or cared how he felt. After Vaughan had apologized, Duke didn't know what to say. He immediately felt bad for raising such a fuss in the first place. It's not a bad thing that someone who loved you wanted to make sure you were healthy and healing properly.

After breakfast, Vaughan and Duke had stretched together; doing some of the basic physical therapy exercises they'd been taught. By the time they got to the ten-pound weights, Duke was already sweating. He quadrupled his effort on his one good hand, putting both weights in his palm and curling them. It looked like Vaughan wanted to object but he didn't. They had instructions not to lift anything over fifteen pounds, so Duke only did one rep. He didn't want Vaughan walking around on eggshells, like Duke would bite his head off at any moment.

As they strolled, Duke stopped and took Vaughan's hand into his and kissed his palm. His man's grin was sexy and assured. "Don't think you can't say what's on your mind, okay. I know I bitched earlier, but I may have overreacted."

Vaughan moved in closer, both of their sweaty chests molding to each other even through the thin tank tops they wore. "You didn't overreact. I was being a mother hen. I want to be your man, not your handler."

"You *are* my man," Duke whispered, backing both of them up. "And for the record. I don't mind being handled."

Vaughan's eyes sparkled with mischief. When Vaughan's back hit the tall fence, Duke felt himself being pulled in tighter. Tilting his head automatically, Duke went in for another taste of his own. Vaughan was the same height and they fit so perfectly together, as if the fates had designed them for each other. It was crazy to think that way, but there had to be some divine intervention, because while Duke wasn't chopped liver, men like Vaughan didn't end up with men like him. One thing for sure was Duke didn't question Vaughan's loyalty or dedication to him, for obvious reasons.

Duke closed his eyes and let Vaughan's strong hands roam his body. "You feel so damn good. Full of tight muscles," Vaughan murmured in between sweet kisses. "I want all of you, Duke. The good, the wonderful, the bad, the ornery; everything that makes you, you. I want it."

Duke held his head back, gazing up at the warm sun. The Atlanta heat had nothing on his man's scorching tongue. Vaughan moaned low and deep in his throat while he sucked on Duke's skin, running that sinful tongue along his Adam's apple before dipping into the dimple just beneath it.

"Fuck. Feels good." Duke's cock was so hard and uncomfortable it bordered on painful. He was constantly getting erections, but no release. Although his abdominal pain had significantly reduced—unless he overdid it—he still wasn't sure how an orgasm would feel. He was sure Vaughan would practically make his head pop off, especially since it'd been far too long since he'd had someone other than himself responsible for giving him pleasure.

"You taste so good, sweetheart," Vaughan marveled in his smooth, velvety tone. "I don't know how much longer I can resist you."

Duke pulled on Vaughan's hair, directing his mouth back over to his ear, back to that spot behind it that made him delirious with want. "Goddamn you," Duke hissed when Vaughan assaulted that spot in the best way.

"I see you guys have worked everything out."

Duke groaned at the deep voice carrying all the way from the other side of the backyard. Vaughan didn't bother letting Duke go but he knew that Judge's tall, brooding figure was watching them. Surprisingly, Duke didn't care how long he'd been watching either. *Good.*

Vaughan licked Duke's lip, sucking it in between his teeth, his hazel eyes locked on Duke. He wasn't stopping anything Vaughan was willing to do to him, regardless of their audience.

"They at it again?"

Duke finally jumped apart at the sound of Quick's voice. He could play exhibitionist with Judge but not with Quick, especially when it was his son that Duke was utterly enjoying. "Jesus."

Vaughan laughed and lightly swatted Duke on his ass before grabbing his hand and walking them back across the yard. His man had so much confidence and swag that it couldn't help but rub off on him. Duke was sure his neck was bright red; he just hoped he could blame it on the heat and exercise instead of Vaughan's ministrations.

"What are you two doing here?" Duke asked for lack of anything better to say after getting caught trying to dry fuck against a fence in the middle of the day.

"I live here," Quick retorted humorously, turning back into the house.

PROMISES

"Do I need a reason to come visit my best friend after he's had life-saving surgery?" Judge added, walking right up to Duke and hugging him. Vaughan was forced to move back to allow for Judge's huge frame. Duke hugged his friend back. Even though he'd come at the most inopportune time, Duke was still glad to see the big lug. He had on his dark jeans and a white t-shirt stretched so tight across his massive chest that it struggled not to tear apart. His beard had gotten longer, and Duke had a quick flash of memory of how much he used to love to pull on it when they fucked. Though they were back to being strictly platonic friends, Duke would never forget what he and Judge had shared for so long. But Vaughan was so much better for Duke than Judge had ever been. Vaughan was a lover, a partner, someone who craved love as much as Duke did. They were perfect together in many ways and he hoped he'd get a chance to show that to the young stud soon.

"I'm gonna go shower," Vaughan announced, giving Judge a side-eye. He looked pissed, but it was hard to tell. Duke wanted to protest his man's departure as Vaughan took the steps upstairs gracefully. He'd promised they'd shower together and take a nap... naked. Now all that'd changed and it appeared neither one of them were happy about it.

Judge pulled out two thick manila folders from his messenger bag and dropped them on the table. Duke took that as his cue to get ready to talk business.

Quick came out the kitchen with a plate of deli sandwiches and salads. "Hey. Where's my boy?"

"He went upstairs to shower," Duke answered, already sifting through the contents of the folder and not liking what he saw. As soon as he heard the water turn on upstairs his thoughts fled from work mode and went to images of a glistening, wet, sexy man who was all his. Duke's cock wept for attention. For only one man's attention. He wanted to tell his friends to leave, not caring if one of them paid the mortgage, and insist they come back in a month because that's how long it would take him and Vaughan to recover from their honeymoon fuck period. At that moment he knew that he had to get out of Quick's house and be alone with his boyfriend before they were caught doing something none of them would ever be able to forget, because the things he needed Vaughan to do to him bordered on obscene, maybe even illegal in some states.

PROMISES

CHAPTER TWENTY-SEVEN

Duke chewed a few pieces of lettuce, his stomach rebelling at the little bit of food he was able to take in while listening to his buddies go over both the bail bond and PI businesses' latest cases. One in particular had Duke sweating; images of baseball bats and boards being slammed down on his body repeatedly forced their way to his mind.

Quick's hand was on his shoulder bringing him back to reality. "Duke. You need to go after this guy."

"Gotta get back on the horse, buddy," Judge added.

"Don't give me those bullshit clichés, Judge," Duke gritted out. He knew how PTSD worked for the most part. He was terrified to go after another bounty. He'd almost died the last time. Was at death's door with one foot over the threshold before god answered his prayer and sent an angel to save him. Now his friends were sitting there trying to convince him that he needed to go after the same guy that had beat the shit out of him and left him for dead.

"He's suspected to have killed again, Duke."

"I thought you said he was already in jail," Duke barked at Quick.

"I thought wrong."

Duke ran his hand through his still-sweaty hair. Which was odd since Quick had the AC pumping harder than in a restaurant kitchen. He was scared. *Fuck me.* "I need time to think, guys." Duke stood up, leaving his partially eaten sandwich and salad.

"Duke. You still have a few weeks of recovery, man. No one's saying go out there tonight. I can put my guys on surveillance, tap phone lines, and interview this bastard's acquaintances. I mean, the whole nine yards. It'll be a clean recovery. Put this piece of shit back in jail where he belongs. And you can show every fuckin' one out there that you're still the baddest bounty hunter on the East Coast. Imagine suffering an injury like you did, and then practically coming back from the dead and taking this asshole out. You're back to being the motherfuckin' man." Judge tried to assure him and it was working. Judge always knew how to give a damn pep talk.

Duke's mouth turned up in a sinister grin. In his mind, Duke knew what Judge and Quick were doing was right. It's the same thing he'd do if one of his guys had been severely injured. He'd try to help them recover physically and then get back on the job so the fear didn't take root and consume them. It was something he had to do. He wasn't ready to retire and he couldn't imagine doing anything else. He needed to put his star back on as soon as possible and get back out there.

"How's Dana? I haven't heard from him since I left the hospital." Duke looked back and forth between his two guys.

Judge sported his usual poker face, making it obvious he was hiding something. But Quick. He was never a good bluffer. His sharp green eyes communicated any and every emotion he was feeling. And at that moment his expression contained a mixture of exhaustion, regret, and apology.

"Spit it out, Roman," Duke demanded.

"It's nothing we need to discuss right now," Quick told him hastily, standing and clearing their lunch dishes. "You barely ate, Duke. You gotta keep up your strength, pal. Vaughan will have my ass in a sling if I don't ensure you eat."

PROMISES

Duke didn't speak as Quick hustled around him. When his friend moved to pick up his salad plate, Duke's hand darted out and grabbed his wrist; the abrupt move forcing Quick to finally look him in the eye. "Does it look like I need you to spare my feelings right now or make sure I eat all my food like a good little boy? I had a mother; I don't need her replaced. I want to know what's going on with my guy and I want to know now. Because if I find out something is wrong, you'll pay first, Rome. I found out about the surgery you tried to hide, I'll find out whatever it is you're trying to keep from me now, too. Only this time I won't let you off the hook so easily."

Judge's hearty laughter broke their tense stare off. "Fuckin' Duke, man."

Quick shot Judge an evil look, prying his wrist out of Duke's grip and dropping into the recliner next to him. "First of all. Dana is healing fine. He's just… he doesn't."

"Quick," Duke growled.

"Just tell him already," Judge urged.

"He's still feeling responsible for your injury. He was one that did the surveillance and he was the one I was helping, the reason I couldn't get upstairs to help you, so—"

"God, that is such bullshit! Why would he think that?" Duke fussed, his anger rising quickly. If all his friends thought him such a badass, then why were they treating him like a little bitch? All the ducking and dodging, and lying to so-called *protect* him was driving him insane "Get Dana on the phone. Yesterday!"

Quick reluctantly but hurriedly pulled out his cell phone and hit a couple buttons.

"No more secrets. I mean it. No fucking more," Duke declared.

Judge and Quick both nodded once, then his friend was handing him the phone: already on speaker. Duke didn't wait for

Dana to say a word. His conversation was fast and to the point, like Dana was used to.

"Hey, man. You feeling alright?"

"Um. Sure," Dana claimed hesitantly, obviously shocked at hearing his boss's voice from Quick's phone.

"Good. Get your ass over here for a mandatory meeting now. I'm at Quick's." Then hung up. Duke would set Dana straight and hopefully they could all go back to their lives.

Vaughan was sprawled across the bed listening to his man's deep voice carry up the stairs to him. He'd left the door open on purpose. He wanted to hear what was going on but he didn't want to go down and interrupt the impromptu business meeting. He'd been more than a little pissed off when Judge put his arms around Duke, almost pushing him out of the way. *He* was Duke's man. His partner. He wouldn't be disrespected. Judge'd had his chance and been too stupid to take it.

Another man had arrived about forty minutes after Vaughan got out the shower. Although Vaughan couldn't see him, he figured the guy was as big and burly as all the rest of the men that worked for Duke, because his voice was deep and frightening even though he wasn't in fight mode. The visitor had started out with apologies, but Duke and his dad cut him off. It was only a few minutes before they were off the subject of fault and back to talking about business.

Vaughan wanted to throw up when he heard that Duke was going back after the man that had tried to kill him. Somehow the asshole had eluded the authorities again and was back on the loose. Why did his man have to be the one to hunt the rabid animal down? Couldn't they send the FBI or some other team to get him? Shouldn't the guy be on the Most Wanted list? He didn't expect Duke to become a desk jockey but he hadn't expected him to try to get back in the field so fast, either. He wasn't sure what to say or do about it. His love wasn't conditional. He had no other option regarding his heart but to love Duke in every way. He'd pray every day that his man was safe when he left his bed to go to round up bad guys. God had answered his prayer before so he'd keep doing it.

He'd been so deep in thought that he hadn't heard Duke come up the stairs or into the bedroom until the bed was dipping down next to him.

"Hey. You feeling okay?" Duke questioned softly, climbing up next to Vaughan and dropping wearily down onto his pillow. He nuzzled in close to Vaughan's left side, running his nose along his man's smooth jaw. "You always smell so good."

Vaughan brushed his fingers over Duke's cheek, along his clammy skin. "You look so tired, sweetheart. That was an awfully long meeting. It's almost dusk."

"My head hurts a little," Duke admitted, draping his arm over his eyes, blocking out the afternoon sun shining through the sheer curtains. "You should really get some darker curtains."

"I won't be here that long. I'll get my own place after I've worked and saved a bit." Vaughan kissed Duke's forehead, his dark brown eyebrows rising when he pulled back.

"What?" Duke peeked from beneath his arm.

"You feel hot. Like feverish hot," Vaughan said.

"I'm just tired. And it's hot as hell outside." Duke looked at him sheepishly, like he knew it was a silly excuse as soon as it left his mouth.

"Yeah. But it's not hot in here." Vaughan got up and went into the bathroom, emerging seconds later with the thermometer and a cool rag. "You can gripe if you want but I'm taking your temperature."

Duke opened his mouth like a good patient. His mood looked like it was already lifting as Vaughan took care of him. His man's temperature was ninety-nine point four, which wasn't

PROMISES

bad but wasn't good. If his temperature got over one hundred, he'd have to go to the hospital.

"I think a cool shower would help," Duke answered Vaughan's concerned expression. "I don't feel like I have a fever. I feel like I had a stressful meeting and I need some rest, is all. Even Charlie showed up, but at least he brought me some things from my place."

Vaughan ignored his excuses and wiped across Duke's forehead, and then peppered kisses down his temple to his cheeks, and finally his lips. Duke opened willingly for Vaughan's tongue, accepting it with excitement. There were mmms and groans while they nipped and bit at each other. "I'm so fuckin' crazy about you." Vaughan accented each word with a kiss. He took Duke's good arm and wrapped it around his waist, letting his casted arm rest untouched on his other side.

Duke held him tight and turned his head to the side, letting Vaughan have his way with him. Demonstrating also that Vaughan would have full control when they were in bed. Most of the time, anyway. Duke trembled when Vaughan bit his earlobe. "Fuck. I'm crazy about you too, Vaughan."

Really?

"More than you were…," Vaughan hesitated and shook his head slightly. "Never mind."

"Tell me," Duke urged, turning Vaughan's head back to look at him. He leaned in and captured those sexy lips, pulling the bottom one into his mouth for special treatment since it was particularly tasty. Vaughan hissed when Duke bit him, then moaned when he licked and sucked away the sting. "Tell me. Now."

"It's silly. And I'm starved," Vaughan mumbled nervously. He turned, eyeing the tray of food Duke had bought up for him since he'd missed lunch. He secretly admitted he liked this side of Vaughan. It revealed his human frailty. That he wasn't as perfect as he portrayed. He got scared, nervous, rattled and… jealous, just like any other man, and Duke wanted to rejoice. He thought he'd never be worthy of someone so composed and put together as the man beside him. But Vaughan wasn't Superman, so Duke didn't have to worry about playing the man in need of rescue.

Vaughan got his lunch tray, and after he was back on the bed eating his salad, Duke got up to shower. He leaned in and whispered in Vaughan's ear, "Yes, I'm crazier about you than I ever was about Judge, and he can already see it, that's why he baits you, handsome. And just so we're clear. I was never in love with Judge. Not like I already am with you." Duke cupped Vaughan's cheek and oh so gently pecked him on his kiss-swollen lips before closing himself in the bathroom. Leaving a speechless Vaughan behind on the bed.

PROMISES

CHAPTER TWENTY-EIGHT

Vaughan woke for the fifth time that night. His alarm clock showed it was just after four a.m. *Great. That time I slept a whole hour and five minutes.* Lying next to a warm, shirtless Duke hadn't stopped his mind from spinning. He had so much rattling around in his head it was no surprise he couldn't sleep. One: Duke had told him he loved him and Vaughan was too shocked to even say it back. He'd been wanting to hear those words for over ten years. Now that they'd been said, he hoped they were true. He needed to trust that Duke was an honorable man and wouldn't deceive him. After having known him most of his life, he'd never heard or seen anything that would make him doubt that trust. Two: Duke's skin was still warm to the touch, so his fever was still there; in spite of the acetaminophen he took before they laid down. Three: How was he going to survive when Duke finally went back to work and started putting his life on the line again? Four: Work. He needed to get started at his new job or he'd lose it before he even started it.

"What's going on, baby? You've been tossing all night," Duke asked in a sleepy drawl. His voice was groggy and scratchy as he spoke against Vaughan's throat. They'd found a sleeping position that worked well for both of them. Duke still had to sleep flat on his back, but Vaughan didn't have much discomfort lying on his side, cradled into Duke's warmth, his one good hand wrapped beneath Vaughan's body, holding him close.

"I'm fine. Just a lot on my mind."

"Mmm hmm." Duke sounded like he was already drifting back off to sleep when Vaughan felt rough fingers grazing his spine. It soothed him like nothing ever had. "Everything's going to be fine, so stop worrying."

"Who said I was worried? I'm not," Vaughan protested huskily as Duke's fingers started to ignite his body to flame: as usual.

"Liar." Duke chuckled and Vaughan's cock pulsed in his thin pajama pants. As if Duke could smell Vaughan's arousal, he leaned in and rubbed his coarse beard stubble along Vaughan's Adam's apple. "I can feel the worry."

"Can you also feel this?" Vaughan whispered, thrusting his rock hard erection against Duke's thigh.

Duke groaned low in his throat. "Fuckin brat," he murmured sexily, descending on Vaughan's mouth, taking what he wanted while making Vaughan forget all about his worries... *Which were...?* Vaughan reached down between them, lightly stroking Duke's furry belly, carefully tracing the outline of his incision. Duke gasped shallow breaths, keeping his forehead in contact with Vaughan's while they both looked down between their close bodies.

Vaughan sucked in a sharp breath when Duke started to unbutton his pajama shirt, pushing the sides open so he could look at Vaughan's chest. He did so much more than just look. Duke followed the same patterns with his fingers over Vaughan's incisions as he'd done his. Both of them peering at the identical scars on their abdomens. It was still such a shock to see.

"I still can't believe you did this. No one has ever done anything like this for me." Duke's voice was hushed, but full of emotion at the same time, and it drove Vaughan crazy.

PROMISES

"I'd do it again, sweetheart." Vaughan tried to sound strong but his voice quivered anytime he thought of Duke dying or not being with him. "I'll do anything if it means keeping you with me. I love you, Duke Morgan. So much more than I thought possible."

Duke's lazy smile was infectious. After a few minutes, they stopped touching their matching scars to pay attention to other areas that were straining for attention. "Touch me," Duke moaned so prettily. "I need your hands on me so bad, baby."

Even though their breathing had accelerated and their chests were rising rapidly, it didn't appear that either of them were in any actual pain. Vaughan reached down and cupped Duke's straining cock through his boxers. When Vaughan felt the moist fabric where Duke's cock had leaked for him he thought he'd lose his load right there. *Oh, my God.*

Vaughan knew it was only a couple weeks before they'd be back to their respective lives, so he needed to make love to Duke as soon as possible. Needed that primal, physical oath. That claiming and marking. Vaughan reached inside Duke's underwear, longing to feel that hardness in his hands again. As his shaking fingers wrapped around the head of Duke's cock, he felt the hard steely length pulse inside his grip.

"Oh, fuck," Duke moaned quietly, burying his mouth in Vaughan's thick chest muscles.

Vaughan gave Duke one long, slow stroke from the base to tip and gathered the precome that had risen to the surface. He refused to let one drop go to waste. Vaughan slowly pulled his hand out, much to Duke's displeasure, and licked the sweetly bitter fluid from his fingers.

"Jesus," Duke hissed, his body a hard, thick mass of muscle in Vaughan's arms as he brought his man almost to the edge before forcing his orgasm back down. Tormenting them both.

Vaughan couldn't have been more turned on if they were actually fucking. The angst between them was becoming extremely hard to bear. They were men in their prime with needs. Fuck that waiting shit. They couldn't possibly be the first couple to have shaved a little time off their recovery period after surgery and given in to the palpable need to come together.

Duke grunted again, and Vaughan could tell his man was fighting to keep the pleasure he was feeling from creeping through the walls and reaching his father's ears. Like a high school kid making out with his boyfriend, who he'd snuck in. If things were different, it would almost be funny.

After Vaughan was certain that he'd got every morsel of Duke's essence off his fingertip he moved closer to let Duke kiss him. The moan that tore through both of them when the kiss started was too loud to even think that Quick didn't hear it. "Shh. Oh god, babe. I can't be quiet. Feels too good." Duke groaned again.

Vaughan laughed sexily into Duke's parted mouth as he gasped for breath. "Why are you shushing me when you're the one that can't be quiet?"

"Fuckin' brat," Duke said, in that velvety tone that made the word a term of endearment instead of a derogatory term for a petulant child.

Vaughan reached back inside for another feel of his lover, his own cock begging for some attention. But he wanted to give Duke all the pleasure he could handle. Vaughan leaned in and licked a long swipe up Duke's neck and sucked hard behind his ear. As soon as he wrapped his fingers around Duke's thick shaft and stroked the ridges of that swollen head, his thumb digging into the seeping slit, Duke's fist tightened painfully on Vaughan's shoulder and his hips bucked as he emptied his release over Vaughn's hand and on to the mattress. A guttural growl followed the second and longest spurt of come and Vaughan clenched his teeth when he felt Duke bite down on his collarbone.

PROMISES

"Duke. Fuck, sweetheart." Vaughan was panting against Duke's ear as he waited for his man to come down from his orgasm. He rubbed up and down Duke's back, hoping like hell that he hadn't hurt him. After his breathing returned to normal, Duke loosened the hard grip and rubbed a soothing hand over the marks he'd probably left there.

Vaughan tried desperately to take deep, calming breaths and will his cock to go down. He didn't want Duke to feel like he had to reciprocate right away. He only had one good arm and he was probably worn out after that ill-advised exertion.

"Damn." *That had to be the best orgasm I've ever had in my life.* "Felt so good."

Duke heard Vaughan sigh and he wasn't sure it was a relief filled sigh or a regretful one.

"Are you okay?" Vaughan inquired worriedly, gently pulling Duke's boxers back over his flaccid dick.

Duke's elated chuckle was laced with humor. "I'm better than okay."

"Mmm. Good. Sleep then. I've disturbed you enough."

Duke grumbled, burying in closer, awkwardly reaching for the elastic on Vaughan's pants. "Wait. I want to touch you, too. I want you to come."

"I'm good, Duke. I promise. We still have to be careful."

"I don't, but you do. That's not fair. I want to see you come." Duke shuffled closer, the best he could, as he gazed at Vaughan's face.

Vaughan stopped Duke's persistent hand and tucked it back under his waist, into their sleeping position. "You *will* see me come, I promise. Just not tonight. Now. Com'ere." Duke was so comfortable tucked against the silky skin all over Vaughan's body that he couldn't fight the sleep any longer. He loved that Vaughan had exhibited some of his dominance and shut down

PROMISES
their playing. He had no doubt that Vaughan would follow through on his promise soon.

PROMISES

CHAPTER TWENTY-NINE

Duke woke to an empty bed in the morning. As he felt around on the cold sheets next to him, he quickly realized how comfortable he was sleeping with someone for the first time in many years. It almost came naturally for the two of them. A quick glance at the clock and he saw it was almost noon. *Fuck!* When was the last time he'd slept that long? His days started early. Crime never slept. Duke got up and went into the bathroom to handle business. When he came out he dressed quickly in a comfortable sweat suit that Charlie had brought over and headed downstairs.

Duke poured himself a cup of juice and went in search of Vaughan. He found him on the phone in Quick's office and as soon as he walked in he realized his man was talking business, sounded like his employer so Duke eased back out the room and sat in the living room. He thought he might go into the office but he knew his presence wasn't needed. He hated sitting around not doing anything. He was a productive man, had been since college, he didn't know how to sit on his ass and do nothing. Maybe a walk around the yard will be good. As soon as Duke stood and zipped his jacket the doorbell rang.

He was more than comfortable being at Quick's and answering his door. But he didn't expect to see Dr. Chauncey on the other side of it with a large black bag at his feet.

PROMISES

The man pulled his shades up into his hair, his bright blue eyes radiating his amusement. "Well. I went to your place and didn't get an answer so figured I'd come here and check with your friend."

Duke was still dumbfounded as he moved to the side and let Dr. Chauncey in. He had on his typical tan Dockers, a blue and white plaid button up shirt tucked in to them, and dark brown Oxfords. Now that Duke was really able to see him out of the confines of a stuffy hospital room, the man was actually quite handsome. He had his dirty blond hair trimmed on the sides, the long side burns graying slightly at his temples, the hair on top just a bit longer.

"Dr. Chauncey, what a pleasant surprise," Vaughan said, shutting the door to his father's office behind him. The smile he gave the good doctor was genuine and Duke finally realized that they'd probably built quite a relationship while Duke was laid up.

"It's okay," Vaughan spoke up again when the doctor looked back and forth between them quizzically. "He knows now."

"I figured as much since he was over here." The doctor came further into the living room casually looking around before he sat down.

Duke couldn't help but wonder why Dr. Chauncey was there, but that was clarified as soon as the man spoke. "Why aren't you in bed Duke? I was told you had a slight fever yesterday. How come I wasn't notified of that until this morning?"

Duke turned and scowled at Vaughan, who quickly threw his hands up, signaling his innocence. "Don't look at me I only told—"

"Quick," Duke grumbled, finishing his man's sentence. If anyone would rat him out to the doc—good intentions aside—it'd be his best friend.

PROMISES

"Yes. He called my nurse today asking some questions about what to pay attention to. He sounded very concerned, so I thought I'd take it upon myself and come check on my patients."

"I'm fine," Duke muttered under his breath. "I had a stressful day yesterday. It happens to everyone."

"Actually. No. People don't get fevers from stress unless they have a condition called psychogenic fever. Then a person—"

"Okay, okay. I got it. My temperature did spike, but it was temporary."

"You should've called last night," Dr. Chauncey argued.

"You told me what to call about. Why would I disturb you in the middle of the night? My temperature never got to one hundred, did it babe?" Duke argued in his defense, looking to Vaughan to back him up.

"No it didn't. And I took his temperature every couple hours."

"Aww. Look at you two." The doctor chuckled. "It sounds like everything worked out for you guys, huh?"

Vaughan smiled so charmingly that neither of them needed to reply. Yeah. Things were awesome.

Duke calmed down as Vaughan came and sat down so close to him he was practically on his lap. The doctor didn't go right into examining Duke, instead they talked about their last couple of weeks recovering and what plans they had coming up. It seemed like they'd been friends forever. The doctor was cool and rather funny. His sense of humor bordered on raunchy, especially when Vaughan mentioned them being allowed to get back to some physical activity in the bedroom.

Dr. Chauncey rolled his eyes. "Young people and their sex drives."

"Tell me about it," Duke chimed in, grinning coyly when Vaughan glanced at him in disbelief.

"You weren't complaining about my sex drive last night."

PROMISES

"TMI!" the doctor yelled, and all of them laughed loudly. They were still laughing when Quick came through the front door looking like an escapee from *Renegade*.

Duke noticed Quick was in his chasing gear—so he called it. His large frame was encased in head to toe leather except for the black t-shirt that had BOUNTY HUNTER printed in bold letters across his broad chest. His gold star was suspended from a long chain and rested between his thick pecs. Duke was ready to start cursing about Quick going on a bounty alone when he noticed that Dr. Chauncey was gaping at his friend. His sharp blue eyes were traveling hungrily up and down Quick's body as he made his way into the living room.

Duke covered his laugh with a mock cough, breaking Dr. Chauncey out of his trance. "Um. Dr. Chauncey."

The man startled at the sound of his name like Duke had smacked him. "Yes. Um. Yeah, Duke. D-did you call me?"

Vaughan stared oddly at the doctor's sudden fluster but Duke couldn't wait to tell his man his new theory about Quick and Dr. Chauncey. He hadn't been sure he'd actually seen attraction in the men's eyes when they were in his hospital room. But now. He was more than sure.

"I didn't know you made house calls, Doc," Quick said casually. Everyone watched as Quick pulled off his mid-thigh leather coat and hung it on the rack by the stairs, now revealing his two holstered chrome nine millimeter handguns. Duke had to admit, they always did look like hot thugs when they were dressed for a chase.

Dr. Chauncey shook his head like he was trying to organize his thoughts. "I don't. I mean, I do. Well, sometimes… only when." The doctor took a calming breath and slowly made his way through his sentence. "I don't typically, but my nurse told me about your call and we'd been trying to reach Duke all morning, so I went to check on him."

Quick grunted something and kept walking.

PROMISES

"Coming to your house isn't a crime is it, Roman?" Dr. Chauncey inquired seductively, although Duke didn't think that's the tone he was going for. It looked like his friend brought out the fire in the conservative doctor.

Quick spun around, looking the doctor in his eyes with that fierce green glare. "Do you want it to be a crime, Cayson?"

"Dad," Vaughan blurted, turning to look at Quick like he'd lost his mind. But Duke had a hard time controlling his laughter, especially when his friend's cheeks turned a light shade of pink before he stormed off to his office and slammed the door.

"What has gotten into him?" Vaughan wondered, looking bewildered. "I'm so sorry Dr. Chauncey, but he never acts like that. I hope there's nothing wrong."

Dr. Chauncey was flushed and wore a morbidly embarrassed look on his face. "I never did like my first name much, but hearing him say it like that makes me downright loathe it." His forced laugh didn't reach his eyes and Duke felt sorry for him.

"I'll check on him." Duke went to stand, but Vaughan grabbed his arm.

"I think Dr. Chauncey wants to check you out so he can get back to the hospital."

Dr. Chauncey threw his hands up, dismissing Duke. "It's fine. Go on and check on your friend. I hope I didn't overstep. Sometimes I just run my mouth with no regard for consequence. Please tell him I'd like to apologize."

"There's nothing to apologize for. I think he just needs a vacation. He's been handling everything for everyone and not taking a second for himself," Vaughan said sadly.

"Hmm." Dr. Chauncey hummed like he was in deep thought. Right before Duke closed himself in Quick's office he heard a compassionate, "That's a shame," from the good doctor.

PROMISES

CHAPTER THIRTY

Duke didn't utter a word when he was inside Quick's office. He eased down onto the sofa nestled close to the window in the spacious room and looked around as if he'd never been in there. He noticed that Quick had added more pictures of Vaughan on the built in bookshelves along the far wall, as well as a few knickknacks.

Quick was rummaging through the stack of papers on his desk, still not bothering to acknowledge him. So Duke spoke up first. "You went after a bounty today?"

"Yes."

"Without consulting me?"

"Yes."

"Quick."

"What?"

Duke was getting frustrated but he stayed calm. If Quick really was warring with his sexual identity, Duke didn't want to add to it.

"What's going on, buddy? You go out on a bounty without backup then you come in here and bite my doctor's head off."

"You're wrong!" Quick barked; slamming his heavy palm down on the cherry-stained oak desk, causing the couple of picture frames there to fall over on their faces.

"About?" Duke asked calmly.

PROMISES

"I didn't have a chance to contact you. I got the tip early and I went for it. The new guy, Markson, that Judge sent over, went with me. The bounty didn't put up a bit of resistance, not to mention the kid was only one hundred pounds soaking wet. And for the record, I didn't insult your doctor. He insulted me."

Duke raised his eyebrows in question. "Oh really. How so?"

Quick bolted up from his seat, waving his fist angrily. "You saw him. Looking at me like that. And saying my name all... like... You know, you heard him."

It took all Duke's will power not to laugh in his friend's face, especially with him looking so serious. Duke covered his smirk with his hands and feigned that he was contemplating what his friend said.

"Don't you fuckin' mock me, Duke. I can see you trying to hide your crooked-ass smile, but that's okay. Laugh all you want, but I don't want him in my house again."

"Okay. Calm down, calm down, please, Quick."

"See! See! You called me Quick. No one calls me Roman. No one! I don't want him calling me that!" Quick was pointing at the door like Dr. Chauncey was standing just on the other side of it.

"First of all. I call you Roman sometimes, but only your friends call you Quick. The doctor is a professional. And second. You can't get pissed because the guy called you by your name." Duke motioned for Quick to sit, and after a few fuming seconds, he finally did. "I think you might be overeacting."

"Whatever," Quick grumbled, running his hand through his long hair in frustration.

"He said your name like it was honey on his tongue, you said his first name like it tasted like shit and you wanted it out of your mouth as quickly as possible." Duke frowned, knowing he had to be truthful. He needed to let his friend know he'd hurt the fragile doctor.

PROMISES

Duke let the silence drag on before he added carefully, "Unless you like the doctor's flirting and don't know what to think of it."

"Duke. Do you want me to put you out on your ass? Surgery be damned. I will literally throw you in my front yard if you say something stupid like that again."

"Ouch." Duke rubbed his chest like his friend had punched him. "Now you're threatening me. Damn, dude. Where's the love? I was on my death bed only four-and-a-half weeks ago, now you're threatening to beat me while I'm down."

"Shut up. Stop being so dramatic."

"Ditto."

"I'm not, Duke. I just don't want him looking at or talking to me like that."

"Very well. I'll let him know."

"Thank you. I'll just wait here until he leaves."

"Cool." Duke got up and walked to Quick's office door. Throwing it open, he bellowed down the short hallway, "Dr. Chauncey. Roman will see you now!"

"You bastard! What the hell, Duke?" Quick said in a stern whisper.

"Oh. The doc wanted to get a chance to apologize for 'speaking without consequence' – he actually said that – so I thought it only fair to give him that opportunity."

"Fine. Just don't leave, alright. I don't want me and him to be alone… ya know… give him the wrong idea," Quick whispered again.

"Of course not." Duke smiled, reassuring his friend

As Dr. Chauncey got closer he begin to smooth down his shirt and push a few strands of hair back in place. Duke turned and noticed Quick straightening up the knocked over picture frames and scrambling to push some of the papers strewn around into neat stacks. When Quick saw him looking at him in amusement, he hastily flipped Duke off right before the doctor appeared in the doorway. Duke moved aside and let Dr. Chauncey in. "I'll just give you guys some privacy."

"Duke!" Quick yelled at a closing door.

Duke was laughing so hard as he left Quick alone with the doctor that he had to clutch his side. He hobbled back into the living room and Vaughan looked at him with humorous curiosity.

"What the hell was all that about?"

"I'll tell you later," Duke said, sitting down next to Vaughan. They shared a few sweet kisses like they'd been apart too long. Duke pulled back and stroked Vaughan's cheek, only to lean in and tenderly kiss him there. "I love you."

"Mmm. Me too. I need to show you just how much." Vaughan's leer was so salacious Duke had to take a couple breaths to will his dick not to fully harden in his thin sweats.

"I got good news." Vaughan beamed after they finished another round of kisses.

"Oh, yeah? Lay it on me. I need good news right now."

"Great. Good news is... we can fuck."

Duke coughed on his own saliva.

"I told Dr. Chauncey the G-rated version of last night's episode and he said it was alright. If you didn't feel any pain, then orgasms are fine. The physical sexual activity should be kept light until we both feel up to handling more."

"So...." Duke wondered what that meant.

"Soooo... it means I can't fuck you as hard as I intended but I'll make it good for you, sweetheart, don't you worry."

Damn. That was hella good news. He felt like he could fuck right that minute. His body was healing every day. The only injury that gave him problems were his still-bruised ribs and the occasional headaches from the concussion. He knew they'd take the longest to heal but everything else was workable. "We need to go to my place... soon."

"Agreed." Vaughan winked.

PROMISES

Before they could discuss that possibility more, Quick's office door flew open hard enough to bang against the wall, startling him and Vaughan.

"Jesus," Vaughan gasped when he saw a red-faced Dr. Chauncey emerge with Quick hot on his heels.

Duke stood up, wondering what the hell he'd done by forcing those two to be in the same room, especially with Quick already wound up.

"Your friend could use a lesson in manners, Duke," Dr. Chauncey said, glaring daggers at Quick.

"I won't be insulted in my own house! Out! Now!" Quick demanded.

Vaughan got up and went over to his dad searching his face like a demon could've possibly taken over his body. "Dad. What is going on? Dr. Chauncey is here because of your phone call to his office. He needs to examine Duke. Why are you going crazy like this?"

Quick turned on his heels and slammed himself back in his office. Vaughan stood there dumbfounded, staring down the hall.

"Duke, will you take off your top please, so I can look at your incisions. I'll just draw some blood and get a urine sample. That should be enough to determine if any complications have arisen." Dr. Chauncey was digging in his bag when he spoke but as soon as he sat up, Duke saw that the man's baby blue eyes were not as radiant as before. Goddamn you, Rome.

Duke walked Dr. Chauncey to the door after he had collected his samples and was finished with the exam. "Dr. Chauncey. I'm really sorry about Quick. He's usually pretty laid back."

The doctor laughed humorlessly. "I guess I just bring out the worst in him."

Vaughan looked as disappointed as Duke while Dr. Chauncey slowly made his way to the front door. It appeared he was trying to save face by offering up some last minute conversation like Quick's words had little effect on him. But anyone with eyes could see it was bogus. Duke couldn't imagine how embarrassing it would be to get kicked out of the home of someone you'd unknowingly flirted with and told to never return. Or to be treated with utter disgust, because that's the look Quick wore.

They all turned in Quick's direction when he came back into the living room and dropped noisily into his recliner, angrily shoving the handle back to kick his size thirteen feet up. Quick grabbed the remote from his armrest and turned the television up so loud that they could hardly speak without yelling. Catching himself staring again, Dr. Chauncey murmured an awkward goodbye to them, turned and left.

Vaughan closed the door and locked it, then turned heated hazel eyes on his father. He marched over and grabbed the remote from his father's hand and turned the television off. "What the hell was that?"

"Mind your own business, son. This has nothing to do with you," Quick ordered.

"What 'this?' What do you mean? What's going on between you and the doctor? Are y'all old high school rivals or what, Dad? Because I've never seen you treat anyone like that, not even the criminals you arrest."

"I said drop it!" Quick yelled. Vaughan reluctantly retreated, brushing past Duke and recklessly taking the stairs two at a time.

"Duke. We're going to your place," Vaughan yelled from upstairs.

Duke didn't answer. Instead he went back over to the couch and sat down with his hands steepled in front of him. "Do you have no respect for the man that saved your best friend's life?"

"My son saved your life and I have all the respect in the world for him."

PROMISES

"Oh, okay. So Vaughan got special treatment through the whole donor process from himself and went inside the OR, pulled his own fuckin' kidney out of his gut and put it in mine?"

Quick glared at Duke but he didn't waver from his friend's sneer for one second.

"There was no MD anywhere in sight," Duke continued.

When Quick finally looked remorseful, Duke took the opportunity. "You hate him that much for flirting with you? I've seen plenty of women and men try to pick you up, you've never acted like this." Duke lowered his voice like he was calming a skittish colt. "I think you like him, Rome. I've known you for twenty years buddy. Something is off with this guy."

Quick shoved his hands back through his hair, pulling hard on the ends. "Damnit."

"How long have you been attracted to men?"

"I'm not attracted to men," Quick growled, slamming his footrest down and standing so fast he almost broke his chair. "And don't say it again."

"Is that so bad?" Vaughan asked from across the room. He was standing on the stairs with a large adidas duffle bag on his shoulder, looking heartbroken. "You almost sound mortified at a man being attracted to another man."

"You know I don't think like that. My best friend and my son are both gay, along with several of my other friends." Quick sighed. "I just don't want to be called something I'm not."

"Gay or bisexual," Duke chimed in.

"Yes," Quick huffed angrily.

"Well if a man hits on you and calls you gay, then you just look him in the eye and call him gay right back."

"Very cute, Duke." Quick went to the breakfast counter, grabbing his keys and phone. "I'm going out for a bit. Since you two are leaving to Duke's, I'll assume you can take care of each other. I'll call later."

Duke had a feeling that was a lie. He'd give his friend a little time, but not much. He had no doubt Quick was confused by his feelings for the doc and as his best friend, it was his job to help him through this, just like Quick had helped him with every situation his heart went through.

PROMISES

CHAPTER THIRTY-ONE

"What was I thinking? What the hell? How could I be that stupid? Shit! Shit!" Cayson continued to beat on his steering while he sat in the McDonald's parking lot a few blocks from Quick's house. He'd been so upset he didn't think he could drive anymore. He was already sick to his stomach from being humiliated and rejected, but the addition of the horrific smells that drifted into the air from the disgusting fast food joint made it so much worse. Over and over he'd reprimanded himself for doing something as stupid as using a patient as a reason to see someone who interested him.

As soon as Cayson got to the hospital that morning, his nurse was in his office going over Quick's message regarding Duke. He tried to keep from fidgeting while she told him what he'd relayed to her over the phone about his patient. Just thinking of the big man he'd met only a few weeks ago had left a most intoxicating impression on him, like nothing had before.

Quick was everything Cayson had ever dreamed of in a man. Big, brawny, and hard-packed with natural muscles from working. And all that sexy ink on those massive arms. The thought of those big arms holding him down made Cayson bristle at what would never happen. Nor would he fulfill his fantasy of running his fingers through Quick's long, thick hair that draped over his shoulders. He longed to tame those beautiful brown locks. Yearned to slowly strip off the sexy-assed leather coat and dark clothes, to get to the man underneath. It was like Roman Webb walked right off the set of his favorite porno site and fell into his life.

He'd never believed in love at first sight, but he did believe in lust at first sight, and he had that in spades for the big guy. Cayson stopped pounding his head on his steering wheel and leaned it back against the headrest. He looked in the mirror, saw the slight reddening on his forehead, and cursed himself again. How was he going to explain that? *I ran into a tree... face first.* Cayson turned his ignition back over but hesitated to put his car in motion.

He wanted to go back and square things with Quick, but what could he say. The man was disgusted by him. Cayson ran his hand over his hair, probably making it stick up like a madman, but fuck it. No one thought he was attractive anyway. Since high school when he'd discovered he preferred to hang out in the boy's locker room rather than stand along the fence behind the practice field and watch the cheerleaders practice. He'd tried sports, but after being pushed and battered enough on and off courts or fields, he realized he'd stick with books... and that's what he did.

His long trek through college had been uneventful and tiring. Even undergraduate wasn't the fun that he'd heard so much about from his high school nerd buddies. College was supposed to change their status from geeks to smart hotties. Needless to say, that didn't happen. While he didn't endure the bullying he had in high school, he was still ignored just as much. Unless someone needed a science tutor, then he got a phone call.

Cayson groaned. He couldn't get Quick's look of revulsion out of his mind. Those piercing green eyes had been his undoing when he'd first met him. Never had he seen a man more gorgeous and so far out of his league. Hell. All of Duke's friends were handsome and hot. He didn't have one visitor that wasn't fuckin' fine as hell. That's why he was still berating himself. Never had Cayson come close to pulling a man as striking as Roman or any of Duke's buddies. *Roman.* Damn even the man's name is sexy. Cayson cringed inside when he thought of how he—like he was special—called the man his given name when everyone else called him Quick. But the man put him in his place faster than Cayson could turn on his charm. More like the charm he wished he had.

He figured whatever the man had going on; it wasn't a good time to be in his company. He'd remember that he was strong, confident and demanded respect for himself and his friend while he was in the hospital, but he was also kind. That wasn't the man he'd just seen. He hoped that maybe it would change, but he had a feeling it wouldn't, because it never did. Of all the men who'd rejected him, no one had ever called him with a change of heart after realizing they'd let a good man pass right by them. And damnit, Cayson was a good man. He worked hard, cared for people and healed them, empathized with them. He wasn't a bad person. Cayson squeezed his eyes closed. *Then why the hell am I so unlovable?*

Leaning back, he replayed the scene in Quick's office when Duke had left them alone.

Cayson looked at Quick like he'd lost his mind when he fussed at Duke for closing the door. Nervously fidgeting with his hands, he stilled them by pushing them into his pockets. Quick was just staring at him like he was a visitor from another planet.

"Can I sit?" Cayson finally asked after realizing Quick wasn't about to help make him comfortable.

"I don't care," Quick grumbled. "But if you think you need to apologize, then save it. It's no big deal."

Cayson sat down gingerly and braced his hands on the chair's arms to keep from reaching out for Quick. When he'd walked into that house in all that fuckin' black leather, the words BOUNTY HUNTER stenciled boldly across his deliciously huge chest, Cayson thought he'd pass out or come. He'd never seen a man look that deadly and delicious all at the same time. When he removed that coat, Cayson immediately noticed the weapons nestled close under Quick's large biceps. He hadn't realized he was fawning until Duke roused him out of the fantasy that was starting to play in his mind again.

A vision of Quick barging into his home and forcing him to the ground, securing his hands behind his back. He could smell the leather as Quick rubbed against him, keeping him pinned under him. *Oh god.* Cayson might've moaned out loud. The dialogue in the fantasy that he was boldly picturing right there in front of the man was even hotter than the image of being taken.

"If you fight me, pretty doctor, it's only going to make me fuck you harder." Quick would warn him in that growly voice right before he—

"What the hell is wrong with you?" Quick stood, his hands on his strong hips, his sharp eyes filled with rage, making his usually meadow green eyes appear more hunter green and meaner.

"Nothing's wrong. I was just—"

"It ain't gonna happen. Whatever you were thinking right then." Quick pointed at Cayson's head. "Not. Gonna. Fuckin'. Happen."

"I wasn't thinking anything bad." Cayson hurriedly tried to recover. "I was trying to come up with a suitable apology for the way I talked to you. I shouldn't have called you Roman. If you prefer Quick, then I will call you that." Cayson tried to look unaffected, but his brain was screaming at him to make it right. *Make friends with them. Let them see how great a guy you really are.* Maybe there was enough room in Duke and Quick's circle of friends for him. He didn't expect to be an honorary member of the club, but an invite to a barbeque or a fight night would be nice.

PROMISES

Cayson bit his bottom lip—another nervous gesture—while he thought of the right words. He was a thinker, typically, and didn't usually act or even speak without thinking it through first. So why did Quick take him so far out of his comfort zone and make him pine for things that would never be within his grasp?

"I didn't mean to make you uncomfortable."

"You didn't, doc," Quick said, his tone unfazed.

"Well then, good."

"If you want to examine your patients, I think you should do it in your own office, not mine." Quick went back to shuffling some papers around as if Cayson was dismissed.

"You're a real asshole. You know that." Cayson regretted it the moment he said it. Because Quick stood to his full height and came from around the desk and stood over him like Cayson was in for the ass whupping of his life, but if he was… fuck it. Might as well have his say first. "You called my office, worried about your friend. When I couldn't reach him to schedule him to come into my office, I came out to check on him. Not all doctors disregard their patients as soon as they exit the hospital doors. Duke will be under my care for a year or more. Since y'all are all so close and you're my other patient's next of kin, I thought we might see each other a few more times."

"You make personal visits to all your patients' 'kin?'" Quick used air quotes around the word kin. "Or just the ones you want to shag? Are you that hard up, doc?"

Cayson could feel the warmth from embarrassment spreading across his chest and rapidly making its way to his neck, and then his face. He had to be red as fuck because his face felt like it was on fire. He was humiliated. Was he hard up? Yes. Was he lonely? Yes. But he didn't have to be made to feel like a pathetic loser. He was too old for that. True, most of his colleagues were married and settled with families, and Cayson craved it, but he'd settle for someone that would just treat him nice. How hard was that? Ask him about his day when he got home. Make love to him after a hard day. Hold him and whisper words of encouragement to him when he lost a patient on the operating table. Those things happened to him regularly, but he dealt with them alone.

There was nothing else he could say. Quick wasn't the man he thought he was. Cayson made to stand but he ended up awkwardly maneuvering around Quick, who was still standing over him. He hurried out of the room, vowing that no matter what, he'd never come back to his house again.

He took care of his patient and got the hell away from where he wasn't wanted. Cayson pulled out his cell phone and called his office, letting the nurses know that Duke's labs needed to be picked up from Cayson's house. Since he didn't have any more appointments and wasn't scheduled for surgery until the following day, he figured a day off might not be a bad idea. He'd call his father and see if he wanted to go fishing or something. Since his mother passed a few years back, it'd just been him and his father. After a while I'd only be him.

Cayson's phone chimed and the name he saw on the caller ID almost brought tears to his eyes. But he must be a glutton for punishment today because he picked up. "Hey, Joe."

"Cayson, what's going on? You busy?"

"Um. Not really." Cayson pinched the bridge of his nose. "Actually, I was thinking of doing something tonight since I don't have to get up early."

"I was thinking of doing you. Come over," Joe ordered. He was an anesthesiologist that used to work at the hospital with him, but right after their first casual hook up, the handsome man had gotten a job at another hospital across town. Duke thought that their few fucks were leading to more but he'd been gravely mistaken. Joe was adamant about not wanting to date, that he was too busy to be tied down. Even though they were both in their forties.

PROMISES

Cayson bit his lip again, afraid to ask his next question. He'd only admit it to himself, but he was terrified of more rejection. If he didn't take control of his life, then it was going to pass right by him. "How about a movie tonight? Then we could go to this nice Italian restaurant I've been hearing a lot about."

Silence.

"Joe. Joe are you there?"

"Yeah. I'm here. Look, Cayson I just realized that I'm on call tonight. I better not."

Cayson gritted his teeth at the slew of curse that lingered on his tongue. "You called me, remember. You called to ask me over to fuck, but when I suggested a date, now you're on call. That sounds—"

"I made a mistake. Got my days mixed up is all. I'll talk to you in a few weeks." And Joe hung up.

Cayson shook his head as he stared at the now black screen of his phone. *Seriously. I can't even get a basic dinner and a movie?* He was going to be alone forever. He hoped Duke realized how good he had it. Because he not only had an amazing man like Vaughan to have his back, but his life was full of friends that adored him. How had Cayson ended up with no one?

I was a good kid. I worked hard at school. I was good to my folks. I'm not mean to people and I try to help anyone that asks me to. Cayson put his car in drive and headed towards his house. One question was in the forefront of his mind and probably would be for the rest of the night. *Why doesn't anyone want me?*

PROMISES

CHAPTER THIRTY - TWO

"I like your place, babe." Vaughan smiled, walking around Duke's condo. It wasn't anything that would make *Ideal Home* magazine, but it was his and it was clean. Duke dropped his own bag by the couch and sat down to look through his mail; Charlie had stacked it on his coffee table.

When he'd finished separating what was important from what was junk, he leaned back and linked his fingers behind his head, resting his throbbing skull against the back of the couch. Vaughan leaned in to read the spines on the vast collection of mystery novels on his bookshelf. He had biographies and documentaries lining the bottom shelves as well. Vaughan kicked his shoes off before coming and settling next to Duke.

"How you feeling?" Vaughan asked.

Duke pulled Vaughan into his side so he could bury his nose in his hair and breathe in his clean scent. "I'm alright. I'm just concerned about Quick. He's fighting this and I don't know why."

"You really think my dad is attracted to men?" Vaughan slowly shook his head like it was inconceivable.

"No. Not men. At least I don't think. It's just Dr. Chauncey."

"He is handsome, but they sure seem to be extreme opposites."

"That's the most fun. I don't think you noticed how the doc looked at your old man when he came in dressed like that the way he was. Like the prim and proper man had always dreamed of dating a bad boy."

"Oh, god," Vaughan groaned miserably. "No. No. No. My dad is not some hot bad boy. Come on, Duke."

Duke laughed. "I wouldn't expect you to think he was."

"He was so upset, though. I hate that. What can we do?"

"We'll pull back. Give him some time to figure shit out in his head first. If he really likes the doc, then he'll bring it back up when he's ready."

"Okay, then. If you think that's best." Vaughan wrung his hands in front of him, a nervous habit Duke had recognized in his man.

"What I think is that we should get comfortable and enjoy each other's company." Duke smiled.

"Sweetheart, that's the best thing I've heard all day. Besides… you know." Vaughan winked and brushed a kiss against Duke's cheek. "I'm gonna go freshen up."

Duke pointed Vaughan down the dark hall. "Last bedroom on the right, bathroom is across the hall, and the linen is under the sink. I'll clean up in my bathroom and meet you back on the couch."

Vaughan's smile bordered on predatory. "Sounds like a plan."

Duke's cock was already half-hard. Just the thought of them being in his home alone was enough to make his stomach flutter with expectation. They also didn't have to worry about anyone overhearing or listening to them. Now that Dr. Chauncey gave them the go ahead for light activity. Light was better than none and he was going to take full advantage.

Duke looked around his living room, picking up here and there. It was only him, so his place never got dirty. He had a nice size microfiber sectional with a chaise lounge on the end. Duke pulled a lightweight quilt from the closet and draped it on the back of the chaise. His most favorite possession—his sixty-five inch 4K 3D curved TV—was perfectly positioned in front of the couch. The television had one of the most amazing pictures he'd ever seen. He was so excited he was almost vibrating. This felt very similar to a date. They'd order in, watch a movie, and then... bed. Duke put a few takeout menus on the coffee table for them to choose from for dinner.

Duke heard the shower going in the hall, so he hurried into his own room and began to strip. His bed was neatly made and he double-checked that he had the necessary supplies in his nightstand. In the bathroom he did what he needed to do to make the evening perfect. Emerging from the shower feeling clean inside and out, Duke looked for something comfortable to wear. He came out the room in a pair of track pants and a sleeveless t-shirt. When he turned the corner, Vaughan was already leaning along the chaise lounge with the Indian restaurant's menu in his hand.

He looked delicious lying there. His hair still damp from his shower and combed straight back. The thin pajama pants were riding extra low on Vaughan's hips, showing off the perfect V and silky treasure trail leading to that glorious cock.

Duke grabbed the remote control and the cordless phone off the end table and sat close to his man. "Did you decide on something?"

"Yes," Vaughan said huskily, leaning over and claiming Duke's mouth in a possessive kiss.

Duke opened and submitted to Vaughan's demanding kiss, trying not to whimper and moan like a starving man, but it was difficult. He felt so good. Tasted even better as Vaughan sucked on Duke's tongue in the most suggestive way. "Mmm. Yes. Oh, god, yes," Duke croaked hoarsely, leaning all the way back so Vaughan could lick him everywhere he wanted.

PROMISES

Vaughan tore his mouth away, gasping for air. Both of them leaning and panting against each other. "You keep making those sounds and we'll be skipping dinner and the movie."

"We have all night," Duke whispered.

"I know." Vaughan ran his hand through Duke's thick gray and black hair. They stayed that way until their breathing came back down. "I've just missed you so much."

"I've missed you too." Duke didn't dare stop Vaughan when he pressed those delicate lips against his again, this time keeping the act gentle and languid. The kiss promised so much more to come.

Vaughan broke away again, his pretty hazel eye full of lust just for Duke. "Okay. Let's eat. The sooner we get on with our night, the better."

They ordered an assorted vegetable appetizer and masala wings to start. They both ordered curry dishes. Vaughan opting for lamb instead of chicken. Duke was delighted to know that Vaughan loved naan – Indian clay oven bread – as much as he did. After ordering four different naans, Duke ended the call.

"Now. A movie." Duke turned to the Pay-per-view section and began flipping through the selections. "Action, drama, comedy, what's your pleasure, babe?"

"How about action?"

"Okay." Duke scrolled down over a few more selections before asking, "How about *Northman: A Viking Saga*? It's set in the ninth century, I think. I saw the trailer. There's lots of fight scenes, killing and the special effects are crazy good."

"Sold. Sounds interesting." Vaughan settled back on the couch and draped the quilt over their lower halves. Duke turned off the lights in the living room, leaving the light on in the narrow hallway. Just enough for them to see each other but not ruin the mood.

They were only a half-hour into the movie when Duke's doorbell interrupted them. Vaughan helped him with the food,

PROMISES

placing all the containers on the small kitchenette set in Duke's eat-in kitchen. They both added large helpings to their plates to take back into the living room and eat in front of the television.

    Vaughan didn't realize how hungry he was until he started eating. It was only six o'clock, but he didn't remember eating any lunch. They ate in silence while the movie played. Every now and then, one of them would reach over and eat something off the other's plate. As soon as they finished dinner, Duke put away the dishes and threw away the leftovers, claiming he didn't like day-old food. Vaughan found that funny and interesting, both of them were learning each other's quirks. Now Vaughan knew that if he ever wanted leftovers, he'd have to snag them before his man threw them away.
    "Come on, let's finish the movie," Duke said, lying down completely and resting his head in Vaughan's lap while he casually finger-combed his scalp.
    When the credits started to roll, Duke was almost sleep. Vaughan could make him feel so peaceful just lightly stroking his head. His touched soothed him. It's what a partner's touch was supposed to be able to do, if love was really involved.
    "Sweetheart. Did you fall asleep on me?" Vaughan said softly.
    "No. Almost, though. I like it when you scratch my head." Duke sat up, stretching his back.
    "Is the knot still on the back of your head?"
    "Naw. Not really. It's tender to push on that area, but the bump has gone down enough," Duke answered.
    He turned off the television and tossed the remote on the couch.
    "Your TV is nice, babe. I haven't seen the curved ones yet. That shit is sweet. The picture is unreal."

PROMISES

Duke beamed. "Yeah. I had to have it. Especially since I'm home quite a bit. It's nice to be able to watch my shows on something nice."

"I think we should change that don't you? I wouldn't mind getting out more myself." Vaughan stood and held out his hand to Duke. As soon as their hands connected, Duke felt an overwhelming surge of excitement pulse in his chest as tiny sparks of electricity lit up his stomach. His cock pressed against his pants, tenting the front of them. He wanted to reach inside and adjust himself but… Oh, what the hell… Duke pulled the elastic and reached his hand inside his pants, unbending his aching cock, and aiming it upwards so it had more room.

"I can help with that," Vaughan offered seductively, pulling Duke closer. He took Duke's hand from inside his pants and replaced it with his own. "Damn, you are hard. Hard as stone, baby."

Duke closed his eyes and swayed with Vaughan's touch. "Oh, hell. I need you, Vaughan. Enough fuckin' waiting."

"Come on."

Duke was careful not to drag Vaughan behind him as he led them to his bedroom, closing them inside the dark room. Before Vaughan could make a move, Duke let go. "Hold on."

Vaughan watched Duke light a couple candles that were on his nightstand. "I had a blackout right before my assault and I had to use these. They've been here ever since. I'm glad I still have them."

"Me too." Vaughan took his t-shirt off and dropped it across the high back chair Duke had in his room. "It makes it more romantic."

Duke stood on the other side of the bed and mimicked everything Vaughan did. When he got to his briefs, Vaughan teasingly ran his finger back and forth beneath the elastic before he slowly pulled them all the way down. His dick sprang free and slapped against his stomach. Duke's gasp was easily heard in the quiet room and Vaughan was glad that his man approved. While he waited for Duke to remove his underwear too, Vaughan gave his long cock a few slow, tantalizing strokes. When Duke dropped his underwear, Vaughan's mouth pooled with salvia at the sight of all that dark hair at the base of Duke's cock. His first thought was of how much he wanted that thick shaft pressing on his tongue. The thoughts that followed where all variations of tonguing, biting, thrusting, and any other means of contact with that almond, tanned skin.

They stood on opposite sides of the bed, both stark naked. Vaughan saw when Duke's eyes traveled to his incisions then back up to his face. He saw all the love and gratitude Duke had for him and what he'd done. Over the previous few weeks he'd begun to recognize Duke's different looks and expressions. He particularly loved the looks that Duke reserved only for him.

Duke pulled back the navy blue comforter on his king-sized bed and climbed underneath, pulling the soft fabric up over his waist. Vaughan did the exact same thing, and then he didn't waste a second of time. He nestled up closely to Duke's left side and threw his leg in between Duke's furry thighs. His cock rubbed deliciously against that hard muscle and Vaughan couldn't stop himself from seeking out more friction. Duke wrapped his arm under Vaughan's body and held him tight while he unashamedly ground himself against him.

"Your body is fuckin' amazing," Duke murmured against Vaughan's cheek. His one hand rubbed up and down Vaughan's back, then over his ass. "Damnit. If I didn't have this cast on, I'd have both hands all over you."

Vaughan's heavy-lidded eyes drifted up to Duke's face. He was lying on his side in their sleeping position, but it wasn't going to work. He needed full access to Duke. Lifting the covers, Vaughan straddled Duke's hips, arms braced on either side of his head. He was careful to keep his ass pressed on Duke's groin, mindful not to put any weight on his stomach. Duke's dark eyes were wide as he watched Vaughan maneuver on him and then lean down to kiss him. The kiss was everything he didn't expect. Soft, sweet, slightly hesitant. He cupped the back of Duke's neck and held him to him until he absolutely had to come up for air.

"Closer. Come closer, baby. I need to feel you against me," Duke begged.

"I don't want to hurt you. I'm heavier than I look."

"Vaughan," Duke rumbled, using his one hand to pull Vaughan's body down on him.

Vaughan still supported most of his weight on his elbows but he leaned in until their chests were together. He kissed him again but he made sure to keep the kisses light, full of love. Vaughan didn't want them to get out of control and end up hurting one another. Duke opened his legs and let Vaughan slide between them, and he immediately began to thrust gently into Duke's balls. Damn, he was comfortable there. Where he'd known for years that he belonged. Loving on Duke Morgan.

"Yessss," Duke hissed. Vaughan reached down and gripped both of their cocks together. His movements still calculated and slow. He was running this right now. If they were gonna indulge, then he was damn sure going to make it safe… but also, so very worth it.

"There's so much I want to do to you, Duke. Oh, my god." Vaughan pushed his lips against Duke's temple and held them there, pressing and mumbling his sentiments. Trying to figure out what word in the English language described what he was feeling for Duke. "I watched you when I was younger. Watched you until I just couldn't anymore, and I told my dad that I wanted to study abroad."

"You were just out of grad school when you went to Europe," Duke said through a whisper that revealed his shock. "That was almost six years."

"Yep." Vaughan ran his fingertips down Duke's cheeks, tucking his chin between his two fingers and tilting him up to look him in the eye. He needed to Duke to know how serious he was about him long before the man needed a life-saving kidney. "In my twenties—early twenties, actually—I'd convinced myself that I was ready to approach you. That you'd finally see me as a man. I'd just finished my master's; I felt so grown up and mature. There were men and women in grad school that still fucked around and did stupid shit. Anytime I thought about things getting tough, and wanting to stop, I thought of you." Vaughan kissed Duke again, keeping it chaste so he could continue speaking. "But when I came back home to North Carolina, I went straight to your office. And I saw you there. It was late. So late that I should've called first. Or texted you. Anything that would've saved me from seeing what I did."

Duke lifted his head and shifted slightly. "Vaughan. What? What did you see?"

Vaughan's caress was gentle and affectionate on Duke's hair, but the next second, Vaughan's fingers curled tightly around the long, silky strands of silver on the top of Duke's head. Anytime he thought of that image it made him see dark things. Made him feel like he could actually be mean. Vaughan clenched his teeth together and thrust his solid erection deep between Duke's thighs. It sought out what it wanted, craved... to claim.

Duke's breath caught and he moaned seductively when Vaughan pressed hard into him. "What did you see, Vaughan? Tell me."

Vaughan slid down lower, so he could lock eyes with his lover. Duke's eyes were a smoldering, rich chocolate brown, but the outer rims simmered with a lighter shade of brown, almost like gold, when Duke was excited... aroused. Leaning in, he took Duke's mouth in a punishing kiss, loving the way Duke gasped and panted into his mouth, straining for oxygen. But Vaughan held him pinned beneath him until he was ready to let him have air. "Let me fix it," Duke pleaded when Vaughan let him breathe.

"You can't fix that." Vaughan licked down the back of Duke's ear, into the nape of his neck. With his firm grip still on Duke's hair he turned him to the side so he could have access to his neck. "I saw him with his hands on you."

"Jesus," Duke groaned. "How long ago was that?"

"Not near long enough." Vaughan bit the side of Duke's neck, hard enough to show he wasn't kidding. The mere thought still drove him insane. Enough that he couldn't stay and watch Duke pine for someone else. Especially a bastard as big and intimidating as Judge.

Duke hissed and tried to pry away from Vaughan's assault. "Fuckin' brat," Duke growled back at him. "Just fuck me already. Then only that image will be in your head from now on."

Vaughan licked at the puffy red welt he'd left on Duke's throat. He burrowed his way back up to Duke's mouth and kissed him gently, whispering to him. "I need to forget it. I need inside of you." He looked down at their joined abdomens, reaching between them to lightly trace their similarities. "No matter what happens to us in the long run. I'm always there." Vaughan pointed at the long incision along Duke's pelvic bone.

CHAPTER THIRTY - THREE

Duke didn't have much left to say. It twisted his stomach to know that Vaughan had come to him before and Duke was with someone else. Damn, that had to have hurt something wicked. He couldn't imagine watching the person you love be intimate with someone else. He wished he could take all that away for Vaughan, but he wouldn't know where to start. He didn't regret his time with Judge. He was there when no one else was filling the void in his bed. But that's all Judge filled. He never even came close to touching Duke's heart, much less filling it.

Duke would only be able to show Vaughan what he meant; how different the importance was of the roles both men played in his life. He turned and positioned himself on his side and pulled a couple pillows down to drape his top thigh over it as he opened himself up for his lover. He stretched his casted arm in front of him and Vaughan settled comfortably behind him, curving his body around him. Duke reached his hand back and shamelessly pulled his ass cheeks apart, showing himself to his man. His most sacred offering. This was the fourth man he'd ever offered it to in his life and he hoped he'd be the last.

"I touch myself like this when you're not with me." Duke said breathlessly, as his fingertips danced across his hole, and every few swipes he'd push his middle finger in, just past the rim.

PROMISES

Vaughan groaned low and proud in his throat. "You think about me when you're in this big bed all alone?"

"Yes," Duke purred. "Only you. I need you so badly there. Just you, Vaughan."

He felt Vaughan place his finger over top of Duke's while he continued to tease himself. "You look so fuckin' sexy doing that. I wanna watch you pleasure yourself one night. As if I'm not in bed with you. I just want to watch while you call my name out when you orgasm."

"Vaughan. Come on," Duke groaned. He'd do anything Vaughan asked, to be honest. But waiting was killing him. Thinking about using his flesh-toned seven-inch dildo on himself while Vaughan sat back with his hard cock leaking on his stomach and watched him. Duke wouldn't last two minutes. He'd feel Vaughan's presence there and he'd explode. He didn't even want a lot of prep now; one or two fingers would be enough stretching. He wanted this wonderful man to fill him and press deep inside him. He pressed his own cock into the soft folds of the pillow but it didn't give him near enough of what he needed. He needed friction, contact. Before he could complain, he heard Vaughan spit behind him then felt the slick feel of two fingers pushing into him.

"You can take it can't you, sweetheart?" Vaughan said behind him. His voice had dipped to that strong, breathless baritone pitch as he pushed deeper into Duke's channel. He closed his eyes and gritted his teeth through the sweet burn. With his own fingers still in the mix he traced his stretched hole around Vaughan's long digits.

"The lube and condoms are in my top drawer," Duke added after enjoying a few more deep strokes. Sighing each time Vaughan pushed against his ass. A few seconds later he heard the top of the lube click and the sound of the liquid squirting from the tube.

PROMISES

"I think it's okay to bypass the condom don't you? I mean. One of my organs is inside you, sweetheart. If I have something in my blood, it's pretty safe to say you probably do, too," Vaughan said, his tone full of amusement and lust.

Duke partly chuckled and part moaned when he thought about the truth in Vaughan's statement right before a blunt tip pushed at his twitching hole.

"Are you ready?" Vaughan licked the shell of Duke's ear, continuing to press inside instead of waiting on an answer.

"Oh, fuck yes. All the way, Vaughan. As deep as you… Ahhhhhh… Fuuuuck." Duke panted harshly as Vaughan continued an endless dive into his body. While his man's cock wasn't stretching him beyond capacity, he was sinking that long cock deeper than anyone else ever had.

When Duke finally felt the prickly hairs at the base of Vaughan's dick, Duke pushed back further, hoping there might be an inch left untapped.

"Easy, baby." Vaughan gripped Duke's hip hard, keeping him securely in place. "I don't want to hurt you."

"Never," Duke whispered, turning his head, seeking out Vaughan's soft mouth. Even at that angle, Vaughan was able to lean over and capture Duke in a searing kiss, his mouth open wide, his tongue plunging deep into his while his cock sat buried to the extremity inside his pulsating ass. "Please keep going."

"Oh, god. I love how you beg. So damn beautiful." Vaughan pulled out a couple inches and pressed back in, keeping the thrusts slow and shallow. Whenever Vaughan would drive all the way back in, Duke would grunt a curse word, and it turned him on like nothing ever had.

With one hand under Duke's neck, his palm against his cheek keeping him turned towards Vaughan's mouth. The other continued to hold Duke's hips. After Duke was able to control himself he felt Vaughan's hand move over and splay across his ass. "I love the hair you have here and around your dark hole.

PROMISES

It's sexy." Vaughan breathed a soft escape of air into Duke's open mouth each time his cockhead sank deeper.

With their foreheads pressed together, Vaughan kept up a steady and smooth rhythm. Duke felt Vaughan reach down and pull the covers back up to their waist. Covering them both and wrapping his arm up and across Duke's chest, securing him to him. Vaughan linked his fingers over Duke's shoulder and pushed him down as he eased up. It was a gentle forcefulness that made Duke see stars. That wonderful cock touching places he didn't think could be reached. It made him cry out to Vaughan for more. Regardless who heard, he made sure Vaughan knew that what he was doing to him had never been done before.

Vaughan rubbed all over his chest. Squeezing his pecs and twisting his nipples, while still keeping his movements slow and stimulating, never amping up the tempo to where things could get rough and frantic. It was so romantic and sensual, perfect for their first time. The room was dim, the candles' flames casting a beautiful luminance on their lovemaking. And that's what it was. As much as Duke loved to be rode hard, he couldn't deny how wonderful the feelings were that he and Vaughan shared. And based on the sounds coming from behind him he was confident that his new lover was pleased.

"Oh, Duke. Damn I've waited so long. Nothing has ever felt this good to me. I love you so much. Come on, sweetheart. Come with me. I need to come inside you." Vaughan's movements became less rhythmic, jerkier. "I feel like I can't get deep enough."

Duke gasped for breath when Vaughan went deeper. "It's deep enough, babe. Trust me. It's so fuckin' deep."

Vaughan's smile could be felt against Duke's cheek. "Yeah. And you're so tight. Like you've been waiting for me." Vaughan pulled all the way out until the tip of his cock was just outside Duke's hole before he eased all the way in to the root.

PROMISES

Duke screamed out, his orgasm slamming into him with full force, completely taking him by surprise. "Vaughan! Fuck! I'm coming!" Duke groaned like he was in excruciating pain but Vaughan was making sounds very similar to his as he felt warmth flood his already hot channel. "Oh, god. I feel you. Feel you inside me."

Duke's confined heat seared Vaughan through his shaft to his aching balls. A spark ignited in his groin and radiated through every part of his body that was in contact with Duke's—which was all of him. Nothing could've prepared him for the real thing. To finally have his heart's desire.

Vaughan held on to Duke for dear life as he let his seed flood him. "Fuck, you've got a sexy hole." Vaughan breathed heavily even though the loving had been slow. His orgasm had stolen his breath away.

They laid there for an unknown amount of time, holding and loving each other.

"Was it worth it?" Duke said into Vaughan's bicep, which was pressed against his cheek.

"Every damn year that I waited for you was worth every second of what we just did." Vaughan eased out of Duke's ass. He watched his come drip out of Duke's hole and slick down the hairs that surrounded his opening. A sight he'd never tire of.

"How are you feeling?" Duke sounded like he was almost asleep.

"I feel like I'm floating. I'll be right back."

"Don't go."

"I'm gonna get us a washcloth and clean you up and then you're going to sleep in my arms until the sun rises."

"Hmm," Duke hummed his approval.

When Vaughan finally finished cleaning himself off and brought a warm cloth for Duke, his man was already asleep. He couldn't help but puff his chest out. Carefully, he wiped Duke's thighs and crease free of his juices, then oh so gently wiped over Duke's stretched hole. He wanted to push his finger back inside and stroke until they were both ready to go again, but he wouldn't dare deprive Duke of some much needed rest.

He blew out the candles and made his way back to the other side off the bed. Again he pulled up the covers and folded himself back over Duke's prone body. *Damn, he's the most beautiful man I've ever seen.* Squeezing Duke tighter to him, Vaughan cleared his mind of all thoughts except Duke and drifted into a peaceful sleep.

CHAPTER THIRTY-FOUR

He felt Duke stirring beside him and it pulled him from a very delicious dream, but when Duke nestled back into his growing morning wood, he quickly realized the real in-the-flesh version was so much better than the dream substitute. Their hips begin to move together as both of them woke from their deep sleep and drifted into sexual abandon.

Duke moaned; pressing back harder and lifting his thigh back over the pillows. Vaughan could still see the slick around his hole. He felt around blindly not even wanting to open his eyes to the warmth of the morning sun he felt on his face. Touch and sound were all he used. He learned the curve of Duke's hips that rose over a firm, fuzzy ass and sloped down to the top of hard, muscular thighs. He trailed up Duke's crease until he felt the tight skin surrounding his way to heaven and pushed in. "Mmmmmmm," he whimpered carnally.

"Make love to me again, Vaughan." Duke's morning voice could be described as nothing less than lewd and X-rated. "Put that long cock back inside me."

"Oh, fuck." Vaughan's eyes rolled behind his eyelids. He fumbled with his cock; anxiously lining it up to Duke's opening. He slid in just as slowly as the night before and the grip Duke had on his shaft was tight enough to make Vaughan hiss at the

PROMISES

unforgiving squeeze. "Fuck. Fuck. Fuck." As he sank into the depth. "Tightest ass ever, sweetheart."

"It's yours. Take it," Duke instructed groggily.

Vaughan slowly dragged in and out, letting them feel all of each other. He pushed Duke's leg up higher and angled his cock inside to peg that spongy gland that had Duke declaring his love for him and cursing him at the same time.

"Harder. Fuck me hard."

Vaughan growled in Duke's ear. "Not now. As much as I want to hear you scream until your neighbors know my name, I'm going to make you wait for that."

Duke snapped his own protest but Vaughan spread Duke's cheeks and pushed in again, pegging and brushing his prostate as he did.

"Fuck, listen to you. Sounding like you're in love with my dick already." Vaughan looked down at their connection. Saw his cock slick and shiny with his own come from the previous night. It was enough to make him shoot off again. He was rocket ship hard and his head was pulsing to the same beat as his dick. "So damn deep inside your tight ass you can barely move."

Duke cursed him.

"All the expletives you can think of won't stop me, sweetheart. I can make you fly." Vaughan buried himself again, grinding himself into Duke's ass, his mouth pressed firmly against his ear. "Beg me, Duke. Beg me to love you, beg me to fuck you." Vaughan thrust deep with each statement. "Beg me for more, beg me to stop."

Duke's body began to shake and Vaughan knew he had him. Had his man where he'd wanted him for years. A shivering, aching, needy mess beneath him, impaled. Long strokes seemed to be Duke's undoing, along with Vaughan's provocative talking.

"I'm not going to bang you out this time, honey. Not yet. Still gonna go nice and easy until you're healed enough to take the kind of fucking I'm going to give you." Vaughan's tone and his words contradicted how he moved. He dug in and out of his lover as slowly as he could muster. But he kept talking about how hard he was going to take Duke's ass. "As soon as this cast is gone and we're both one hundred percent healed, I'm going to get that dildo you tried to keep hidden in your nightstand drawer and I'm going to watch you fuck yourself with it while I feed you my cock."

Vaughan caressed down the side of Duke's face to his lips while he continued to love him from behind. "I'll try not to fuck the hell out of this perfect mouth, but I make no promises."

Vaughan's balls pulled up high against his body when Duke pulled Vaughan's middle finger into his mouth and began to suck it like he'd do his dick. He swirled his tongue around the tip of his finger before pushing the entire digit back down his throat, deep enough to tickle his esophagus.

"Oh, you bastard," Vaughan whispered harshly, his hips snapping on their own. So he wasn't the only one that could play dirty. Duke squeezed his ass muscles tight and wrenched a wail from Vaughan that was so extreme, he had to bury his face in the back of Duke's hair to scream his release.

"That's better. Come hard for me," Duke coaxed in that sexy southern twang, sounding the most satisfied Vaughan had ever heard.

He finished grunting and sputtering around his orgasm like he'd never come before. "So perfect." He nuzzled between Duke's shoulder blades, tracing the muscles he found there with his tongue. "You're perfect."

Next thing he knew Duke was asleep again. Well he knew how to make his man rest. While he cleaned them up again, he thought he'd have to make it up to Duke for him not getting to come, but as he wiped up his mess he saw the large damp spot in front of Duke and the dried residue on his cockhead. His man *had* come. Was Vaughan that consumed by his own orgasm that he hadn't even realized it? *This is going to be so much more fun than I thought*. Still in the same position, Vaughan held Duke as he slept.

PROMISES

CHAPTER THIRTY-FIVE

It was a Saturday night. Quick sat on his patio sipping his fifth beer, not counting how many he'd had at the little bar across the street. His son had gone over to his best friend's house again. They'd been on their fifth or sixth date now, who knew. It seemed like they were always doing something together while they were on the final stretch of their recuperation. Duke's cast was off and both of them were passing their check-ups with flying colors, their bodies almost back to top shape.

Vaughan's medical leave was up and he was scheduled to report to his new job on Monday. Quick wasn't sure he'd see him before then since he'd been practically living with Duke. His son and best friends were lovers… that was still going to take some getting used to. Even though Vaughan had told him years ago about his feelings for Duke, Quick honestly thought he would find someone else before he finished law school and came back.

He couldn't have been more wrong. His son was even more in love. When he'd first learned about it, Quick had called it a puppy love or infatuation. Duke was a good-looking man. All testosterone and muscles. At first he'd thought *he'd* been attracted to Duke but when they got to know each other more, Quick realized it would never work. There were only a few men that Quick had ever been attracted to, but it never amounted to anything, so why tell his best friend?

    Quick never considered himself gay. He'd never been with a man. Didn't even crave it actually. But lately there had been a stirring in his gut that he couldn't shake. It hurt. And as much as Quick wanted to pretend he didn't understand why, he was too smart to play dumb. He thought about Dr. Cayson Chauncey again. Replayed the argument they'd had in his office. Over and over. He'd hurt the sexy doctor. *Sexy?*

    This wasn't good. He knew it. But every part of him screamed at him to do something. Make all the negative feelings he had go away. However, he simply couldn't bring himself to call him, not even to apologize. It wasn't necessarily his pride that prevented him from doing it; it was the assumption that Dr. Chauncey would probably slam the door in his face or tell him to fuck off. He could imagine the proper man all pissed and angry. Those blue eyes blazing with pent up rage and lust.

    Oh, fuck. The way that man had looked at Quick when he came in dressed in his gear. It made his chest constrict remembering the want and need he saw in the sweet doctor. But for all of that to be displayed in front of Duke and his son was too much. He was a private man. His personal life was just that… personal. Yes, he had friends, but they were grown men. They didn't discuss their romps anymore. This wasn't junior high.

    Maybe it was best to leave it alone. He didn't need to see the doctor anymore. Duke didn't need an escort with him to his doctor's appointments. He was more active than Quick had been over the past week. His friend went to work out daily and then god only knew how active his nights were. Quick shivered. He didn't want to picture any of that.

    It was time for him to move on with his life. He and Vaughan had an amazing relationship. He still found plenty of time for the old man and it made him feel much better that all of them were getting back to normal again, but he couldn't expect Vaughan to stay with him until the end of his days and keep him company. Quick needed to find his own company to ease the loneliness of the long nights. That were getting lonelier and lonelier. But his son had his own life to live.

Just call him.
No.
He won't be mean. He's too sweet to be mean.
Yes he will. He hates me now. Legitimately so.
You saw how he looked at you. Have you ever seen so much desire in anyone's eyes?
Well if it was there, it's damn sure gone now.

Instead of sitting there and listening to the devil and angel on his shoulders argue back and forth, Quick got up to get himself something a little stronger to drown out the noise. He didn't want to hear it. No matter what, he wasn't going to pursue the doctor. He wouldn't know how, anyway. The man deserved so much better than a roughneck with only a high school education. The doctor—surgeon and lifesaver—was out of his league. It didn't matter either way, because Quick had blown it, and for no good reason.

Standing there propped against his counter, he was lost in the quietness when his business phone rang. He moved as quickly as his inebriated legs would carry him and grabbed his cell from the patio table.

"Quick," he answered tiredly.

"We got him," Judge said with no preamble, getting right to the point.

"Who?" Quick said, sitting down before he lost balance. His head was swimming and the floorboards of his deck felt like they were rolling back and forth under his ass. Yeah, he was drunk.

"That bastard that got Duke—Aaron Williams. The bounty that had almost killed him. I've had my guys on his last known acquaintances for a while. And you won't believe it, but the overconfident motherfucker is still in Atlanta."

"Fuck." Quick gripped his hair and tucked it behind his ear. He tried to think, but Judge's rough voice cut into his musing.

"He needs to get this guy. Duke hasn't been in the field since that day," Judge stated.

"He had surgery, Judge. He had to recover, man. Are you trying to say—?"

"I know that! He had laparoscopic surgery seven weeks ago. He *is* healed. Even his cast is off now. He's back in the office. He's lifting weights and buffing back up, exercising, fucking...."

Quick all but growled and Judge laughed him off.

"I'm just saying. He's stalling. He's passed up two bounty recoveries that would've been real easy for him but he's afraid, Quick. And you know it. We got to get him back out there. Soon!"

"Okay, okay. But first off, how good is this intel? None of us are going back into a gang war zone. No amount of bail is worth what we went through."

"Agreed. But you know he needs to get back out there. Whether it's to take down Aaron or any other random bounty. He just can't stay huddled up in that office. The recon is spot on. My guys are the fuckin' best. One of them is an ex-SEAL. He knows his shit. Aaron has been there for two days and it doesn't look like he's about to run, either. My guy said he looks comfortable, like he might be settled in and staying a while. It's an old girlfriend's house. She works at a grocery store all day and he's there while she's out. There's limited in and out traffic and no children living there. It's as good a time as any to get him."

Quick knew Judge was right. Duke couldn't cower in his office. He was a bounty hunter. It's what he'd done all his life. He wouldn't be fully healed or whole until he faced his demon again, only this time he'd kick his ass. "I'll call him in the morning."

"No!" Judge snapped. "Call him now. We go in the morning. You know how this goes. That guy looks like he's stable but he could bolt at any minute. We're not his only enemies, I'm sure."

"In the morning! Wait... who is we?" Quick asked.

"Yes. You. I'm going, too and so is one of my guys."

"You haven't done bounties in months. Duke's gonna think you're there to watch over him. He won't like it."

"I'm still a hunter. Always will be. And I will be there to provide backup whether Duke likes it or not. I don't give a damn. Now call him. We go at 0600." Judge hung up.

Quick huffed a tired sigh. He wasn't in the mood to make the call, especially after midnight, but it had to be done. If the situation were reversed, Duke would be all over him about getting back on the horse. So he'd do it for his friend.

He dumped the rest of his rum and Coke down the drain, since it appeared he was doing to have an early morning, and pressed the speaker button on his phone. As soon as Duke's groggy voice answered, Quick jumped right to business.

"Judge just call me."

"So? This better be good to wake me. I was sleeping peacefully."

I bet.

"I don't know how good you think it'll be but I think it's great. Judge and his PI guys have got a solid lead on Aaron Williams. Judge wants to go after him in the morning."

"What the hell do you mean Judge wants to, and what the fuck do you mean in the morning? Why is he even calling you? I run the bounty business!" Duke was certainly wide-awake now, as his thick country accent blasted through his Bluetooth speaker.

PROMISES

"Duke, please. You know this is right. Just think for a second. You're feeling fine. He's still our bounty. We got good intel that our guy is in a non-hostile location and we have sufficient back up. There's no reason not to get this asshole."

Duke huffed but he didn't object.

"Time to face your demons man."

"I could say the same thing to you, Rome. You don't have to face your demons so why should I?"

"What demons?" Quick barked.

"Don't play stupid. You know what the hell I mean. You're not facing your shit, so I don't have to either."

Quick balked. "What are we, in grade school, dude?"

"That's how you're acting."

"Fine. We'll face our demons together. You first... then me."

"Promise."

"Promise."

"Deal. I'll see you in the morning." Duke hung up.

That was a little too easy. He'd been expecting an hour-long conversation spent trying to convince his friend to take his revenge, but Duke eagerly agreed after Quick gave him what he wanted. Quick stared at the phone wondering if he'd just been had.

Dr. Cayson Chauncey was by no means a demon but if he rejected Quick half as hard as he'd rejected the doctor, the man could level him. And it'd fuckin' serve him right.

CHAPTER THIRTY-SIX

Duke let Vaughan squeeze him to him, needing his man's comfort. They'd been lying there asleep in each other's arms, exhausted from their lovemaking, as the smooth sounds of jazz filtered into their bedroom along with the moonlight, lulling them into a magical post coital bliss.

It was obvious Vaughan had heard the conversation between Duke and his dad. Duke could feel the worry drifting off his lover. "It's going to be alright, V."

"I know it is. I just want you to be careful."

"I have too much to live for not to be more careful than I ever have in my life." Duke pulled closer and leaned up to kiss Vaughan's lips. "I love you."

Vaughan whispered sensually, "Je t'aime aussi, amoureux."

Duke fondled his aching balls. He wasn't sure if he had any seed left in there but damn if he didn't crave release again. They'd both become insatiable animals as their bodies returned back to normal and their strength had increased. "You drive me crazy when you speak French."

Vaughan made sure every part of them was connected as he moaned softly in Duke's ear. "Qui vous tourne le plus? Moi de vous parler ou de faire l'amour avec vous."

Duke gripped Vaughan's long cock and pulled on it. "V, that sounded beautiful. What did you just say?"

PROMISES

Vaughan rotated his hips, pushing his cock harder into Duke's large palm. He moved until he was on top of him, pressing all the weight and muscle into his own. "I said. What turns you on more? Me talking to you or me making love to you?"

Duke grabbed a handful of Vaughan's ass and yanked him tight in between his legs, spreading them wide, letting his man know the obvious answer to that question. "Damn, you feel so good. I can't get enough of you."

Vaughan thrust harder. They were already naked from their earlier lovemaking. As soon as they got inside Duke's house they were on each other. For some reason the dim lighting of the romantic restaurant Vaughan took him too had put him in an extremely passionate mood. His man had fed him, wined him, and wooed him until Duke was nothing but a puddle of in-love mush in the palm of Vaughan's hand.

Duke held on tight—so relieved that the restricting cast was off as Vaughan took him for another hard ride.

"You're not too sore are you?" Vaughan was already pushing back inside him, knowing Duke wouldn't deny him. He hadn't said no once in all their weeks together, he wasn't about to start.

Pushing back against Vaughan's strong hips was all the answer his man needed as he began to pound into Duke like he'd promised him he would. Duke had always been there for everyone else. Fulfilling countless promises to others without taking anything for himself. Finally someone had promised him something and followed through on that promise. Vaughan was in love with him. Duke had no doubt in his mind. They had the most special connection a couple could have and because of that, Duke knew they'd go the distance. It's why he'd been hesitant to get back in the field, leaving the chases to a few newly hired recruits. He didn't want to risk losing Vaughan. But he knew his

PROMISES

friends spoke the truth, he had to get Aaron Williams, or else it would haunt him, his life, and his dreams forever.

"Oh, god. Don't stop, Vaughan. Don't ever stop. Feels so good," Duke grunted around Vaughan's punishing thrusts.

Damn, the man knew how to give Duke exactly what he needed. Vaughan could make the sweetest, slowest love to him, making his body float above them and watch how stunningly they came together. And then there were times like right now. When he loved to be controlled in the bed and Vaughan gave just the right amount. Enough for Duke to feel dominated but not emasculated.

"Fuck! Harder. Make me remember what I'm fighting for, baby. Make me think of you all day tomorrow."

"Ahhhh. Duke, mon amour." Vaughan was panting in his ear, his body rubbing lusciously against his own sweat-dampened skin.

Duke could no longer hear the smooth jazz that was coming from his neighbor's house, only the sounds of their sex. "I'm gonna come, V. Fuck me good. Come with me."

Vaughan's pretty hair was slicked back from his face with sweat and exertion, his golden skin flushed and moist as he pushed his body to give them what they both craved. Duke knew the telltale signs of Vaughan's impending orgasm. His body stiffened, his cock got unbearably hard, and his face transformed into an angelic mask of pleasure right before he exploded inside Duke's body.

Vaughan fumbled for Duke's cock while his own orgasm tore threw him. Vaughan only got a chance to give Duke a few strokes before he threw his head back against the pillows and cried the sounds of his orgasm into his lover's throat. Jizz splattered between them and Duke's body jerked violently with each spurt of the creamy liquid, making his eyes roll back in his head and his body shake with desire.

PROMISES

"Oh, my god," Duke whispered. Vaughan chuckled in that sexy way as he gently lowered Duke's legs and settled back between them. After a long while their breathing had evened out and the world came back into focus. They stared at each other for a long time, gently touching and grazing each other's mouths, before Vaughan finally broke the silence. "I'll be waiting for you in our bed tomorrow night. Come home to me, Duke. Promise me you'll always come home, and I'll love you forever."

He'd keep his head down in the fight tomorrow. There was no way in hell he could ever abandon the man in his arms. Not even by dying.

Duke cradled Vaughan's head to his chest, letting him hear his heartbeat: only for him. "I promise you, Vaughan. I'll always come home to you. I've waited my whole life for this, I'll be damned if I'll lose love now."

Vaughan had set his alarm for five a.m. so he could be sure to kiss his man before he left for work. He tried not to worry that Duke was going after the same man that had almost killed him. Tried not to think about all the shit they'd just overcome because of that shithead. Listening more intently, he heard heavy footsteps outside the bedroom, like pacing. He got up and put on his robe—more and more of his possessions had been making it to Duke's house daily—and sought out his love. Duke had a travel mug of coffee in his hand that he sipped from with each lap he made. "Babe, what's wrong?" Vaughan asked around a yawn, while rubbing at his tired eyes.

"Nothing. I'm fine. What are you doing up? Did I wake you?" Duke sat down at one of the stools underneath the breakfast bar in the kitchen and picked up his half-eaten toast.

"I'm up because you're no longer in bed. You look upset." He stood behind Duke and massaged his shoulders, his hands gripping the large muscles the best he could in an attempt to settle Duke. He couldn't go out there like this. Vaughan stopped rubbing and came around to Duke's front, opening his legs and easing in between them. Duke set his cup down and looked up into his eyes, and Vaughan could see so much there. The love, the nerves, fear, and a little excitement just beneath all that.

"You're gonna kick ass out there today." Vaughan kissed Duke's mouth, slipping his tongue in for a quick taste of Duke's tongue and the strong, black coffee that lingered there. He wouldn't go back into what they'd discussed the night before. Nothing more needed to be said, and most of all, he didn't want to distract his lover. Instead he'd occupy him with something else.

Vaughan wrapped his arms tighter around Duke's neck and rotated his hips, pressing his sensitive cock and balls against Duke's leather pants. Fuck if he didn't look sexy in his gear. Weapons were strapped to his back and a shiny gold star was suspended down his thick chest resting over his sternum. Vaughan already had ideas of Duke wearing that outfit in their bed. The smell of leather always did crazy things to him.

"Feels good, babe," Duke murmured against Vaughan's cheek, both of his hands held Vaughan's ass, massaging the smooth globes as he writhed against him. Even though Duke had on thick leather pants, he could still feel the bulge between Vaughan's legs, could feel the hard, thick length stabbing him through the thin robe he wore.

"You feel good too," Vaughan added.

They sat that way for a while. Vaughan straddling Duke's lap while his man rested his head against his shoulder breathing him in. It seemed to do the trick. Duke appeared more comfortable and less fidgety. So Vaughan took advantage. He'd keep his lover's mind on something else. Rotating his ass in the other direction, Vaughan pressed down harder, placing the crease of his ass right over Duke's considerable bulge.

"Ahh, fuck," Duke groaned, holding Vaughan's hips tight.

PROMISES

"Did I tell you how fuckin' sexy you look in all this black and leather.? It's really doing it for me."

Duke grinned up at him, winking slightly. "You into leather?"

"I'm into anything you're in," Vaughan said, licking Duke's earlobe. His own cock was rock hard and sticking out of his robe. Instead of ignoring it, Vaughan reached down and fisted his length, seductively watching Duke's dark eyes lower to view the act. Vaughan pulled on it slowly, not on a quest to finish, only to distract his man. It was working. For both of them. Vaughan's ass clenched tightly when Duke thrust up to meet it.

"That's it. Just like that." Vaughan sighed. Duke's strong biceps bulged while he maneuvered Vaughan's ass exactly how he wanted him. It was really doing a number on his head. He loved being in control in bed but seeing Duke like this was a lot. His man looked downright bad as fuck.

"When you get home, I want you to keep all this on." Vaughan ran his hands down the jet-black BOUNTY HUNTER t-shirt and skimmed across the leather gun holster, on down to the butter-soft black leather pants. "I want you to bend me over your bed and take me like the king that you are. You go beat that fucker's ass that had the audacity to try to take you out, then you can come back and howl your victory into the night while you fuck your man hard and fast."

"Damn, Vaughan." Was all Duke was able to gasp before the hard knock at the front door alerted them that it was time. His father was here to get his lover. Easing off of Duke's lap he stood and straightened his robe. Duke held his neck and leaned in to kiss him again. "There's not a person on this earth that can keep me from coming home tonight. I want you." Duke squeezed one side of Vaughan's ass. "I want this so bad."

"It's yours. Always will be." Vaughan gave Duke one last kiss and left Duke to answer the door while he went back to the bedroom. He didn't need to watch him leave. Didn't want to,

PROMISES

either. He'd prefer to watch him walk back through the door after he did his job. When the front door closed, Vaughan tied his robe tight around him and got back in the bed. He wished he had work to do, but he wasn't due to start until Monday. He could go exercise but it was six in the morning. He couldn't just lay there and think about possibilities. He needed to stay positive. He reached over and grabbed his pain pills and took a couple, swallowing them dry. They would help his mind to stop wandering and get back to sleep. Hopefully when he woke, it would be from Duke's hands rousing him.

PROMISES

PROMISES

CHAPTER THIRTY - SEVEN

Duke stood in the parking lot of his business sipping an energy drink, neither he nor Quick filling the silence with useless conversation. Instead, they watched as Judge pulled up in his huge Dodge. Two men the size of Dallas Cowboys linebackers bounded out of the truck and fell in behind Judge. Damn they looked scary as hell and Duke had to admit that he didn't mind those big motherfuckers tagging along.

"Hey man. You're looking good." Judge gave Duke a one-armed hug and introduced his two guys. "Duke this is Bradford King, we call him Ford and his brother Brian King."

Duke stuck his hand out. "It's good to meet ya. Thanks for coming along. It wasn't necessary, but still appreciated."

The brother that spoke up first was only a fraction larger than the other was. They both had dark hair and even darker eyes. Ford had a full beard while Brian chose to keep his to designer stubble length. "We did some private work for Judge before he asked us to accompany him on this bounty. He told us about your perp and we're the ones that found him. I guarantee you the intel is good. My brother is the best."

Duke nodded and turned to look at the brother—Brian—that had yet to speak. He held eye contact but his mouth was pinched closed so tightly it looked like it'd need to be pried open with a crowbar for the man to speak.

PROMISES

Duke asked Brian, "Was there anyone else in the house? Children, elderlies, women?" They'd already discussed this by conference call earlier in the morning, but better sure than anything.

Brian nodded his head yes, but didn't elaborate. Duke stared at him then turned back to look at Judge. Something was off.

"Brian doesn't speak. He's as smart as they come and wicked strong, but he prefers not to talk."

Prefers... not can't. Duke looked back at the big man standing just slightly behind his big brother, a little to the right of him. Ford turned and looked behind him and his brother signed something to him. *So that's how he communicates. As long as someone can understand him, it's fine with me.*

"Brian said there is a heavyset woman living there too. She works at a gas station during the night and sleeps most of the day."

Duke's heart rate kicked up at the mention of a woman. It was more than likely the same one that had played a major part in his ass-kicking last time. So both of them were there. Duke thought he'd be more nervous, but he wasn't, just anxious as hell. Ready to conclude this chapter of his life. He wanted those crackheads to pay, to be behind bars where they belonged.

Dana pulled into the parking lot, his Chevy Nova blasting some kind of pop instrumental. When he killed the engine, the noise level went back to tolerable, and he approached them, looking rested and as well as Duke. Dana didn't like to wear the leather so he chose dark jeans and a matching jean jacket over his BOUNTY HUNTER t-shirt.

The six of them stood there, waiting on Duke's final command. Their team was all back together again, plus a couple new additions. It'd been a while since Duke was in the field with Judge. He had no doubt they'd prevail. Then he had a heck of a reward to claim when he was done.

PROMISES

Eyes were trained on him. Duke fastened his bulletproof vest and the others started to check their weapons and making final preparations to leave. Judge laid a map on the hood of Dana's car since it was the lowest; everyone else had huge trucks taking up most of the parking lot.

"We've already been through this, but once more won't hurt." Judge pointed at a place on the map. "We'll enter through the back of this neighborhood. Brian says that there's little to no activity at this time of day.

Of course not. It's the ass crack of dawn. Everyone should be asleep.

Duke continued to listen, fine with letting Judge run this part of the op, but it was understood that Duke would secure the bounty; everyone else was there for backup.

"Duke, Quick, and I will enter through the front. Dana, Brian, and Ford will come through the back all on the same count. Don't underestimate this guy. He's a cold-blooded killer."

"How the hell did he make bond?" Ford asked after Brian signed it to him.

"He's a known gang banger and killer but he's never been convicted of murder. Only on petty drug charges and one breaking and entering."

Once everyone was confident of their duties, they loaded up into two trucks and started the trip to Allendale and Alston, located in one of the highest crime neighborhoods in Atlanta. Duke rode shotgun in Judge's truck with Dana in the back and Quick drove his truck with the two sumo brothers.

Duke took a deep breath as the scenery started to change the closer he got to the 'hood. Homes that once stood three stories high were now abandoned, crumbling, and boarded up. Men and women both stood on the corners waiting for their next customer. Duke ignored it all. He had no quarrels with them. As long as they let him come in and do his business, he'd leave their territory and hope to not return. Anyone that got in his way would meet whatever consequence he saw fit.

"You ready, boss?" Duke opened his eyes. When did he close them? Judge and Quick were watching him closely. Duke took the safety off his Glocks and opened the door. There was their answer. He was more than ready.

Duke got on his radio. "On my count. Three and we're inside."

He got his ten-four responses and the three of them begin approaching the house from the front, knowing Dana was on top of things in the back.

"Ready on your count, Duke." Dana's voice echoed through the radio.

Duke counted into the radio. When he got to three, Quick busted through the front door and at the same time, the back door flew open hard enough to take it off the hinges. One of the brothers must've done that.

Duke was inside now. His heart was beating faster than it ever had, but he kept his hands steady and his eyes trained forward. There was nothing downstairs. A few pieces of furniture, including a ratty recliner that sat in front of a small, old-style television that was still on.

Quick and Judge were both yelling, "BAIL RECOVERY AGENTS! WE'RE ARMED!" Duke joined in and the three of them were taking the stairs fast while three men remained downstairs. Duke used his hand signals to motion for Judge to check the bedroom on the left and Quick the one on the right. Duke headed to the last bedroom and after he finger-counted to three, they each kicked at the door in front of them.

The bedroom was larger than it appeared. Judge and Quick both called clear into their microphones, but Duke was stunned into stillness at the scene before him. Duke had his gun trained on Aaron Williams' forehead, his trigger finger poised, ready to pull and put an end to all this.

PROMISES

"Drop the weapon, Aaron. It's over," Duke hissed. He wasn't even yelling. He was calm and in control.

"Stay back. I'm getting out of here whether you like it or not." Aaron looked like he was high, drunk, stoned, tripping, and anything else drugs could do to you. The bedroom stank to holy hell and the man looked like he hadn't showered in weeks. The same applied to the woman he held in front of him; his 9mm pointed at the back of her skull. It was the same bitch that had beat him. Her eyes were wide, bloodshot, and glazed. Duke wondered if she really knew what was going on.

Duke heard his name called and he answered right before Quick and Judge made it down the hall and into the room.

"What the fuck?" Judge snarled, standing close to Duke. His own weapon raised and ready.

Quick spoke into his own radio, "We have a hostage situation. Stand down."

Duke knew he was talking to his guys downstairs. Stand down for them really meant be on high alert and approach cautiously.

"You and your team got seconds to get the hell out of my house before I kill her."

Duke took a couple of steps closer, his gun gripped so tight his hand began to cramp but he didn't dare ease up. "Kill her," Duke growled. "I don't give a fuck."

Aaron looked shocked for a split second. But he tightened his hold on the woman's neck while he aimed his piece at Duke, then Judge, then Quick, then back to Duke. This man didn't know what he wanted to do. His eyes darted all around the room like he was hallucinating. They needed to end this fast. Aaron was too fucked up to do any real damage.

"Take him, Duke," Quick whispered sternly. "Get that fucker."

"Help me," the woman cried in the man's arms. She still had on her gas station smock and her wild hair was all over her head like she'd literally been yanked out of the bed. "Please, help! My brother is crazy! Don't let him hurt me! I don't want to die!"

"Neither did I, bitch. But it didn't stop you from trying to beat me to death," Duke countered, getting angrier by the second. The woman's eyes widened, then narrowed like she was trying to recognize Duke and couldn't. Figured. She had no clue who he was. What she'd done to him. Fuck her.

Sirens were approaching outside and the second Aaron turned to look out the window all three of them pounced. Duke went for Aaron's arm that held the weapon and pulled it above his head, punching him hard in the midsection to hopefully make him release the weapon. The gun fired twice in the air and Duke struggled to keep the barrel up. He threw a few elbows to the man's jaw while slamming his arm against a dresser, trying to dislodge the weapon.

Quick jumped for the lady, removing her from the situation, throwing her body to the matted carpet. Judge had Aaron around his neck, trying to weaken him while they wrestled with the gun. Another shot was fired and Quick yelled out, gripping his shoulder. The woman was bucking hard beneath his large body, and Quick's face was full of pain and anger as he fell against the wall.

"Rome!" Duke screamed.

"I'm all right." Quick grimaced, trying to right himself. Duke noticed the blood on the wall. Fuck. Quick was hit.

The woman jumped up and headed for the door but was detained by one of the big brothers before she could get out of the room. Duke watched Brian's impassive face as he used some military style restraint hold and brought the screaming bitch down to her knees. He didn't hurt her but he was determined not to let her get the upper hand. With her hands secured behind her back, Brian ignored all the curses and angry slurs as he propped

PROMISES

her against the wall, never uttering a word. He made it look so damn easy.

Duke and Judge continued to wrestle with Aaron, who was even stronger than Duke remembered. Judge kept one fist around the guy's throat while he pummeled the guy's ribs with the other. Duke knew those blows had to do some damage because Judge was hitting the man hard enough to jolt all three of them. It had to be the drugs and adrenaline pumping through the guy's system that kept him upright so long. When Brian joined in, they were able to get the gun away from the perp without it firing again. When he was down, Judge allowed Duke to put the cuffs on him. Duke was breathing hard, but he got to his feet and yanked Aaron up with a little assistance from Brian. Once Duke was sure their bounty was secured, he passed him on to Judge and ran over to his best friend.

Quick was sitting on the floor with his back leaning against the wall. Sweat ran down his temples and Duke could see his friend trying to keep his composure. Duke yanked off Quick's leather coat and pulled the short sleeve of the t-shirt up. The bullet looked to have grazed his friend on his shoulder. It took a pretty decent chunk of flesh as it passed through, but didn't look to have done a ton of damage.

"How's it look? It's not the muscle is it?" Quick panted.

"Doesn't look like it." Duke said, applying pressure with a towel that Dana brought him. "It's bleeding a lot, Rome. You'll need stitches for sure."

"Fuck." Quick grunted, lifting himself up from the wall with one hand.

"Suck it up, ya big pussy," Judge ordered.

Quick flicked Judge off but the smile curving his lips was reassuring. His friend was fine. Thank goodness. That whole situation could've gone differently. Duke's hands shook. He was scared, but it was all right. It was over. He walked behind Quick as they made their way back downstairs and outside. The neighborhood was lit up with red and blue lights, including an ambulance and a couple fire trucks.

Dana stood with the two brothers while they gave the police their bounty paperwork. One of the cops offered to transport their bounty for them but Duke refused. He let Judge load Aaron Williams into the back of his truck; he was taking the shithead in himself.

He walked around to the back of the ambulance where Quick was sitting on the stretcher and the young EMT was applying another bandage to the still-bleeding wound. Duke told Quick he'd meet him at the hospital after he dumped their bounty *under* the jail.

"I'm good, pal. I'll get a ride home. Don't worry about bringing me my truck" Quick's eyes were drooping and Duke frowned at the paramedic.

"It's just the adrenaline wearing off, sir. He's fine. Vitals are good."

Duke gave the paramedic the okay and turned to leave. He sent Vaughan a quick text that he'd be home shortly and everything was okay. He'd tell him about Quick's little bullet graze after the man was home and resting. No need for Vaughan to be worried and race up to the hospital for nothing.

Duke shook his other guys' hands, thanking them for the support. Ford walked up to Duke with his brother close behind. "We wanted to say we appreciate the opportunity to work with you. Judge keeps us pretty busy with recon, but my brother and I wanted to extend our services to your bounty hunting business. We're damn good trackers. I think we'd be beneficial to you in your office here."

Duke didn't even have to think about. "Agreed. Now that I've seen you two in action. I can use a couple of guys like you. I think Judge said you were ex-SEALS?"

"Yes. When my brother was medically discharged five years ago, I left with him. I couldn't stay there without him."

PROMISES

Brian didn't speak up, of course, but he looked like he agreed with what his brother was suggesting. "You want to work here in my office too?" Duke asked, looking at Brian.

The man simply nodded. Although he didn't speak, Duke knew the man was capable. He'd seen it. "Okay, then. Be in my office on Monday at eight. We'll go over some things, but I warn you, it's going to be crazy. We're getting ready to get back into full swing now and it's gonna be long hours. Are you up for that?"

Ford smiled and it brightened the man's face, making him look approachable and handsome. Brian stuck his hand out for Duke to shake, then turned and left. That was his goodbye. Ford added, "We'll see you Monday. Have a good weekend, Duke."

Oh I plan too.

Judge looked at Duke for a while before he pulled him in for another one-armed hug. Their unspoken words were enough. Judge had been right. Duke needed the closure of getting this bounty. He felt so much lighter and carefree. With Aaron and that woman loose on the streets, Duke would've continued to have nightmares. Now, he was at peace with it all.

He could go home and claim his reward. Duke smiled.

PROMISES

CHAPTER THIRTY-EIGHT

"Sir, it's against policy," the paramedic pleaded, trying to get Quick to stay on the stretcher.

"I can walk just fine. There's nothing wrong with my legs." Quick jumped down out of the ambulance, still holding the numerous gauzes the EMT put over his wound, and headed into the emergency room. He walked up to the counter and the nurse's eyes practically bulged out of her head as she took in Quick's appearance, probably due to the weapons. After she was done gawking, she ushered him into the triage room and started a chart on him.

"I'm afraid it may be a little while. We're short-staffed and flooded with flu victims."

"Great," Quick murmured.

"You can sit here for now." The round-faced nurse pointed to one of the many stretchers that were lined up in the busy hallway. "Unfortunately there're no more rooms available. The doctor will get to you as soon as he can. We've called for more doctors to come down, but I can't guarantee how long that will be."

Quick waved her away. "It's all good," he said, and leaned back on the stretcher with one arm draped over his eyes, blocking the irritating fluorescent light directly over his head. He let his long legs drape over the sides, since he was too tall for the bed. People hustled back and forth in the hall but Quick was too tired to care.

"Quick. Quick. Wake up."

Quick knew exactly who that timid voice belonged to. He wanted to pretend he was still asleep but his arm had started to ache the longer he laid there. He had no clue when he'd fallen asleep, but he was still exhausted.

"Quick. Open your eyes. It's Cayson... Dr. Chauncey."

He finally pried his eyes open and sure enough, there he was—the star of Quick's erotic dreams—staring down at him through those beautiful baby blues. "Quick, what happened?" The doctor was looking at the small file that had been placed at the foot of his stretcher. The man's eyes widened and Quick had a hard time taking his eyes off the doctor.

"You were shot!" Dr. Chauncey yelled, and a few of the staff stopped their hustling to turn and look in their direction.

"Tell everyone, Doc." Quick smiled.

"Sorry." Dr. Chauncey bit his bottom lip, embarrassed, and Quick wanted to pull that abused piece of flesh into his own mouth and lick the sting away. Suck it until the doctor moaned for him to never stop. "Are you in pain?"

"Nope," Quick lied.

"Mmm hmm. I forgot you're a real tough guy. This big gash in your arm doesn't hurt a bit, huh?" Dr. Chauncey rolled his eyes. He looked at Quick for a few seconds like he was trying to determine the best thing to say next. Quick watched him tug at the collar of his gray sweater like it was choking him. When Dr. Chauncey finally cleared his throat and said his piece, Quick was beyond relieved. "I can take care of it for you if you don't mind. But I understand if you prefer another doctor."

Quick grinned and winked at the sweet doctor. "I don't mind at all." Quick was so tired when he came in that he didn't think about the possibility he'd run into the doctor down in the ER but it appeared he was one of the extra doctors called down

PROMISES

to help. Quick gave the man one of his most charming smiles, disregarding his arm burning like a zillion bees had stung him. He wanted to show the man he wasn't the big jerk he'd encountered at his house. It was just a bad day. Everyone was entitled to a few of those.

Dr. Chauncey wasn't able to hide his surprise. "Okay. I can be professional, Quick. Come on into room six, and I'll fix you up in there."

Quick followed the doctor into one of the private rooms and closed the door. When they were alone, Quick realized how much height he had over the doctor. That alone turned him on. When he stood in front of the bed in the room, Quick looked down at the doctor, standing extra close to him. "You can call me Roman."

Dr. Chauncey looked at Quick like he'd lost his mind. "I can?" he said wistfully.

"Yes, you can," Quick mumbled softly. His deep voice still overpowering in the small room.

"Okay Roman." Dr. Chauncey's face was slightly pink, his pretty cheeks flushed with excitement. Quick could see it as clear as day. It was amazing. Even though he felt the throbbing in his arm, he couldn't have been happier. Dr. Cayson Chauncey was right in front of him. Helping him, caring for him. Quick's chest expanded with relief. He'd been beating himself up for weeks over how he'd treated the doc. All because the man had caused feelings to stir inside himself that he hadn't felt in entirely too long.

But he had a second chance to apologize to the doc and a chance to maybe do other things. Quick had made a promise and he was going to honor that promise... right now.

The End.
Part Two to be cont....

PROMISES
Quick still has to follow through with his promise next....

Bonus Scene .... Keep reading!!

PROMISES

BONUS SCENE

Duke made fast work of completing Aaron's paperwork. By the time they'd finished with intake and booking, Aaron's big ass was crying like a punk bitch. Begging not to be taken back to jail. Those must have been some damn powerful drugs the man took if they turned you from a whiny ass girl to a heartless thug with the capacity to kill. Knowing Aaron was that distraught only made Duke want to celebrate harder. All those weeks of hell he had to go through, including the suffering of the love of his life, he would admit he was enjoying a small bit of consolation. He'd gone back to his office to get a few files together for the new employees he had coming in on Monday and to prioritize some outstanding cases.

By the time Duke go home, it was after the dusk. He opened the door to his condo and noticed how dim it was inside. He could smell food and under the delicious aroma was the smell of vanilla candles. Duke put down the dozen roses he had in his hand and went to pull off his coat. His smile was stretching across his face as he called for his lover.

"Babe. I came home, just like I promised." Duke called out, hanging up his heavy leather coat and picked up the flowers, heading further into the condo.

When he opened his bedroom door, Duke had to grasp the knob to keep his legs from giving out. Vaughan was in the

PROMISES

middle of his large bed in nothing but a black g-string that failed miserably at holding in that long, hard cock.

"Jesus," Duke whispered.

Vaughan turned onto his side, propping his head up with his hand. "The flowers are beautiful. Thank you."

Duke forgot he even had the bouquet in his hands. He went over to the dresser and set them down gently, then turned back to the work of art in the middle of his bed.

"Well, are you going to stand there and look at me or are you going to join me?"

Duke snapped out of his trance and slowly began to remove his weapons. He tucked them into his nightstand drawer and then reached for his t-shirt. He had to fumble with it a few times before finally removing it. His mind was a completely scattered mess. No one had ever done anything like this for him. He wasn't only talking about his boyfriend surprising him by wearing the sexy underwear for him. But everything. The caring for him, cooking for him, staying home, and keeping the bed warm for him. He'd never experienced it in all his years. Now he was beyond blessed. It was almost like his heart was overwhelmed.

Duke went for the button on his pants when Vaughan made him stop. "Wait a minute. Take the pants off real slow, sweetheart."

Duke tried to be sexy as he slowly removed the rest of his clothes. He never considered himself overly seductive or good at bedroom games, but hopefully Vaughan was willing to teach him. Duke stretched out on the bed and wrapped his man in his arms, squeezing him tight.

"I'm so glad you're home." Vaughan kissed Duke like he hadn't seen him in weeks. When they finally came up for air, Duke was hot and breathless.

"Damn, I wish I could come home to this every night."

PROMISES

"You can," Vaughan whispered. "My dad doesn't expect me there much anymore. Besides, he's pretty happy with his hospital experience today. Hopefully he'll have his own company soon."

"Oh, really?" Duke looked surprised.

"Yeah. But we'll talk about that later. There's something more important you should be thinking about right now, love."

Duke laughed lightly. "And that is?"

Vaughan nibbled on Duke's cheek before he answered. "Me."

"I'm always thinking of you, babe. That won't change… ever."

Vaughan straddled Duke's lap, fitting his cock right against his crease, rubbing Duke's sensitive dick against the tight fabric of the thin string nestled between Vaughan's soft ass cheeks.

"I love you."

"Yes." Vaughan groaned. Duke's mouth dropped open when Vaughan reached under the pillow and got the lube. He rubbed a considerable amount on Duke's length and he had to grit his teeth to keep from pushing his cock faster into that tight fist. Because there was no way in hell he was coming before he got inside Vaughan's warm body.

His eyes sprung open when Vaughan eased the dark string between his ass to the side and let Duke's cock rub deliciously against his tight star. When his lover began to sink down onto him, Duke grabbed his waist and held him still, just barely able to keep his eyes from crossing. "Oh fuck. Fuck. Wait baby. Let me prepare you first."

Vaughan held still. The head of Duke's dick just past his entrance. "I've been preparing myself all day."

Duke sounded like he was a woman in labor the way his breathing escalated almost beyond his control. "You've been here doing—"

PROMISES

"That's right. I've been here fucking myself with that big dildo you got in your drawer, just so you could sink into me and fuck me like the man you are." Vaughan's eyes were a stunning hazel that shimmered radiantly as he continued to sink onto Duke's thick cock.

"Oh, my fuckin' god." Duke twisted and hissed. "Oh, you're still so goddamn tight."

"That's it baby. Go as deep as you can." Vaughan grimaced. His beauty was a sight when he was like this. Impaled on Duke's cock, his strong thighs twitching and burning with strain to keep him from sinking down too fast. "You're so big."

"Take all of me, Vaughan," Duke pleaded. He sat up and put his arms around Vaughan's waist, holding him tight to his body. Needing the contact and the anchor.

As soon as Vaughan's ass was pressed against Duke's groin, they both released a contented sigh while Vaughan's body adjusted to him. "Ahhhh. Fuuuuck. Vaughan, baby. Ride me."

Vaughan gave Duke's rock hard cock a few shallow thrusts, getting them both ready until finally his man rose up and slammed back down on Duke's dick so hard he screamed out into the dark room. Vaughan did it again and again. Until Duke was barely holding on, his head bowed with his chin touching his chest. Vaughan kissed the top of Duke's head as he bounced up and down on him and Duke grunted with each pounding his lap took.

He should've known Vaughan would be a controlling ass bottom as much as he was a controlling top. "You watching my ass swallow your dick, sweetheart?" Vaughan huffed, never losing momentum. He wasn't going crazy on him like Duke knew he could, but he was damn sure fucking him good enough to make him beg for more.

Duke whined. "Please don't stop. Don't ever stop, V."

"Never." Vaughan slowed his pace and changed up the tempo. Moved his hips in a slow winding grind, like he was stripper. His beautiful body fit him perfectly. All that toned muscle over flawless golden skin made Duke feel like he was fuckin' his own personal god. When he was able to catch his breath albeit only briefly, he realized that the intensity of the slow drag up and down his wet cock was just as erotic as the fast-paced fucking. Only the slow was more sensual, more intimate. He adored how Vaughan could fuck him like he was being punished in the best way and he could make such slow sweet love to him that Duke felt like the most beloved man in the world.

"Oh babe. I'm gonna come. I can't hold it. You feel too damn good." Duke's face was still buried in the small thatch of slick hairs on Vaughan's chest. He twisted his head back and forth, his lips brushing against his lover's hard sternum as he spread his legs and held on for the ride. And oh did his man ride him.

His balls tingled and pulled up snug to his body. Duke spit in his palm and grabbed Vaughan's pale cock that was sticking out the side of his tiny g-string. It only took a few strokes before Vaughan was painfully squeezing Duke's shoulders and spraying their chests with his come, groaning Duke's name over and over in his ear.

"Yes, baby. Fuck yes." Duke made sure that Vaughan was spent before he licked his fingers clean and held on to that toned ass, thrusting up into him with everything he had. He was no longer responsible for whatever came out of his mouth as his orgasm shot to the surface at a mind-altering speed. Without a second thought, Duke flipped them both over, Vaughan sinking face first into the plush mattress.

"Fuck me," Vaughan said shakily, staring back at Duke with eyes half hooded from his release, his hand underneath him lazily pulling on his semi-hard cock.

Duke knew he only had a few seconds before he was going to explode. It'd been way to long. He sank back fast and deep

PROMISES

into Vaughan and hammered into his perfect ass like it'd been years since he'd topped. God, it had.

He used both hands to hold Vaughan in the perfect position so he could pound him how he wanted him. Duke was showing any and every one that he was still the motherfuckin' man and anyone who questioned it or challenged it would find out the hard way.

"You are mine. All. Fuckin'. Mine," Duke said between thrusts.

"Yes!" Vaughan yelled beneath him. "Fuckin' show me."

Trying desperately to keep his eyes open to watch the erotic scene, Duke pushed in as deep as he could possibly go and howled his release deep inside his lover's ass. Bellowing his victory. He pressed his forehead against the back of Vaughan's neck and jerked with each pulse of his cock. Flinched with each spurt of his seed. Fuck. It was so primal. Duke felt like a completely new man.

Though Vaughan loved to top and top Duke hard, he wasn't threatened by letting Duke lead sometimes. Knowing he'd need it. Needed to flip his own dominant switch on every now and then. Letting them know Duke was still an alpha. Always would be.

The End

There will be more of Duke and Vaughan in Promises Part II

ALSO BY A.E. VIA

NOTHING SPECIAL SERIES

Nothing Special (Nothing Special #1)

Embracing His Syn (Nothing Special #2)

PROMISES

Here Comes Trouble (Nothing Special #3)

Don't Judge (Nothing Special #4)

PROMISES

BLUE MOON SERIES

Blue Moon II: This Is Reality

Blue Moon III: Call of the Alpha (COMING SOON)

You Can See Me   (STANDALONE)

ID
PROMISES

Printed in Great Britain
by Amazon